He was a warrior with the look of the hawk, or a great jungle cat

A molded breastplate, apparently made of the same kind of material as his helmet, encased the upper half of his strangely elongated torso and bore strange, twisting, interlocking Celtic designs. Spurs jangled at the heels of his knee-high, black leather boots, an accessory that should have struck Lakesh as absurdly superfluous, but for some reason seemed perfectly in keeping with the man who wore them.

A metal gauntlet of a gleaming silvery alloy covered the man's right hand and forearm, reaching up almost to the crook of his elbow.

At first, Lakesh did not recognize him, although his translucently pale face, the blue-white hue of skim milk, struck a distant chord of recognition. Then his wide, slanted eyes flamed up with a molten orange shimmer and Lakesh knew who he was. He didn't have the time or opportunity to speak his name.

From behind him, he heard Brewster Philboyd blurt in sheer terror, *"Maccan!"*

Other titles in this series:

James Axler
Outlanders

MAD GOD'S
WRATH

A GOLD EAGLE BOOK FROM
WORLDWIDE ®

TORONTO • NEW YORK • LONDON
AMSTERDAM • PARIS • SYDNEY • HAMBURG
STOCKHOLM • ATHENS • TOKYO • MILAN
MADRID • WARSAW • BUDAPEST • AUCKLAND

First edition February 2004

ISBN 0-373-63841-8

MAD GOD'S WRATH

Special thanks to Mark Ellis for his contribution to the Outlanders concept, developed for Gold Eagle.

Mountain and hills, come, come and fall on me
And hide me from the heavy wrath of God
                              —Christopher Marlowe
                              1564–1593

The Road to Outlands—
From Secret Government Files to the Future

Almost two hundred years after the global holocaust, Kane, a former Magistrate of Cobaltville, often thought the world had been lucky to survive at all after a nuclear device detonated in the Russian embassy in Washington, D.C. The aftermath—forever known as skydark—reshaped continents and turned civilization into ashes.

Nearly depopulated, America became the Deathlands—poisoned by radiation, home to chaos and mutated life forms. Feudal rule reappeared in the form of baronies, while remote outposts clung to a brutish existence.

What eventually helped shape this wasteland were the redoubts, the secret preholocaust military installations with stores of weapons, and the home of gateways, the locational matter-transfer facilities. Some of the redoubts hid clues that had once fed wild theories of government cover-ups and alien visitations.

Rearmed from redoubt stockpiles, the barons consolidated their power and reclaimed technology for the villes. Their power, supported by some invisible authority, extended beyond their fortified walls to what was now called the Outlands. It was here that the rootstock of humanity survived, living with hellzones and chemical storms, hounded by Magistrates.

In the villes, rigid laws were enforced—to atone for the sins of the past and prepare the way for a better future. That was the barons' public credo and their right-to-rule.

Kane, along with friend and fellow Magistrate Grant, had upheld that claim until a fateful Outlands expedition. A displaced piece of technology…a question to a keeper of the archives…a vague clue about alien masters—and their world shifted radically. Suddenly, Brigid Baptiste, the archivist, faced summary execution, and Grant a quick termination. For Kane there was forgiveness if he pledged his unquestioning allegiance to Baron Cobalt and his unknown masters and abandoned his friends.

But that allegiance would make him support a mysterious and alien power and deny loyalty and friends. Then what else was there?

Kane had been brought up solely to serve the ville. Brigid's only link with her family was her mother's red-gold hair, green eyes and supple form. Grant's clues to his lineage were his ebony skin and powerful physique. But Domi, she of the white hair, was an Outlander pressed into sexual servitude in Cobaltville. She at least knew her roots and was a reminder to the exiles that the outcasts belonged in the human family.

Parents, friends, community—the very rootedness of humanity was denied. With no continuity, there was no forward momentum to the future. And that was the crux— when Kane began to wonder if there *was* a future.

For Kane, it wouldn't do. So the only way was out— way, way out.

After their escape, they found shelter at the forgotten Cerberus redoubt headed by Lakesh, a scientist, Cobaltville's head archivist, and secret opponent of the barons.

With their past turned into a lie, their future threatened, only one thing was left to give meaning to the outcasts. The hunger for freedom, the will to resist the hostile influences. And perhaps, by opposing, end them.

Prologue

A silence as deep and still as the white pumice deserts of the Moon's Mare Imbrium draped the tomb of Maccan. When Eduardo Vega caught that singularly sepulchral concept slinking through his consciousness, he tried to stomp on it and crush it out. The big, vault-walled room was *not* a tomb, he told himself fiercely, only a storage chamber. The star shine flowing down from a round skylight in the high, arched roof proved that without a doubt, even though it glinted dully on two objects resembling high-tech Egyptian sarcophagi.

The filtered illumination struck highlights on the stacked metal crates and the hand tools scattered atop the long trestle tables. Most of the crates were stenciled with the legend NASA and a few others read DEVIL/Manitius Base. Pieces of machinery lay scattered on the floor. Various areas around the warehouse were piled with debris, separated by their materials for future recycling.

The walls, ceiling and floor of the storage chamber formed one continuous surface to make a huge, hollow ellipse that measured out to a hundred feet in diameter. When in it, Eduardo always felt as if he were

trapped within the center of an impossibly gargantuan ball.

From the curving walls of the chamber jutted plat-
forms connected by a series of cage-enclosed lifts and
crossed girders. Tall, Y-shaped induction pylons
sprouted from the floor, but their ceramic surfaces
were blackened with soot. Between two of the pylons
stood a pair of oblong pedestals, nearly seven feet
long. Four small pyramids crafted from pale golden
alloy were placed at equidistant points around them.
Resting on pedestals were smooth, crystalline ovoids
made of translucent materials, both of which canted
at forty-five-degree angles.

Climbing off the stool on which he had half dozed
for the better part of an hour, Eduardo wiped his eyes
with the heel of his left hand. From his right wrist a
radiophone dangled by a leather strap. He squinted up
at the skylight. Space looked unchanging. The deep,
jet-black emptiness, alleviated only by the bright, tiny
pinpoints of stars, was the canopy of eternity overhanging the Manitius Moon base. He snorted at his
own poetic turn of thought.

The radiophone suddenly crashed with a blend of
static and an angry male voice. "Eduardo! Goddamn
you! Eddie!"

Eduardo winced at Morisette's tone as he thumbed
the transmit key. "I'm here, Gabe. What's the problem?"

"You're ten minutes overdue for your check-in! If
I come down there and find you asleep again—"

"You'll what?" Eduardo broke in harshly. "Court-martial me? No, wait, you can't do that, 'cause I'm a civilian, just like you are. Exile me to Earth? Oh, that would be a fucking shame, wouldn't it? I couldn't pull guard duty in these lovely surroundings anymore. Oh, boo-hoo, that would just shatter me!"

The comm accurately transmitted Morisette's deep sigh. "You drew the short straw this week, Eddie."

"Don't remind me." Eduardo tried to smooth some of the sharper edges of anger from his voice. "I don't see any point in posting guards here. That elf-eared son of a bitch isn't going anywhere."

In a tone of aggrieved patience, Morisette retorted, "You know damn well we're not worried about him going anywhere...but keeping somebody else from coming along to fetch him, to wake him up, is the mission statement."

Eduardo snorted in derision at Morisette's use of military jargon. "Oh, please. Saladin is dead. If Mac has any followers left, they're out scrounging in the Wild Lands. They wouldn't come back here."

"That's why we post guards, dumbass. To make sure they *won't* come back. I'm tired of arguing with you. Just be a little more on the ball when the next check-in time comes around."

Morisette signed off with an autocratic click. For a moment Eduardo wrestled with the urge to reestablish radio contact just so he could tell the man to kiss his ass, both in Spanish and French.

The urge passed and Eduardo began to make a circuit of the room, trying to work a kink out of his back in the process. As he passed one of the stasis canisters, he caught his reflection in the rounded crystalline cover. He glimpsed a middle-aged man slightly below medium height, wearing a dark brown coverall. His complexion was of a similar hue and his long black hair framed a deeply scarred face.

The scars had been inflicted well over a year ago by a carnobot under the control of Megaera, but she was thoroughly dead, killed—according to Brewster Philboyd—by Maccan himself. He could only hope the mechanoid that had permanently disfigured him was equally inactive, as well.

He glanced over at the second cryostasis canister and repressed a shiver. If the storage room could be called a tomb, then that particular stasis unit was a coffin or a sarcophagus. But neither the hollow chamber nor the canister was exactly what Eduardo found himself mentally identifying them as.

The big room was little more than a warehouse, holding the odds and ends left over from the construction of the Moon base two centuries earlier. The colony wasn't much to see, but it represented twenty-some years of tremendous labor, conducted largely in secret between the 1970s and the late 1990s. Most of the base had been hollowed out of the rock of the regolith, the inner wall of the Manitius Crater. A network of conduits and ventilation shafts supplied air to most of the colony, and machines called grav-stators transmitted Earth-normal gravity fields.

Out on the flat plateau on the floor of the crater, a sprawling solar power station had been built. This was an arrangement of metal frames holding reflective semiconductor chips that stored and converted solar energy to electricity. Much of the solar power was directed toward the big hydroponic gardens enclosed within the main part of the base. The individual sections were roofed with domes of transparent plastic. Plants of all kinds grew in beds of fertilized soil. For many years the vegetable gardens had served as the source of most of the food for the colony.

Eduardo swallowed a sigh, thinking back to the long months he had lived on the lunar colony before entering cryostasis to relieve some of the strain on the base's limited resources. After the nukecaust of 2001 forever separated three hundred and thirty human beings from the world of their birth, they'd had no choice but to make the colony self-sustaining. At first the base personnel fabricated everything they needed— or they'd tried to do so. Fortunately, even before the nukecaust, rich veins of gold, copper and iron ore had been discovered and mined in areas outside the Manitius Crater. Then other items had been found and the reasons to continue with the manufacturing process had become less immediate.

Thinking about those other items caused the flesh between Eduardo's shoulder blades to prickle. At the faint scuff of a footfall, he whirled, every nerve end tingling. Someone was walking down the narrow passageway just outside the open hatch.

Swiftly he returned to his stool, reaching for the pulse-plasma emitter leaning against the bulkhead. The weapon, known colloquially as a quartz cremator, looked like the skeleton of a rifle made of polished glass overlaid with ceramic. The sectionalized barrel terminated in a long cylinder made of a crystalline substance. He cradled it in his arms as the footsteps, interspersed with the clink of metal, grew louder. Despite realizing that whoever strode down the corridor wasn't making any effort to be stealthy, a sense of imminent peril crept over Eduardo.

He rested his fingers on the firing plate just as a figure appeared in the hatchway. He heard a startled intake of breath. "For God's sake, Eddie—"

George Neukirk gaped at the quartz cremator with wide, alarmed eyes. Eduardo gusted out a profanity-seasoned sigh and lowered the weapon. "For God's sake yourself, George. What the hell are you doing here? I thought you were down in Cerberus."

Neukirk nodded and stepped farther into the room, his eyes darting nervously from Eduardo to the pulse-plasma emitter. He was a short, chunky man with seamed, weather-beaten features and a white crew cut. He wore a gray, zippered coverall cinched at the waist by a wide leather tool belt. Wrenches and various sizes of screwdrivers dangled from it.

"I'm up here servicing a replacement TAV," he replied in his gravelly voice. "One of the two Mantas flown to Cerberus was shot down over India a couple of weeks ago, remember?"

Eduardo nodded. "Right. Grant was the pilot."

Neukirk shrugged. "Just figured I'd stop by and say hello before I gated back. Thought you might want some company."

"Thanks," replied Eduardo sardonically. "But I've

got company." He turned, gesturing to the cryo canister. "Mac's a great conversationalist."

Neukirk's chuckle sounded forced. "He did have the gift of gab."

Eduardo walked toward the unit. "Beats me why Kane doesn't just drag this thing out to the surface and open it up. Mac wanted to die anyhow."

"There was some discussion along those lines," Neukirk said. "But everybody thinks Mac might be a good source of information...providing he can be controlled."

Eduardo nodded distractedly, stopping beside the sarcophagus. Beneath the crystal cover, it seemed filled with a cloudy substance like smoke that had been frozen in midswirl. He touched the transparent surface, and the vapor within the ovoid immediately cleared.

Within it appeared Maccan, his long fingers curved like talons, the tips flattened against the inside of the lid, his eyes wide and wild but unseeing. His expression was locked in a contortion of fury. All the color seemed to have been leached from his body. His form had the appearance of pale blue ice, not only in color but composition. Even a spattering of blood on the side of his face was black, like splashes of ink. The blood had trickled from a wound Kane had inflicted.

Eduardo could see that Maccan, even lying half prone, was a little over six feet in height, but so exceptionally lean he appeared even taller. Absently he noted that the man's torso seemed strangely elongated but perfectly in proportion with his slender arms and legs.

His limbs were encased in a black, skintight covering, and an assortment of brightly colored cloths decorated his almost emaciated frame, giving him a scarecrow-like appearance. A yellow rag around his hips served as either a sash or a belt, and another length of bright green fabric was knotted around his left thigh for no apparent purpose.

Maccan's face was long and bony, his chin a jutting V under the smaller V of his pursed lips. His long, narrow nose looked delicate, with tiny nostrils. His eyes were abnormally large and back-slanted, but without the epicanthic folds of the Asian. Because of the polarizing effect of the stasis chamber, Eduardo couldn't tell their color, only that they were dark. His smooth skin was marred by a curve of scar tissue along his right cheek.

The man's unnaturally long fingers bore many sigil and talismanic rings. One was a loop of iron embossed with a cup-and-spiral glyph. Another glittered with a hexagonal red stone. Each ring was fashioned from a different substance—crystal, metal, gems and even what looked like polished, lacquered wood.

A mane of iron-gray hair grew outward from a point on his forehead and swept down from high, flat temples. It was brushed back behind his ears to fall in a loose tumble around his shoulders. Maccan's ears were positioned very low on his jawline, and though they lay close to the sides of his head and weren't large, they tapered to upswept points.

"Sometimes," Neukirk murmured from behind Eduardo, " I wonder if we weren't better off not reestablishing contact with Earth."

Eduardo removed his hand from the humped crystal cover and the smoky vapor within it immediately swirled around the figure of Maccan again, obscuring it from view. The stasis unit was an encapsulated survival system that froze a subject in an impenetrable bubble of space and time, slowing to a stop all metabolic processes. He grasped only a little of the technology involved, but he knew it was of extraterrestrial origin.

Turning to face Neukirk, he asked, "What do you mean?"

Neukirk reached behind him with his right hand. "I mean—" he whipped his hand back around "—knowing about postnuke Earth put all sorts of ideas in my head. Like how to get the hell away from it."

Eduardo's thought processes felt paralyzed, numbed by bewildered shock when he finally realized the rail pistol gripped in Neukirk's hand was trained on him. The pistol held the general configuration of a revolver, but instead of cylinder, a small round ammo drum was fitted into the place where there would normally be a trigger guard. The gun had no trigger, just a curving switch inset into the grip.

The slender barrel stretched to nearly ten inches in length. Made of a lightweight alloy resembling dulled chrome, the rail pistol utilized a system of tiny electromagnets to launch an explosive projectile of tungsten carbine at a fantastically high muzzle velocity. A unit of energy inside the grip propelled the projectile out of the barrel at a speed of nearly 15 miles per second. In a vacuum, the velocity would be closer to 35 miles per second, with absolutely no recoil.

Eduardo was intimately and uncomfortably familiar with the destructive effects of the long-barreled hand weapons. Not too long ago, he'd used one of the rail guns to destroy a marauding carnobot. He inhaled deeply and as he exhaled, he demanded, "What the fuck is this about, George?"

Neukirk gestured with the pistol. "Drop the cremator, Eddie."

Eduardo hesitated for only a second. He dropped his emitter to the deck. Responding to another jerk of the rail pistol's barrel, he stepped away from it. "Why are you doing this?"

Neukirk grinned, showing the edges of his teeth. "I'm asserting myself." His voice sounded like two steel plates striking one another edge-on. "I've been one of Maccan's people for months, nearly a year."

Eduardo's lips worked as if he was trying to spit or to scream. Finally he managed to husk out, "Maccan's a maniac, George! He wanted to kill himself and take the whole damn solar system with him!"

Neukirk nodded agreeably. "I'm not saying he's perfect, but since the DEVIL platform imploded, he probably won't be so fixated on suicide."

"You'll give him a hobby?" Eduardo demanded. "Like what, knitting?"

"We already have something ready to occupy his attention."

"'We?'" Eduardo echoed incredulously. "You've hooked back up with those idiots who believe he's a god?"

Neukirk shrugged. "He's not a perfect god, I'll

admit. But he's about the most reasonable facsimile I'm liable to run into in my lifetime."

Eduardo squeezed his eyes shut, feeling terror knot in the pit of his stomach like lengths of slimy rope. Hoarsely he said, "Mac is just as likely to tear your eyes out as thank you if you revive him. What can you gain from freeing him? He wants followers, not colleagues."

Neukirk's lips compressed. "There are less worthy pursuits for someone of my intelligence and talent."

Opening his eyes, Eduardo uttered a sneering laugh. "Name two, Georgie."

Neukirk's face twisted into a something ugly. "I've only got time for one. Goodbye, Eddie. "

He squeezed the trigger switch of the rail gun. A pellet no larger than a shirt button sped from the long barrel with a sound like a piece of wet cloth being ripped in two. It punched Eduardo in the chest and exploded at the instant of impact, pulverizing his clavicle and all the bones in his rib cage. The detonation was not necessary, since hydrostatic shock instantly stopped his heart. He careened backward, his feet completely leaving the floor.

Arms and legs flailing, blood foaming from his mouth in a crimson fountain, Eduardo Vega flew nearly half the length of the chamber and almost through the hatch. He struck the deck with a wet slap, his body twisting and writhing, legs kicking feebly.

His legs were still twitching in post mortem spasms when seven people strode into the storage facility, all of them looking around alertly. They wore steel-gray

armored EVA suits, known in the old NASA vernac-
ular as "hard" suits. Designed for high-impact resistance and to deflect the penetration of micrometeorites,
the extravehicular activity suits were the late-twenti-
eth-century versions of medieval battle armor. However, none of the people who marched into the
warehouse—four men and three women—wore the
helmets.

They paid no attention to Eduardo's corpse except
to shift position to keep from bloodying their boots in
the dark, wide pool spreading out around his body.

A woman marched up to Neukirk. "You sure you
know how to operate these units, George?" Despite the
feminine timbre of the voice, her tone was harsh, both
an inquiry and a challenge.

Neukirk turned toward her, forcing a smile to his
face. "I'm not like you, Shayd, or the rest of your
crew. I was born in a world of technology, so I don't
fear it as something arcane I can never master. Besides,
keep in mind I was in cryostasis myself for most of my
two hundred years on this turd ball."

Shayd stiffened at the patronizing bite in Neukirk's
response. Nearly a full head taller than Neukirk, she
was a good deal leaner and longer of limb, as well. Her
angular, café-au-lait face was set in a grim mask, her
long, yellow-streaked hair tied up in a knot atop her
head.

Her large pewter-colored eyes regarded him unblinkingly. Faint scars showed on the left side of her
face, one of them bisecting her eyebrow.

A ten-inch bowie knife lay in a canvas scabbard

across her belly. The square butt of a Gyrojet rocket pistol protruded from the top of a vacuum-formed plastic holster attached to the right thigh of her space suit. The pistol looked like a toy made of stamped tin, but it fired 13 mm rocket rounds. The percussion primers of the projectiles were surrounded by a ring of four canted exhaust ports that propelled the round. The Gyrojet was a weapon perfectly suited for combat on the surface of the Moon, inasmuch as its range and penetration power were far greater than those of a standard firearm in an atmosphere.

Nodding curtly toward the sarcophagus holding Maccan, Shayd snapped, "Prove it."

She didn't need to suggestively finger the butt of her pistol to emphasize the request. The cold gleam in her eyes was only slightly less subtle than a direct threat.

Feeling his throat constrict from tension, Neukirk slid the rail gun back into his tool belt and turned toward the canister. He bent and felt around the base. He found the tiny inset keypad and tapped in a sequence.

The smoky vapor beneath the crystal cover suddenly began to swirl and billow. A second later it disappeared completely, as if it had been sucked into a vent and ejected. The transparent sheathing suddenly split in two, the halves sliding apart silently and withdrawing into a pair of almost invisible slots. The warehouse echoed with a protracted hiss, like air escaping from a faulty valve.

A blue-hued light shimmered from within the stasis canister. Shayd stepped forward, eyes reflecting the light raptly. "What's happening?" she asked Neukirk.

Before he could respond, a lean figure sprang out of the sarcophagus as if launched by a catapult. It roared in blind, mindless fury, eyes gleaming with the color of freshly spoiled blood. Shayd and her companions dropped to one knee, bowing their heads in reverence. After a numb handful of seconds, Neukirk did the same, surreptitiously peering upward as Maccan swept a wild, disoriented glare around the warehouse. Neukirk felt cold sweat spring out on his hairline as the burning scarlet eyes fixed on him.

Maccan, last of the Tuatha de Danaan, the mad god of the ancient Celts, reached out a long arm toward him, fingers stretching wide to encircle his neck. An animalistic growl hummed in his throat.

Shayd murmured tensely, "You'd better start talking about this mirror matter theory of yours, George. And make it damn fast."

Maccan heard the woman's words and his hand froze inches from Neukirk's neck. The growl faded and the red flame in his eyes dimmed slightly. Tentatively touching the wound on the right side of his head, Maccan asked, in a hoarse, confused whisper, "What was that again, George? Mirror matter?"

George Neukirk cleared his throat and began speaking.

Chapter 1

Kane awoke to the raucous squawk of birds, the nostril-clogging smell of must and an excruciating pain in his head. Mentally he explored his body, trying to determine where it was presently located and the extent of the damage inflicted upon it.

Slowly he came to understand that he lay on his back with his arms tucked at his sides and his legs together. Several small sharp objects dug into his buttocks and the backs of his thighs. He didn't stir, trying to isolate and identify everything he heard, smelled, tasted or felt. He decided to check out his vision last, not wanting to open his eyes until he was sure of where he was and what was happening.

After a few moments of lying completely still, he grudgingly realized he had no choice but to accept the fact that he had no idea in hell of what was going on. What he could identify was the cawing and screeching of gulls and the rhythmic boom of the surf. The dull ache in his left arm was the result of blocking a blow. Small rocks most likely pressed into his backside, so that meant he lay outside.

He felt a stiffness in his face, a bruise throbbing along the right side of his jaw, spreading out from the side of his head. The rest of his anatomy possessed the general feeling of having been methodically pounded with a sledgehammer.

Kane remembered only vaguely how his body had come to feel like a tenderized steak. His primary recollection of the attack was its savage speed, the quick rush of bodies, angry grunts, blinding pain in the side of his head like a drill-punch boring in, then the sensation of falling. He had no idea of how long he'd been unconscious. He, Grant and Brigid Baptiste had come a long way over the past couple of days, and the meeting at the cove was supposed to be the culmination of the journey from Montana to the northern California coast.

His eyes stung from sweat collecting in pools in their sockets. The heat was intense, but the temperature gave him some idea of the time. The sun had just begun to rise when he'd walked down toward the shoreline for the rendezvous.

Respiration labored, he wondered why, if he was lying outside, the air seemed so thick and stuffy and why it required such effort to drag it into his straining lungs. By fractions of centimeters, he slitted his eyes open, then squinted against a confusing pattern of interlocked light and shadow. After a second or two of blinking, the pattern came into focus and he realized a bag of a burlap material covered his head.

Heart pounding from a surge of claustrophobia, he resisted the desperate impulse to reach up and snatch the bag away. He continued to lie still. Patience was a habit instilled in him during his Magistrate training and later pounded into him by its exercise and the often grim object lessons of comrades and enemies who failed to practice it.

A soft male voice, sounding surprisingly cultured and even sympathetic, said, "Hardly an auspicious beginning. Partly my fault. I hope you don't hold it against me."

Kane didn't move or otherwise react, despite the spurt of adrenaline the voice triggered. Although a gambler and percentage player by nature, a calculator of risks and safety factors, Kane retained vivid memories of the consequences of his own unrestrained moments of impulse. Most of those moments were commemorated by the scar tissue imprinted on various parts of his body.

The voice spoke again, this time edged with impatience. "I know you're conscious. You can get up. You're not tied."

Kane considered the man's words, then slowly reached up and peeled the stifling bag up and off his head. His right arm felt disquieting light, and he realized his Sin Eater had been removed. He pushed himself to a sitting position, setting his teeth on a groan of pain. The movement ignited little hot flares all over his body. He flinched away from the blinding glare of the sun, hot as any dawn could possibly be on the shores of the stretch of northern California coastline once called Crescent City.

He glimpsed gulls wheeling on outspread wings, riding on the thermal currents arising from the juncture of the beach and the thundering sea. They soared gracefully through the smoky spume raised by the nearby breakers. He saw very little except sand, rocks and the long line of combers smashing against seaweed-draped boulders.

As Kane glanced down, he saw a pair of shiny white shoes planted firmly in the sand near his own booted feet. His gaze slowly climbed from the shoes to a pair of denim-clad, sharply creased legs and then up to the man's face, smiling down at him.

It was a very handsome face, topped by longish, carefully styled black hair and adorned with a neatly trimmed, waxed mustache. His eyelashes were unusually long and delicately curved, veiling a pair of limpid brown eyes. His face bore a deep bronze tint, but Kane suspected the tan didn't derive from lying on the beach but from regular exposure to a sunlamp.

He wore a blue yachting blazer with an elaborate crest embroidered on the breast pocket, and in his right hand he held a tiny, battery-operated fan with plastic vanes. As it emitted a faint buzz, he passed it over his face. Kane repressed a snort of derision. Breeze Castigleone didn't look like the boss of the Snakefish barony's Tartarus Pits. In fact, he didn't look like the boss of much of anything, unless it was a clothes closet. Still, though he should have looked ridiculous in his boating ensemble, for some reason Kane could not quite identify, he did not.

Kane shook his head to clear it, opened his mouth and worked his aching jaw. At length, he said casually, "You were right. Hardly an auspicious beginning. But you were wrong when you said it was partly your fault. In my opinion, it was *all* your fault."

Castigleone teeth gleamed wolfishly in the bright sunlight. "You objected to being searched, Mr. Kane."

"I objected to being felt up by that gimp of yours. Where is he?"

Castigleone gestured with one perfectly manicured hand. "See for yourself."

Kane followed the hand wave, slowly inching around on the rock-strewed sand. The man he had referred to as a gimp sat placidly on a low boulder behind him, huge hands resting on his knees. He was nearly six and a half feet tall and looked three-quarters of that wide, at least through the chest. His complexion was about the color of a charcoal briquette.

One finger was missing from his right hand and part of an ear had been cut from the left side of his shaved head. That side of his face was bisected by a crooked, puckered weal that lifted the corner of his mouth up in a permanent grin. His left eye looked as if it was covered by a gray film. His chest was broad enough to force his arms out at the elbows. He breathed through his mouth because of the mashed condition of his nose. Blood flowed from both nostrils, soaking his white T-shirt with a random pattern of crimson.

"My compliments," Castigleone said in a voice purring with amusement. "You're the first man I've ever known who made Belevedere bleed."

"Do I get a prize for that or what?" Kane asked sourly.

"Not from me, sec man," announced a strident female voice from his left. "I would have ended up the same as him, but I was just a little too fast for you."

Carefully, Kane hitched around, noting the strong Russian accent in her voice. It sounded just a little too strong.

"Meet Tashlyn," Castigleone said genially.

Tashlyn stood about two yards away, leaning negligently against a rock. She wore a sleeveless black silk tunic with a Mandarin collar. Below its gold-edged hem she had nothing on but a G-string, a black, patent-leather V gleaming at the juncture of her thighs. A pair of black net stockings covered her long, muscular legs. The boots on her feet bore high stiletto heels, and Kane recalled the drill-punch sensation on the side of his head, but he decided the time wasn't right to raise the issue.

Her hips were ample and tapered to a tiny waist. The curves above her waist were equally ample, even lush, but the same could not be said about her face. A coat of chalk-white makeup had been applied thickly to her skin, as well as vivid red lipstick and two perfect circles of a crimson cosmetic on her cheeks.

Her eyes, which stared unblinkingly at him from between two wings of glossy midnight-blue hair, were outlined with enough black mascara to paint a Sandcat. False eyelashes long enough to sweep clean the beach fluttered like spider legs in the light breeze. Her penciled eyebrows, angled to form a pair of diabolical arches, completed her look.

Tashlyn would have appeared hilarious to Kane if he had seen her in a barony or even an Outland ville. But standing here in her rig in the bright glare of the early morning sunlight, with salt spray forming a faint vapor around her, she exuded an air of the demonic.

She held a long-handled club in her right hand, a flexible truncheon nearly two feet long made of cross-stitched leather, one end as big around as his fist. He guessed it was filled with buckshot and he figured its vigorous use was responsible for giving his body the overall feeling of being hammered. In her left hand she held his Sin Eater, still snugged within its power holster.

"Two strong-arms from two different directions," Kane observed dryly. He turned back to Castigleone. "You don't like to take any chances, do you?"

Breeze Castigleone chuckled. "Actually, I do, but not with a man of your accomplishments and reputation. In dealing with you, I'd be a fool to be anything other than overcautious. Your fame—or your infamy—has spread far."

"I'm on the level," Kane said flatly.

"That remains to be seen. You may get up now."

"Do it slowly," Tashlyn called, waggling the end of her truncheon at him.

Kane did as she said, not because she intimidated him, but because his head swam dizzily when he moved too quickly. He climbed to his feet, silently enduring a spasm of pain mixed in with a little vertigo. He was aware of Tashlyn looking him up and down, but he made a casual show of brushing sand from his clothes and arms.

A tall, lean man, Kane stood an inch over six feet, his thick dark hair touched by the sun at the temples and nape. His face was sun-bronzed, making his light blue-gray eyes look paler than they actually were. A thin hairline scar stretched like a white thread across his left cheek. The general aspect of his physique was of a timber wolf, with most of his muscle mass contained in his upper body above a slim waist and long legs. He wore an olive-drab T-shirt tucked into camouflage pants and high-laced jump boots.

Pretending to massage the right side of his head, he gingerly touched the Commtact, feeling for the flat curve of metal behind his ear and hidden by a lock of hair. Not hearing any voices or even a crackle of static since rousing, he assumed the little comm unit had been damaged in the attack.

"Looking for this?" Castigleone asked. Sunlight winked from the small bronze-hued curve of metal he bounced gently on his right palm.

Kane didn't respond, gazing at the little device. The Commtact fit tightly against the mastoid bone behind the right ear, attached to implanted steel pintels. The unit slid through the flesh and made contact with tiny input ports. Its sensor circuitry incorporated an analog-to-digital voice encoder that was embedded in the bone.

Once the device made full cranial contact, transmissions were picked up by the auditory canals. The dermal sensors transmitted the electronic signals directly through the skull casing. Even if someone went deaf, as long as they wore a Commtact, they would still have a form of hearing.

The Commtacts were still being field-tested, since to make them operational, surgery was required and few people in Cerberus wanted to make that sacrifice.

But the surgery to implant the sensors was very minor, only a matter of making a small incision behind the ear and sliding the Commtact under the skin. Kane's implantation had been performed over three weeks ago under the supervision of the Cerberus medic, Reba De-Fore. There had been almost no pain or any awareness of the device after the incision healed. Its presence was only a small, barely detectable lump that was invisible once Kane's hair fell over the spot.

The Commtact's five-mile range was superior to the hand-held trans-comms. The range of the radiophones was generally limited to a mile, but in open country, in clear weather, contact could be established at two miles.

Kane wasn't so much reviewing the Commtact's capabilities, as wondering how Breeze Castigleone could have possibly known he wore such a unit.

Castigleone chuckled and tossed it toward him. Despite his surprise, Kane snatched it out of the air. "Tasha came across it by accident when you were searched, Kane. She removed it just to be on the safe side."

"Do you know what it is?" Kane asked.

Castigleone shook his head. "Not exactly, but I assume it's some sort of comm. I didn't want you sending or receiving messages from your companions until I had the chance to make sure you weren't carrying anything we couldn't deal with." His smile became a rueful grin. "Like I said, overcautious."

Kane nodded. "To a fault."

He glanced past Tashlyn, his eyes following a trail

of glistening pebbles at the shoreline. They led to a crowded labyrinth of black rotting timbers half a klick away. The bright morning sunlight made the ancient marina look unreal, like a stage setting. Through the open boathouses he saw the partly submerged and barnacle-covered hulks of ships.

Beyond the dock massed a number of seagoing craft, most of them dating back to the years immediately preceding the nukecaust. He saw sailboats, cabin cruisers and even a few barges. Only a few vessels floated high in the water. At least half of the derelicts were waterlogged and nearly submerged, little more than mounds of jetsam rising from the surface of the sea. Some were canted on their sides; others were capsized completely.

"Interesting how you're able to get out of the Pits to conduct business," Kane commented. "Doesn't Baron Snakefish mind that his Pit boss leaves Tartarus unattended?"

Castigleone only shrugged. Named after Tartarus, the abyss below Hell where Zeus had confined his enemies, the Pits were the planned slums of the baronies, melting pots, swarming with slaggers and cheap labor.

Many years before, the barons had decreed that the villes could support no more than four thousand residents, and the number of Pit dwellers could not exceed one thousand. Part of every Magistrate's duty was to make Pit sweeps, seeking outlanders, infants and even pregnant women and either ejecting them from the barony or killing them.

Despite the ruthless treatment of the Pit dwellers, one constant in all of the nine villes was a Pit boss. By no means an official title or position, Pit bosses nevertheless served a purpose of varying degrees of importance, depending on the ville.

Part crime lords, part information conduits and part procurers of luxuries, most barons tolerated Pit bosses as long as they knew and kept their place. If they maintained a certain order among the seething masses in Tartarus, Magistrates were inclined to overlook limited black-marketeering or the elimination of troublesome elements.

Not only did Breeze Castigleone not look anything like a Tartarus resident, but he also didn't resemble any Pit boss Kane had ever met. But Kane knew Castigleone hadn't risen to prominence in the Tartarus Pits of Snakefish on his looks and fey manner alone.

He possessed a cunning and absolutely ruthless brain, which in tandem with his talent for manipulation and unlawful acquisition of goods made him something of a genius. He had also, in the very recent past, somehow managed to smuggle a great number of death-dealing ordnance out of the Magistrate armory and into the possession of an old enemy of Kane's.

The old enemy was dead now—or so Kane fervently hoped—but the mystery of how Castigleone had accomplished the deed and whether he could repeat it remained to be resolved.

"Do you think we can get down to business now?" Castigleone asked impatiently.

"Sure." Kane turned toward Tashlyn, extending a hand. "My side arm, if you please."

The woman's painted lips curled back over her teeth in a theatrical sneer. "In your dreams, sec man."

"Sec man" was an obsolete term dating back to preunification days when self-styled barons formed their own private armies to safeguard their territories. It was still applied to Magistrates in the hinterlands beyond the villes, so Kane figured Tashlyn was a native of the Outlands, not Russia. The accent was an affectation, probably an imitation of one she had heard in an old vid dealing with spies or vampires.

Still, Kane didn't like the term. Even though he was no longer a Magistrate, he still considered it an insult, but he didn't allow the anger building within him to show on his face. "I'm not dreaming, Tasha. Give me back my gun or I'll take it from you, Belevedere notwithstanding."

He took a menacing half step toward her, and Castigleone interposed, "I'd prefer you weren't armed during the initial phase of our negotiations."

Eyebrows knitting together at the bridge of his nose, Kane spun toward him, mouth opening to voice a profane rejoinder. The rejoinder clogged momentarily in his throat when he saw Breeze Castigleone had exchanged his miniature fan for what appeared to be a miniature pistol. The auto derringer wasn't really miniature and its stainless-steel frame made it look very business-like. He guessed the pistol was an old Semmering American derringer, loaded with a single but nevertheless deadly .38-caliber round.

Kane forced a mocking smile to his face and held

up the Commtact. "You didn't want me sending any messages to my companions with this, right? Well, since my companions haven't heard from me in a while, I'm sure they're on their way here." He waved toward dense stands of sycamore trees about half a mile away, the trunks snarled with undergrowth. "Hell, they may be watching us right now."

Castigleone glanced toward the trees with a skeptical arching of eyebrows, but he said nothing. Kane continued, "If they see me standing here with your painted-up gaudy slut holding my gun, and you with a gun on me, there won't be a single solitary phase of negotiations at all, initial or otherwise."

"I see." Breeze Castigleone gestured with the derringer to the Commtact. "Then I suggest you contact them and let them know everything is under control. That is, if you actually have companions anywhere around."

"Gee," said Kane blandly, "you mean you want me to *lie* to them? Won't my pants catch on fire?"

Castigleone frowned. Kane maintained an unblinking gaze on the man's mustached face, adding, "You claimed my reputation made you overcautious. If you know that much about me, then you know my reputation is shared with a couple of other people, too, right?"

Grudgingly, Castigleone nodded. "Right."

"Then I would think you'd want to be *triply* overcautious. I showed my good faith when I met up with you alone, at dawn. In my estimation, it would be an exceptionally good idea for you to show yours."

Tashlyn stepped forward, slapping the end of her

truncheon suggestively against a thigh. "You're bluffing, sec man." Her words came out as a contemptuous growl. "Fuck your reputation. Even if you're who you say you are, I don't think you have any friends anyplace. You're just another fugitive from the barons with a price on your head."

The shot could not have been timed better, although Kane found fault with the aim. The hard, flat crack of sound against the brazen sky was almost swallowed by the heavy thunder of the surf. The .50-caliber bullet kicked up a spurt of sand a yard from Tashlyn's left foot. A poor shot for Grant, but Kane figured the round had been fired from the big Barrett sniper rifle strictly for effect.

The effect was immediate and pretty much everything Kane could have hoped for. Belevedere rose from his boulder with a grunt of surprise. Tashlyn skipped backward several feet, bleating in wordless alarm. Only Breeze Castigleone didn't move. His frown molded itself into a resigned smile. He placed the derringer in his blazer pocket and held out both hands toward Tashlyn. "Give Mr. Kane his gun, Tasha, sweetheart. We don't want him or his companions to think we're unfriendly."

The chalk-and-vermilion-faced woman hesitated for a moment, then she hissed in disgust and tossed the power holster. Kane caught it easily in his left hand. With his right, he fitted the Commtact back into place behind his ear. "Now," he declared matter-of-factly, "when I tell them everything is under control, my pants won't catch on fire."

Chapter 2

Grant pushed aside a leafy bush and scanned the beach with somber dark brown eyes. Their color seemed more of an angry, dangerous black in the mottled sunlight. He held his head as if he were listening for something other than the squawking of seabirds and the boom of the surf.

He kept the stock of the heavy Barrett rifle jammed firmly against his right shoulder and his finger resting on the trigger guard. He gazed steadily through the twenty-power telescopic sight at the four figures outlined sharply against the beige sand and blue sea. The dazzling light reflecting from the ocean in a glimmering wave pattern forced him to squint.

"What's going on?"

Grant didn't remove his gaze from the scope to glance over at Brigid Baptiste, lying on her stomach beside him, but peering through a compact pair of binoculars.

"I don't really know," he replied, softening his lionlike growl of a voice to a rumble. "But it looks like my .50-cal calling card has made everybody a lot more friendly. Kane has his Sin Eater back."

Grant's long-jawed face was twisted in a scowl.

Droplets of perspiration sparkled against his coffee-brown skin like stars in a night sky. Standing four inches over six feet tall, Grant was an exceptionally broad-chested and -shouldered man, with a heavy musculature.

Gray sprinkled his short-cropped, tight-curled hair at the temples, but it didn't show in the sweeping black mustache that curved fiercely out from either side of his grim, tight-lipped mouth. He wore camou pants and an olive-drab T-shirt. His own Sin Eater was strapped securely in its power holster around his right forearm.

"And it looks like Kane is fiddling with his Commtact," Brigid replied, still peering through the eyepieces of the microbinoculars. "He doesn't seem to be seriously injured."

Her thick mane of red-gold hair fell from beneath the long-visored, olive-green cap on her head. Tied back in a ponytail, it flowed down the center of her spine nearly to her waist. Her delicate features had a set, almost feline cast to them. Her complexion, fair and lightly dusted with freckles across her nose and cheeks, held a rosy hue.

Her eyes weren't just green, but were a deep, clear emerald, glittering like jade. Tall and willowy, with long, taut legs, her slender, athletic figure reflected an unusual tensile strength. Her arms rippled with hard, toned muscle. The unflattering khaki shirt, whipcord trousers and high-topped jump boots she wore did little to detract from her undeniable femininity.

An Iver Johnson TP-9 autopistol hung in a slide-draw holster at her hip and a Copperhead close-assault subgun was slung from a strap around her shoulder.

Still peering through the rifle scope, Grant commented, "If he *is* hurt, I think he gave as good as he got."

"I don't like the looks of that big guy," Brigid breathed. "He seems a little put-out with Kane."

"Yeah," Grant grunted. "But Kane has that effect on most people, if you haven't noticed."

She grinned bleakly, continuing to study the scene through the binoculars.

Grant shifted the Barrett, pushing the rifle forward on the built-in bipod, settling the buttstock firmly in the hollow of his shoulder. Chambered to take .50-caliber ammo, the weapon possessed massive recoil, which only made sense, since it had been introduced two centuries before to take out armored targets and blast holes through concrete walls.

A burst of static filled his head and then he heard Kane's voice echoing inside his skull.

"Testing," Kane intoned. "One, two, three. Testing."

"Got you," Grant said softly. "Calibrate the aud pickup for Brigid, too."

Brigid tapped her right ear. "My Commtact is already calibrated. Reading you, Kane."

"As you may already know, I've been formally welcomed by Boss Breeze Castigleone and his chamber of commerce."

"So we see," Brigid said wryly. "Are you all right?"

"I got slapped around a little while Breeze verified

my bona fides," replied Kane, "but nothing feels like it was knocked too loose. You're here a little earlier than I figured."

"When we lost contact with you," Brigid responded, "we decided not to wait with the jeep and came down to find out what was happening. We've only been here about five minutes."

"You timed it just fine," Kane's voice said. Through the scope and the binoculars, Grant and Brigid watched him turn in their general direction and wave. "Breeze wants you to come on down. There's no reason to hide anymore."

"Is it safe?" demanded Grant.

"As far as I can tell," Kane said in a studiedly neutral tone.

"If it's not safe, if you think it's a trap," stated Brigid, "wave twice."

Kane didn't wave. Instead he said, "I think we're all right for the time being."

Brigid adjusted the focus of the binoculars, trying to bring the four figures on the shore into sharper relief. She swallowed a yawn, tired from the past few days of the hard overland journey from the Darks. Even traveling by jeep, one of the several vehicles that was part of the Cerberus rolling stock, the trip was difficult. However, she reminded herself, the journey itself was less difficult than getting word to Breeze Castigleone he had buyers for his merchandise. If the potential customer hadn't been Kane, he would have no doubt refused the meeting out of hand, suspecting that Baron Snakefish might be pulling a sting.

Brigid didn't know much about the ville of Snake-fish, or the baron who had taken its unique and grotesque name as his own, except that he had participated in the siege of Cobaltville during the so-called Imperator War. All of the nine baronies in the continent-spanning network were standardized, so there probably wasn't much to know.

However, Snakefish possessed a certain historical significance, inasmuch as it had been an important commerce center on the Cific coast in the century following skydark. Although roughly half the state of California lay beneath the sea, the region around the ville had received only a light once-over with neutron bombs. Much of the mammalian life was killed off, but many of the structures remained standing.

Several of the structures were part of a gasoline-processing complex, which in the decades following the holocaust made Snakefish one of the wealthiest villes in the country, at least by the standards of Death-lands. Other than having access to a resource that was more precious than the gold, the ville was the birth-place of a bizarre religious sect that worshiped the giant mutie rattlesnakes in the area. The religion and the source of the ville's wealth vanished at about the about same time, when sabotage caused the fuel refinery to explode. The ville itself burned to the ground, taking with it a goodly number of its two thousand inhabitants.

One of the few survivors was determined to rebuild the ville, to restore its former glory as the primary power on the far western coast. During the process, he took the name of Snakefish for himself. By the time of the Program of Unification, the new ville of Snakefish, although scarcely as prosperous as its predecessor, was a power to be reckoned with. It and its baron were absorbed into the ruling baronial oligarchy.

Grant gusted out a sigh, breaking her reverie. "It probably makes more tactical sense to drop the three of those slaggers in their tracks."

"Probably," Kane agreed inanely, his voice sounding strange, filtered as it was through the Commtact. "But it's a little difficult to cut a deal with corpses."

Brigid could sense Kane's suppressed smile even if she couldn't see it clearly. The painted woman with her ridiculous clothing made her shiver, while the huge black man with the bloody nose made her queasy. "Who are those other two?" she asked.

Kane's distant figure pointed first to the big man then to the woman. "Belevedere," he said. "Tashlyn. Breeze calls her Tasha."

There was moment's silence, then they heard Kane say, "They just want to know who they're dealing with before they come out." He paused and added, "Breeze wanted to know why I told you that."

Grant pushed himself to his knees, pulling the sniper rifle to him and folding up the bipod. "Tell him we're on our way."

He slid the rifle into its felt-lined leather carrying case and zipped it shut, then rose, angling it over a shoulder. Brigid climbed to her feet and checked her pistol to be sure it was loose enough in the holster to be drawn easily, but not so loose it would fall out if they had to start moving fast.

"Ready?" Grant asked.

She shrugged. "Not really, but when has that ever made a difference?"

Grant's lips twitched under his mustache in a fair imitation of a smile, then he pushed aside the foliage and stepped out. He and Brigid marched deliberately away from the tree line toward the four figures silhouetted against the bright blue of the Cific. The two people put on sunglasses to protect their vision from the shimmering glare.

Brigid briefly wished she and Grant had packed out more ordnance from the jeep, but she tried to convince herself that grens and other firearms wouldn't be necessary. As it was, the vehicle was parked beneath a canopy of camouflage netting nearly five miles to their rear.

Hitching her gun belt high, she asked, more or less rhetorically, "Do you think we can trust them?"

Grant countered darkly, "According to what we learned while we were in Ultima Thule, Castigleone supplied some of the material that Zakat used when he tried to loosen the Antarctic ice sheet. So what do you think?"

Kane heard both the question and response, but he wisely refrained from offering his opinion. When Grant and Brigid walked to within a score of yards of the four people, Breeze Castigleone all but ignored her, but flicked his appreciative gaze up and down Grant's massive frame.

"The boss likes big men," commented Tashlyn to no one in particular.

"And really painted-up ladies, too," Brigid murmured. "No accounting for taste."

She subvocalized only so Grant and Kane could hear her, but apparently the woman guessed her remark was disparaging and she speared Brigid with a venomous stare. Brigid, her eyes masked by the dark lenses of sunglasses, kept her expression blandly neutral.

Castigleone flashed the two newcomers a toothy, welcoming grin. "Former Magistrate Grant and ex-Archivist Brigid Baptiste, the other two components of the much-debated triumvirate of terror. It's a great honor to meet all of you."

"We're here to do business, not to be honored," Grant retorted flatly.

Breeze nodded. "Just so. But we can be civilized while we're doing it."

He turned and waved an arm toward the distant dock stretching out from the marina. Almost immediately a dinghy swung around the far end of it, riding on the swells. The faint sound of a low-powered outboard engine reached their ears. Only one man appeared to be aboard, sitting in the stern and piloting the craft in their direction. Kane estimated the boat to be around twelve feet long, just barely big enough in beam and length to accommodate the six of them.

"We need a boat to look at the merchandise?" inquired Kane suspiciously.

Castigleone smiled thinly. "We do indeed. How

else do you think I've managed to keep it hidden from Baron Snakefish's foxhounds for so long?"

"I assume you mean his Magistrates," Grant remarked.

"Of course."

The dinghy motored into the shallows, foam frothing from the prow, and the pilot cut the engine. He was a middle-aged, seam-faced man with the rawboned look of an outlander. Everyone, Castigleone included, waded out and climbed aboard the dinghy. As Kane estimated, the fit was tight, particularly after Belevedere hauled himself into the craft. Despite the cramped quarters, Kane was encouraged since almost no maneuvering room remained. Of course, he reminded himself sourly, that could turn out to be a double-edged sword.

Brigid, jammed up beside him hip and thigh, gingerly touched the contusion discoloring the right side of his head. The brine made it feel raw and sticky. "You sure you're okay?" she asked lowly.

"Just the prerequisite postambush concussion," he answered with a wry smile. "Really, I'm fine."

She returned the smile with a weary one of her own and glanced away. Kane guessed she recalled the serious head injury she had suffered less than a year before. The only visible sign of the wound that had laid her scalp open to the bone and put her in a coma for several days was a faintly red, horizontal line on her right temple that disappeared into the roots of her hair. Her recovery time had been little short of uncanny. Kane was always impressed by the woman's steel-spring resiliency.

The pilot restarted the engine with a yank of the cord and turned the boat back toward the marina. He gunned the engine, the dinghy bouncing roughly on the chop, until Breeze ordered him to ease off on the rpm.

Instead of tying up at the pier or within one of the boathouses, the dinghy rounded the berths and navigated among the derelicts. Many of the old craft were little more than algae- and barnacle-encrusted hulks. The masts of sailboats rose from the sea like a forest of defoliated trees. Other vessels appeared relatively intact and some of the larger wrecks were pressed closely together. Gangplanks made of lashed timbers joined them to one another.

The dinghy chugged under the bow of a half-sunken, rust-pimpled old steamer and pulled alongside an ancient barge. It was secured to another barge by a bridge made of welded lengths of anchor chain. The broad deck of the barge was piled high with all manner of flotsam and jetsam—sticks, seaweed, logs, old fuel barrels and just about every conceivable kind of trash.

Kane gazed speculatively at the collection of debris and his pointman's sense, his sixth sense, rang an alarm. The skin between his shoulder blades seemed to tighten, and the short hairs at the back of his neck tingled. What he called his pointman's sense was really a combined manifestation of the five he had, trained to the epitome of keenness. The pattern of garbage seemed a bit too mannered, not as haphazard as on the first, casual glance.

Looking up into the azure sky, he imagined what the graveyard of ships and the barge might look like to the pilot of a Deathbird. He decided it would look pretty much the same from the air as it did from the boat—uninhabited and uninhabitable.

The hull of the dinghy bumped against the side of the barge. Moving swiftly, without having to be ordered, Belevedere tied the boat to a stanchion and the pilot cut the engine. Breeze Castigleone gestured expansively to the barge. *"Mi casa es su casa."*

Kane didn't ask him what he meant by the cryptic comment, but Brigid inquired skeptically, "You expect us to believe you live here?"

Castigleone shrugged. "It's my oceanside resort, you might say."

Brigid, Grant and Kane clambered aboard the barge. They made no move to help Castigleone or his crew disembark, but they didn't ask for a hand up, either.

Grant surveyed the detritus on the barge's deck with his eyebrows drawn together at the bridge of his nose. He inquired, "The merchandise?"

Castigleone marched across the deck toward an upended oil drum and a tall framework of rusty angle iron. He barked, "Belevedere! Come here, boy!"

Belevedere hustled swiftly forward, falling into step behind the mustached man. Tashlyn and the dinghy's pilot lingered near the three outlanders, but Kane figured their proximity didn't derive from enjoyment of their company.

Belevedere heaved away the fuel barrel, revealing

a drum-and-winch assembly bolted to the deck. A heavy hemp hawser was wound around the drum. At the same time, Castigleone kicked aside a scattering of rotted canvas and lifted a long but slim I-beam from the deck. He fitted it in the framework as a crossbar. A block and tackle dangled from its center.

Brigid, Grant and Kane watched with keen interest as Castigleone took the end of the rope, which was tipped by a metal hook, and pulled out a dozen or so feet of slack. He threaded it through the pulley system and kneeled over a staple-shaped handle protruding from the deck.

Belevedere picked up a cold-rolled iron crank handle and inserted the flanged end into the notches at the side of a drum. At a nod from Castigleone, he began to vigorously turn it. The rope went taut and the crossbar sagged, creaking a little under a great weight.

Mystified, Grant murmured, "What the hell is this now?"

A circular steel enclosure slowly rose from below the barge deck. As Belevedere hoisted it out foot by foot, they saw that it resembled a steel cylinder about seven feet long and four feet in diameter.

Castigleone gestured, waving them over, As the three outlanders joined him, Breeze said jauntily, "You'll be among the very few who ever actually peeked into my vault of wonder."

"'Vault of wonder'?" repeated Grant caustically. "What's so wonderful about blasters and grens?"

Castigleone smiled thinly. "I suppose that depends on your definition of magic."

As the tube slowly cleared the metal collared opening in the deck, Brigid eyed it closely, noting an almost invisible seam running from top to bottom and a series of tiny hinges. She also saw that its surface was not damp or streaked with rust, so the vault's hiding place, although below the waterline, was not actually in the water.

Sweat poured down Belevedere's face as he labored, cutting runnels through the dried blood on his chin. Kane's pointman's sense refused to relax. He cast a casual over-the-shoulder glance toward Tashlyn. Her body language, her posture, telegraphed tension. She absently tapped the truncheon against the side of her leg.

It occurred to him that he hadn't tested the action of his Sin Eater's power holster since Tashlyn had returned it to him. She could have disabled the actuator mechanism while he'd lain unconscious.

He cut his eyes over to Grant. His Sin Eater was strapped securely to his right forearm, but he held the Barrett inside its zipped-up case angled over his shoulder. If circumstances changed quickly, as they often did in the Outlands, then Grant would expend precious seconds freeing up his gun hand.

The best bet if matters took an ugly turn would be Brigid Baptiste's Copperhead. Less than two feet long, with a 700-round-per-minute rate of fire, the magazine held fifteen 4.85 mm steel-jacketed rounds. The grip and trigger unit were placed in front of the breech in the "bull-pup" design, allowing for one-handed use. An optical image intensifier scope and laser autotargeter was fitted on the top of the frame. Its low recoil allowed the Copperhead to be fired in a long, devastating, full-auto burst. All of the Cerberus exiles were required to become reasonably proficient with firearms, and the lightweight "point and shoot" subguns were the easiest for the firearm-challenged to handle.

With a grunt of exertion, Belevedere hoisted the steel cylinder a foot or so clear of the deck's surface and held it in position, his biceps bulging as if they might burst. The boatman came forward and wrestled the enclosure away from the opening, and Belevedere gave the crank a half-reverse turn, bringing it to rest gently on its flat bottom.

Breeze Castigleone ran his hands over the surface. "Be prepared to have your minds staggered and your eyes dazzled."

"We better have something after all the trouble we went to," Grant growled.

Castigleone threw him a fleeting smile as he touched the cylinder. The curved side facing them swung outward on its hinges. Breeze stepped back, pulling it with him. "Abracadabra—"

Two Magistrates in full body armor stepped out of the cylinder, bores of their Sin Eaters trained directly on Brigid, Grant and Kane.

"Hey, presto," Castigleone murmured.

Chapter 3

Everybody looked at each other as if in a tableau. Kane and Grant were intimately familiar with the Magistrate polycarbonate body armor, since they had worn the molded suits themselves for many years.

Jet-black, only the small disk-shaped badge of office attached to the rounded left pectoral showed any color. The emblem, depicting a stylized crimson, balanced scale of justice superimposed over a nine-spoked wheel, symbolized the Magistrate oath to keep the wheels of justice turning in the nine baronies.

The helmet was also of molded black polycarbonate that conformed to the shape of a man's head and exposed only a portion of mouth and chin. The red-tinted visor was slightly concave. The Magistrate armor had been designed for more than strictly functional, practical reasons. The two helmeted men were symbols of awe, of fear. They looked strong, fierce, implacable and not altogether human.

Kane and Grant weren't intimidated since they had manipulated the psychology of anonymity many times in their years as hard-contact Magistrates. However, facing the hollow bores of two Sin Eaters, they respected how swiftly the weapons could spit a torrent of 9 mm hollowpoints.

As surreptitiously as he could manage, Kane flexed the tendons of his right wrist. The big-bored automatic handblaster had no trigger guards or safety, and the pistol fired immediately upon the touch of his crooked index finger. The sensitive actuator ignored all movements except the one that indicated the weapon should be drawn.

Nothing happened, as Kane had halfway expected. Either the tiny electric motor or the actuator had been disabled.

"Nobody move," announced the Magistrate on their right. His voice held no emotion, sounding like the hollow echo of distant kettle drum. "Don't even breathe deep. That includes you and your crew, Castigleone."

Kane, Brigid and Grant obeyed the order, all of them knowing that even if they squeezed off the first shots, the body armor would protect the Magistrates from serious injury.

"Back up," the Mag said, gesturing with his Sin Eater. "Keep backing up until I tell you to stop."

The three did as they were told, and the Magistrates stepped out of the enclosure. The armored man who gave the orders exuded an air of detached professionalism, not resorting to bombastic threats or gloating speeches. He was a little over medium size with the thick, square body of a man who intimately knew the ways of close and bloody combat.

Kane and Grant guessed he was probably a veteran officer of some authority. As a general rule, only inexperienced rank-and-file Mags acted like sadistic thugs, little better than the "sec man" pejorative applied to them.

"Stop now," the Magistrate said. "Castigleone, take Grant's rifle and Baptiste's Copperhead."

Kane experienced a brief surge of surprise, but he realized in retrospect it would have been more surprising if the man hadn't recognized them. He and his two friends had topped the baronies' Most Wanted lists for some time now, particularly after the assassination of Baron Ragnar nearly two years before. Tales of the renegades' exploits circulated through the Outlands, giving rise not only to rebellious thoughts but also to outright acts of resistance. To kill a baron was tantamount to killing a god and if a god could be assassinated by mortal hands, then the tyranny of the nine barons could no longer be maintained.

Breeze Castigleone opened his mouth as if to object to the Mag's order, but turned to Tashlyn. "Tasha, get their weapons and—"

"No," snapped the Magistrate, his voice rising a trifle. "I told you to do it, Pit boss."

Castigleone swallowed hard, his face paling by several shades under the tan. Reluctantly he stepped forward and took hold of the leather-encased Barrett leaning against Grant's right shoulder. Studiously avoiding eye contact. Breeze took the weapon, then moved over to Brigid. She relinquished her subgun without a murmur of protest or the flicker of an eyelash.

Castigleone slid away, gusting out a sigh of relief

that his trim body was no longer in front of two Sin
Eaters. He handed the rifle to Tashlyn but kept the
Copperhead.

"Grant, Kane," the Magistrate continued, "I want
you to remove your side arms. Just drop them."

Kane and Grant hesitated and the bore of the Mag's
pistol shifted to Brigid. "Must I make an example of
her?" His tone held an undercurrent of cold conviction. Both men instantly realized he wasn't running
a bluff.

Doing as they were told, they unbuckled the straps
and fastened the Velcro tabs on the power holsters.
They let them thump to the deck at their feet.

"Very good, gentlemen," the Magistrate said. Perspiration trickled down his cheeks from beneath his
visor. Both Grant and Kane knew from uncomfortable
experience how hot the armor and its Kevlar under-
sheathing could become in high temperatures.

"You have the advantage of us," Kane commented
mildly.

The man's mouth quirked in a half smile. "Which
is quite the feat, from what I hear. My name is Hauk.
This is Loxley." With one hand, the Mag undid the un-
derjaw locking guards of his helmet and tugged it off
his head. Loxley kept his on, as if he didn't want to
show his face regardless of how much he sweated.

Hauk's face was that of a man in the prime of his
life—a hard life. His features were regular and unex-
ceptional. If not for the deep cicatrix scar creasing his
left cheek from the corner of his gray eye to his chin,
he wouldn't have drawn any attention in a crowded

room. His blond hair was pulled back and knotted at the nape of his neck.

"Does my name mean anything to you?" he asked, his eyes darting from Grant's face to Kane.

Brigid answered the question, after swiftly reviewing her mental index file, recalling all the data she had studied about the nine baronies. As a former archivist in the Cobaltville Historical Division, Brigid's knowledge on a wide variety of subjects was profound, due in the main to her greatest asset—an eidetic, or "photographic," memory. She could instantly and totally recall in detail everything she had read, seen or experienced, which was both a blessing and a curse.

"You're the Snakefish Magistrate Division administrator," she intoned. "Or you used to be."

Hauk nodded in acknowledgment. "Very good."

Absently, Kane noted that Hauk's hair wasn't quite regulation length. But he also knew that ville division administrators were allowed a certain leeway with the rules as long as they performed their jobs to the baron's satisfaction. Hauk also looked a shade too young to be a division administrator, no more than thirty-five or forty, but then Kane had never gained a truly clear understanding of the criteria by which such transfers were granted.

Although Magistrates were legally allowed to marry and to produce legitimate offspring only when they held an administrative post, being appointed as an administrator in any of the ville divisions wasn't exactly a promotion, nor was the transfer completely based on age. The quality of service was the most important consideration. Kane could only assume that Hauk had personally involved himself in their apprehension because Baron Snakefish might have been disappointed in the quality of his service as of late.

Recalling the sinking of the baron's beloved and virtually irreplaceable CG-47 cruiser in the bay of New Edo, as well as the loss of its entire crew of Mags, Kane wasn't surprised by Hauk's presence. Although Baron Snakefish had ordered the attack on New Edo, he certainly held the Magistrate Division commander responsible for its success or failure.

Hauk continued, "You're probably wondering why a Mag Division administrator is out here, participating in the apprehension of three renegades."

"Actually," replied Grant with a remarkable mildness of tone, "I'm pretty sure we can guess."

Hauk arched a challenging eyebrow. "Do tell."

"Back during the Imperator War, we three caused you and your baron a big loss in men and ordnance. I imagine your ville's armory was pretty well cleaned out after the battle of Area 51 and the siege of Cobaltville."

Hauk's expression hardened. "The same could be said for a couple of other baronies, too."

Grant nodded in agreement. "Yeah, but I doubt any other barony suffered the loss of a predark battle cruiser with all hands. After that disaster you were either disciplined by Baron Snakefish or removed from your position. Either way, you need to get back into his good graces and there's no better way than to bring in the three of us in shackles."

Hauk spoke quietly, biting out every word as if he resented each syllable that left his lips. "You're pretty damn close. You're off a bit on a couple of points, but they're minor. Overall, you've pegged the situation correctly. I almost forgot you and Kane used to be Mags yourselves."

"We haven't," commented Kane grimly.

Since both men had spent most of their lives as Mags, forgetting wasn't likely to happen, despite how fervently they sometimes wished they could. At the onset of the Program of Unification nearly a century before, the Magistrate Divisions had been formed as a complex police machine. Kane and Grant had served as cogs in the merciless machine. They had been through the dehumanizing cruelty of Magistrate training, yet the two men had somehow, almost miraculously, managed to retain their humanity.

For the past two years, they had exercised their humanity by doing their very best to not just dismantle the machine, but to utterly destroy it and scatter the pieces to the four corners of the world.

Hauk didn't respond to Kane's remark. "I gave the specific order to have you three hunted down. That's the important thing."

"The old 'if you want something done right' thing?" Grant inquired.

"Something like that," replied Hauk.

"You weren't the first Mag Division administrator to give an order like that," Kane pointed out. "And you're not the first Mag Division administrator to come after us personally."

For the past several years, all of the nine villes in the continent-spanning network had engaged in a cooperative search for the three of them. The search had concentrated mainly in the old military redoubts scattered across the face of America. The subterranean installations, constructed two centuries before to house the most advanced scientific miracles of the day, had been sealed for generations, since the Program of Unification.

Over the past year or so, the redoubts located in ville territories had been methodically visited and inspected by the respective baron's Magistrates. More than one redoubt had shown signs of occupation, as if the quarry had known it was being sought and had moved from redoubt to redoubt to escape capture and to confuse the trail. "I can understand that Breeze got word to you about us contacting him to arrange a buy of his merchandise," Brigid said, "But I can't understand why he did it, or what he hopes to get out of it."

"Last question first since it's the easiest," Hauk retorted. He raised his gaze a trifle, looking toward where Breeze Castigleone stood behind and a little to the left of Kane. "You can field that one, slagger."

Castigleone shuffled his feet uncomfortably, cleared his throat and intoned bleakly, "My life. That's what I get out of selling you to Baron Snakefish. My life and those of my strong-arms."

"Straightforward enough," Kane declared approvingly. "And pretty much what all of us expected to hear." He stared levelly at Hauk. "What's the rest of it?"

Hauk's frozen facial muscles finally displayed a hint of emotion. His lips curled in a sneer, as he answered, "We had a Mag go renegade, Kane...that's something you should be able to relate to. Chaffee by name. When the baron was trying to restock the ville's armory—like you said, we lost a lot of ordnance over the last six months—I assigned Chaffee to inventory and restocking detail.

"He decided he didn't like the detail, didn't like being a Mag and didn't like living in the ville anymore. So he started selling arms to Breeze here, because Breeze fed him a line about arranging a new life in a new place for him."

Grant nodded in understanding. "You assigned the Mags to come after us and then you assigned Chaffee to the armory. Yeah, I can see where the baron might start wondering about your powers of judgment. Particularly when the ville's armory is involved."

Every one of the nine villes possessed a huge storage facility secured behind a massive vanadium-alloy sec door. Each was filled with enough death-dealing ordnance to outfit a midsize army. Only direct voice authorization from Baron Snakefish would allow admittance into the vault.

Each chamber contained rack after rack of assorted weaponry; everything from rifles and shotguns to pistols, mortars and rocket launchers. Crates of ammunition would be stacked to the ceiling to allow for the parking of armored assault vehicles, including Hussar Hotspurs and Hummers, not to mention disassembled Deathbirds.

Almost all of it was original issue, dating from right before skydark. The planners of the old COG—Continuity of Government—programs, had prudently recognized that, unlike food, medicine and clothing, technology—particularly weapons—if kept sheltered, would endure the test of time and last generation after generation. Arms and equipment of every sort had been placed in deep-storage locations all over the United States, within vaults filled with nitrogen gas to maintain below-freezing temperatures.

Unfortunately the COG planners hadn't foreseen the nukecaust to be such a colossal overkill that the very people the Stockpiles had been intended for would perish like all the other useless eaters. Some survivors of the nuking and their descendants had carved out lucrative careers looting and trading the contents of the Stockpiles. Hordes of exceptionally well-armed people had once rampaged across the length and breadth of the Outlands.

When the Program of Unification was instituted nearly a century before, one of the fundamental agreements had been that the people must be disarmed and the remaining Stockpiles secured. Of course, to institute this action, the barons and their security forces not only had to be better armed than the Outland hordes, but they also had to know the locations of the Stockpiles. The barons were provided with both, and far more.

Rather than address Grant's observation, Hauk lifted his left shoulder in a dismissive shrug. "Chaffee got sloppy and left a trail, which I followed to the Tartarus Pits and Breeze. He couldn't tell me where Chaffee and all the matériel had gotten to, but as perfect timing would have it, he told me Kane had just gotten word to him about being in the market for stolen ordnance. And I knew where there was Kane, I'd probably find Grant and Baptiste, too."

Brigid smiled wanly. "Yes, I'd say that *is* pretty perfect timing. For you. Pretty lousy for us."

Hauk's sneer turned into a frown. "My question is how you knew about what Breeze and Chaffee were doing."

Imitating Hauk's own negligent shrug, Kane said, "There's nothing mysterious about it. Chaffee's allies told me about Breeze's little experiment in free enterprise."

Hauk nodded. "I see. And how did you come to know Chaffee's allies? Where are they? Where is he?"

Grant rumbled, "Beyond your or anybody's reach. We were told by a reliable authority that he's dead. He was double-crossed and killed."

Hauk snorted. "That figures. And it's fitting. I have a lot more questions—a whole lot more—but they can keep until you're all in the interrogation cells on E Level."

Everyone on the deck of the barge knew the place Hauk referred to. The barony of Snakefish, as the eight others, had been consolidated by the Program of Unification into a network of city-states: walled fortresses that were almost sovereign nations. They were named after the barons who ruled them and each conformed to standardized specs and layouts—fifty-foot-high walls with Vulcan-Phalanx gun towers mounted on each intersecting corner. There was a single legal way into and out of the villes; the path was deadly to anyone who didn't have business walking it.

Inside the walls, the ville elite lived in the residential Enclaves, four multileveled towers joined by pedestrian walkways. A certain amount of predark technology was available to the elite, the so-called "high towers." Since ville society was strictly class-and-caste based, the higher a citizen's standing, the higher the residence in one of the towers. At the bottom level was the servant class; those who lived in abject squalor in the Pits, which were consciously designed as ghettos.

The residential towers were connected by major promenades to the Administrative Monolith, a massive cylinder of white stone jutting three hundred feet into the air, the tallest building in the villes.

Every level of the Administrative Monolith fulfilled a specific ville function. The base level, Epsilon, was the manufacturing facility. At the bottom of E Level there was a sealed-off section where convicted felons were held pending execution.

Although ville laws were complex, convoluted and often deliberately arbitrary, violators were never sentenced to a term of imprisonment in the cell blocks. Locking away a criminal either for rehabilitation or punishment was not part of the program. Perpetrators of small crimes, those involved in petty thefts or low-level black-marketeering in the Tartarus Pits, were sentenced to permanent exile in the Outlands.

People convicted of high crimes against the ville itself were served termination warrants and executed. If they were suspected of participating in activities that fit the baron's exceptionally loose definition of sedition, they were detained indefinitely, questioned incessantly, tortured viciously.

Rumors were whispered about prisoners in the E Level section being flayed alive, their entrails unwrapped, their bones carefully broken into many, many pieces. The practices reserved for women were particularly vile. Grant, Brigid and Kane knew the rumors had a very strong foundation in fact.

"I know I'll probably regret asking this," Kane said, "but how do you figure just the two of you will be able to get us to those cells? The ville is about 180 miles away, right?"

Loxley spoke for the first time, his voice as melodious as a wood rasp being dragged over wet gravel. "We can just fucking shoot the three of you in your heads, how about that?"

Grant smiled at him pityingly. "That'll make it a little hard to interrogate us, won't it?"

"Shut up," Hauk growled to Loxley. To Grant, he said, "It won't be a problem."

Neither Grant, Brigid nor Kane were inclined to question him further, particularly when they saw the small, cold smile crease Hauk's lips. "Signal them, Loxley."

In a loud, authoritative tone, Loxley said into his helmet comm link, "Ready for pickup. We have the packages."

Within a handful of seconds, two tiny flecks of jet-black outlined against the vast tapestry of azure appeared in the sky. The three outlanders instantly identified the waspish configuration of Deathbirds swooping from the shoreline on a direct course with the barge.

Chapter 4

Kane wasn't surprised by the sight of the Deathbirds cutting across the sky like a pair of hungry vultures. By now, it was almost de rigueur for Mags, whatever or wherever the ville, to call in air support when they thought he and his friends were cornered. It was becoming a predictable pattern, but opting for aerial travel wasn't surprising.

The black choppers were the only form of air transportation to make a comeback after the nukecaust and they were the sole property of the ville's Magistrate Divisions. Painted a matte, nonreflective black, the choppers's sleek, streamlined contours were interrupted only by the two ventral stub wings. Each wing carried a pod of missiles. The multiple barrels of the chin-mounted chain gun in its swivel turret winked dully in the sunlight.

Even though he was familiar with them, Kane couldn't deny that the Deathbird attack helicopters were frighteningly efficient pieces of machinery. They were modified AH-64 Apache attack gunships, and most of the ones in the Magistrate Division fleets had been reengineered and retrofitted dozens of times.

Thirty feet long, fifteen feet high, the maximum

speed of the insect-like choppers was 185 miles per hour. In the hands of an experienced pilot, they could maneuver like hummingbirds, up, down, sideways, backward, all very swiftly and fairly quietly. They could fly day or night in just about any weather, and the twin tail rotor blades crossed one another at fifty-five degrees to reduce engine noise.

The turboshaft engines possessed exhaust suppression ports to further silence the craft. Their exterior armor could withstand hits from high-explosive rounds up to 25 millimeters.

Nevertheless, Kane, Brigid Baptiste and Grant knew from experience that regardless of how formidable the machines were, they were still mechanisms operated by human beings. They were vulnerable to a few carefully calculated offensive maneuvers.

"Looks like you have it all covered," Brigid said conversationally, "except for what you have in mind for Breeze and his crew."

Hauk acted as if he hadn't heard. "Step out farther so the pilots can see you."

None of the three moved. Kane sensed Breeze Castigleone, Belevedere and Tashlyn becoming more tense and nervous with every inch the Deathbirds progressed. "You didn't answer the lady's question, Hauk," Kane said.

The Magistrate's lips curled back from his discolored teeth in a silent snarl and he lunged forward, driving the barrel of his Sin Eater hard into Kane's midsection. The air left his lungs in a grunt of pain and he doubled over, but by sheer force of will he kept himself from falling to his knees. He knew if he did, he'd receive a Mag-issue boot with its steel-reinforced toe in the mouth.

Squinting against the amoebae-like floaters swimming across his eyes, Kane said through gritted teeth, "There's your answer, Baptiste. Breeze and his crew are dead."

He turned his head, trying to focus on Breeze through the blur of his vision. "You didn't buy your life when you sold us out, Breeze...you just bought yourself a little time. And now that time is up. It's been pointless knowing you."

The shadows of Deathbirds crawled across the deck of the barge, intersected, converged and separated again. The spinning vanes created a down-wash, sucking up the warm air and created a stifling semivacuum, full of swirling bits of trash and loose pieces of wood.

Grant turned his head to look toward Castigleone. "You must have had a general idea that Hauk would pull something like this. Once we're aboard the Birds, this whole place will be flash-blasted—and you with it."

Hauk waved up at the choppers, and they began to drop gracefully toward the stern of the barge, about thirty feet away. The gunships came to rest on their landing skids with barely a bump. The Magistrate pushed the bent-over Kane toward them. "Go."

Kneading his midsection, Kane forced himself to straighten, gritting his teeth against the flare of pain igniting in his torso. He turned his back on Hauk and Loxley, and declared, "Breeze, you'd better make up your mind about who you want to throw in with. You don't have a lot of time to think it over."

Growling in frustrated fury, Hauk grabbed Kane by the longish hair at the back of his neck and at the same time kicked him behind the right knee. His leg buckled and he would have fallen on his face, if not for Hauk's agonizingly tight grip on his hair.

"Shut the fuck up!" he roared hoarsely. "He's not going to do anything but stand there like he's been told!"

Tashlyn, her eyes wide with fear, blurted, "Kane's right, Breeze! They'll kill us! They can't afford to let us live now—"

Hauk grimaced and turned his Sin Eater toward the woman. He tapped the trigger stud once. The sound of the shot was very loud. The 9 mm Parabellum round smacked into and through Tashlyn's lower belly, just above the top edge of her G-string.

The woman didn't cry out, but her body was jolted backward, tottering on the stilt heels of her boots. The shock of the bullet's impact traveled down her arms and sent her club twirling from her fingers. The weighted end of it struck Loxley's Sin Eater, knocking it to one side, his finger reflexively constricted on the firing stud.

A 3-round burst pounded into Hauk's armored back, the triple sledgehammer impacts staggering him. He howled in surprised pain. The polycarbonate deflected the bullets, kept them from penetrating, but it couldn't absorb all the kinetic energy. Almost all the wind was driven from his lungs.

As a horrified Loxley frantically shifted his pistol away from his superior officer, Grant hit the man's exposed chin with his left fist and kicked the man's ankle with his right foot.

Dazed and off balance, the Magistrate nearly fell right into Grant's arms. Grabbing for the swinging gun, Grant closed his right hand on the barrel and jerked it skyward. At the same time, he drove the crown of his head into Loxley's nose.

Blood spurted in crimson streams from his nostrils with such violence, droplets spattered on his helmet visor, obscuring his vision. The Magistrate careened backward, arms windmilling as he tried to keep his balance. He toppled rear-end first into the opening from which Breeze and Belevedere had drawn the metal cylinder.

As Loxley's body disappeared, Hauk managed to drag a lungful of air into his laboring chest. He blinked repeatedly against the pain haze clouding his eyes— then gaped at the hollow mouth of the derringer gripped in Breeze Castigleone fist. The bore was no more than five inches from his face.

Pulling himself up to his full height, Hauk demanded contemptuously, "And what do you plan to do with that little toy, slagger? You think I'm going to surrender?"

Breeze Castigleone shook his head. "No...I think you're going to die, you woman-killing bastard."

Hauk's eyes widened in startled comprehension when he realized the Pit boss was not bluffing. Castigleone planted the bore of the Semmering derringer under Hauk's exposed chin and squeezed the trigger.

The report, muffled as it was by flesh and bone, had a flat, lackluster quality to it. There was nothing lackluster about the effect of the .38-caliber, steel-jacketed round. It punched a path through tissue and jaw, driving up through the roof of the mouth and deep into the brain.

Hauk crumpled without a sound of surprise, pain or protest. Kane, Grant and Brigid saw the raw, crimson-edged, ragged wound where his chin had been. A sooty halo ringed the lower portion of his face. He stared upward at the bright sky without blinking.

Brigid Baptiste, although surprised by the suddenness of the Mag's murder, wasted no time in gaping at the body. Nor did she attend to Tashlyn, who writhed on the deck, doubled up around her belly wound. Spinning on a heel, she snatched her Copperhead from where Castigleone had dropped it.

She wasn't callous or even really dispassionate about the injured woman, but she had learned to prioritize over the past couple of years, particularly when her life or those of her friends might be at stake.

Kane scooped up his Sin Eater and kicked the leather-encased Barrett toward Grant. He felt terribly exposed, but the pair of Deathbirds weren't in position to hit much of anything with their onboard weapons, not even the chin-mounted miniguns. That situation could change within a couple of seconds, once the pilots recovered from the shock of Hauk's murder.

A body shifted behind the smoke-tinted foreport of the nearest Bird, and the hatch popped open. Brigid clamped her subgun to her shoulder and squeezed the trigger, spraying the chopper with 4.85 mm rounds. She was careful to fire only a couple of short 3-round bursts. If she held down the trigger, she could burn through an entire magazine in nothing flat. Sparks jumped from the metal chassis amid the clanging clamor of bullet strikes. The chopper hatch closed again.

Kane struggled to strap his Sin Eater's power holster to his forearm, at the same time watching Breeze Castigleone drop his derringer and kneel beside Tashlyn, cradling her head in his hands. Belevedere, blinking around in a daze, took up position behind him as if his huge body would serve as a bulletproof bulwark.

Tashlyn, her lips working as she mouthed silent pleas, stared up at Breeze with pain-glazed eyes. Her hands cupped her lower belly, blood bubbling out between her fingers.

Kane secured a buckle of the holster, a swift glance showing him that Tashlyn had only disconnected the spring cable from the electric motor. She had lacked the knowledge to do more extensive damage to the weapon. It was the work of only a few seconds to reconnect the cable, and he did so with feverish haste. While he worked, Baptiste kept the Magistrates penned up inside the Deathbirds with short bursts from her Copperhead. At the same time, Grant unzipped the carrying case for the Barrett.

Kane reconnected the cable in the holster mechanism and the tiny electric motor whined as he tensed his wrist tendons. Sensitive actuators activated flexible cables in the holster and snapped the Sin Eater smoothly into his waiting hand.

He felt about five times better almost immediately. Turning to Castigleone, he said, "We've got to find cover before the Birds—"

The remainder of his words were swallowed up by the sharply-pitched drone of the chopper engines as they hit high revs. First one Deathbird, then the other, lifted off from the deck of the barge, the vanes beating at the air furiously. Both inscribed high and fast trajectories across the sky. Kane fired one round apiece, but knew his snap-from-the-hip shots missed both helicopter gunships entirely.

The boatman made a shambling, clumsy run for the area on the barge where he had moored his dinghy. He hadn't crossed more than fifteen feet of deck when one of the Deathbirds rotated in the air, its chain gun opening up with a rattling roar. Little spear points of flame flickered from the spinning, multiple barrels.

A hailstorm of .50-caliber lead pounded into the man, breaking his body open, tearing away chunks of clothing, flesh and bone. Flying ribbons of blood mixed with fragments of exploding deck. As his maimed body fell, the chopper's spinning rotors carried it swiftly out of weapons range.

Grant cursed as he brought the Barrett to his shoulder. "We're their meat now."

Kane stepped over to Castigleone and Tashlyn, casting a shadow over the woman's face. She gazed up at him, started to speak, then began to vomit all over herself. She tried to turn her body to ease the spasms but she was unable to move. Castigleone held her head until the sickness passed. She gasped fitfully, and Kane knew the woman wasn't going anywhere ever again. Her spinal cord had been severed by the bullet.

"I asked you a question, Castigleone," Kane said quietly.

Breeze blinked up at Kane, tears brimming in his eyes. In a voice so choked by rage and grief it was nearly incomprehensible, he replied, "Next barge over. Get to that. You'll find all the merchandise I have left under the tarps."

Kane reached down to drag the man to his feet. "Show us."

Castigleone slapped his hand away. "I won't leave Tasha."

Looking at Tashlyn's face, Kane could only assume her complexion was ashen underneath the coating of cosmetics. However he had no difficulty reading death in her eyes.

"If you don't come with us," Kane stated flatly, "you'll die with her."

Breeze shrugged. "I'm a dead man anyway, Kane. I can't ever go back to Snakefish and I sure as shit don't want to try my luck scavenging in the Outlands."

Kane saw the two Deathbirds hovering and rocking on air currents like a pair of angry wasps. "At least you'd be alive."

"I'm not interested in just surviving," Castigleone retorted. "Even leeches can do that. Quality of life is more important to me than quantity."

Grant slid closer to Kane, rifle still at his shoulder

as he tracked the gunships through the scope. "If that's the case," he rumbled, "then your quantity is about to get pretty damn low."

Brigid picked up Grant's Sin Eater and joined them, anxiously eyeing the black choppers as they kept well out of firearm range. She was all too aware of the absence of anything to put between her and her friends and the FLIR lenses of the Birds.

"We need to start moving," she announced tightly.

Breeze nodded toward the vessel tethered to the barge. "That's your best, your only, hope. For whatever it's worth, I hope you make it."

Kane glanced dubiously toward the makeshift bridge stretching over the water, then back at the Deathbirds. They circled in a wide, figure-eight pattern, the standard prelude to a strafing run. To Castigleone he said, "They won't ignore you to follow us, you know."

"Believe it or not," Breeze Castigleone replied, "I'm not sending you ahead as stalking horses, to lead them away from me and my people."

Kane thought his words over for a moment, then stated, "For some reason, I believe you."

Grant said gruffly, "You and Brigid get going. I'll cover you."

Kane hesitated, then wheeled toward the heavy anchor chain between the two barges. The links of the chain were as thick as Grant's wrists and scabbed with rust. He hoped it would provide a degree of traction. Brigid followed at his heels, holding both her Copperhead and Grant's power holster.

"Do you want me to go first?" Kane asked her.

Brigid looked at the chain, gauging the slack, then over her shoulder at Deathbirds. "After you."

Kane didn't argue. Running on the balls of his feet, he crossed the chain bridge. It sagged only a little under his weight, but he made it to the next barge without a misstep. Brigid followed him swiftly, the sun striking flame-colored highlights from her mane of hair as it streamed out behind her.

Neither Grant nor Kane displayed much apprehension about the black choppers circling high overhead. Brigid supposed both men had been through so many harrowing experiences, as Magistrates and after, that life-threatening situations no longer upset their emotional equilibrium. But she knew her assessment was a false one, despite the fact they were hardened veterans of dozens of violent incidents. They had been raised to be killers, after all—to kill anything or anyone that threatened the security of Cobaltville.

Once she joined him on the deck of the barge, Kane shouted, "Grant! Come on, goddammit!"

Before Grant could answer, much less comply, the helicopter gunships swooped down out of the sun, rotors thundering, machine guns hammering.

Chapter 5

One of the Deathbirds took a fifty foot lead on the other. The slugs spit by its minigun scooped foaming spray out of the water in geysers. They struck the deck plates, glancing off with constellations of sparks. The rattle of impact was like a steady drumroll against tin.

Grant chambered a round from the Barrett's box magazine into the breech. His left hand cradled the thirty-three-inch barrel, while his right curled around the pistol grip backing the trigger guard. He placed his eye against the scope and centered the crosshairs of the Barrett on the Deathbird's tinted foreport, above the flickering, rotating chain gun. He preferred a clean shot at the fuselage since the massive wrecking power of the .50-caliber round would obliterate the delicate inner workings of the machine. But, under the circumstances, the cockpit and the pilot therein would have to suffice.

The second Deathbird swooped lower, pinpoints of fire rippling in a rotating sequence from the chain gun in the chin turret. The staccato reports sounded like stuttering thunderclaps. Fountains of water burst up all around the barge. Taking a deep breath and holding it, Grant called on his training, achieving a form of autohypnosis known as the Mag mind, a technique that emptied the consciousness of nonessential thoughts. It allowed his instincts to take over. The sounds around him faded to nothing, and he closed his awareness even to the presence of the steady jackhammering of the minigun.

The image of the Plexiglas port behind the scope's crosshairs leaped into clear, sharp focus. Grant carefully squeezed into the trigger pull. The crack of the sniper rifle shattered the bright morning air. He moved his shoulder expertly, taking the recoil, not otherwise shifting position. Through the sniperscope Grant saw a white, stellated star appear on the Plexiglas and the pilot's body jerk.

The gunship performed an abrupt, almost frantic figure eight from west to east, banked sharply to starboard, veered wildly up, then sharply down. The Deathbird's companion was forced to execute a clumsy evasive maneuver to avoid a midair collision. Engines whining with stress, it rose quickly.

Grant couldn't be sure if the steel-jacketed bullet had penetrated the pilot when it pierced the cockpit, but the black chopper performed a clumsy pirouette, listing from side to side. Vanes and rotors beating the air, it lost altitude, hung motionless for a moment, then dropped.

It nose-dived into the ocean at a forty-five-degree angle, barely ten yards away from the stern of the barge, the smashing impact sending up a cascading wave of foam-edged water. Two of the vanes snapped from the turboshaft with a sound like gongs being struck. The blades pinwheeled crazily in opposite directions.

While the sea still roiled and splashed over the side of the barge, Grant spun and ran across the bridge spanning the water between the two vessels.

"Bagged another Bird," Kane said with a wry smile. "Another notch for you."

"Don't buy me a drink yet," replied Grant worriedly. "One Bird can still blow the shit out of the place and us with it."

Kane eyed the circling chopper speculatively. "He may not want to risk it. His orders were to bring us in alive, not lose his machine. He could just decide to cut his losses."

"I guess it depends on how angry we made him," Brigid interjected. "Or scared."

"Hopefully he's thinking about all the awful stories he's heard about us," murmured Grant, settling the stock of the Barrett against his shoulder, but not peering through the scope. "Maybe that'll be enough to drive him off. Or he could be calling for ground support."

Looking over at the other barge, Kane saw Belevedere lift Tashlyn into his arms as if she weighed no more than a child. He followed Breeze Castigleone to where the dingy was moored. "He wasn't sending us out as stalking horses," Kane commented sourly, "but he's not about taking advantage of the window of opportunity we opened for him."

"Under the circumstances," inquired Brigid, "wouldn't you?"

Kane considered the question rhetorical, so he didn't answer it. Instead he gave the deck of the barge a quick visual inspection, noting the various shapes humped up beneath tied-down canvas coverings. He strode quickly toward the nearest one. Grant and Brigid followed him, Grant walking backward, rifle at the ready, his eyes still on the distant Deathbird. It was so high, the chopper looked like a black speck, a water beetle floating on the surface of a calm pool.

The canvas covering was attached to bolts screwed into the deck, lashed down by rope drawn through eyelets at the corners. "Let's see what kind of merchandise Breeze was selling," he said.

Pulling her folding K-Bar knife from the snap-button sheath on her belt, Brigid slashed through two of the ropes. Kane pulled the canvas away and saw what he expected to see—an array of drab, military-green plastic crates stacked on the deck. Most of them were stenciled with the insignia of the Magistrate Division.

Kane toed a long, narrow case that appeared to be the standard dimensions to contain a pair of LAW rocket launchers. He was a little surprised when it didn't budge, since most of the launchers he had handled were fairly lightweight. Taking the knife from Brigid, he inserted the point into the seal and pried. The lid popped open with surprising and suspicious ease.

Kane stared down at the contents of the case, not really understanding what he was looking at for a long moment. The container held a collection of stones, all of them about the same size, ocean-smoothed rocks obviously taken from the beach.

Kane picked one up, then another and gaped at them in angry disbelief. He husked out, "That lying son of a bitch—!"

Grant, alternating his gaze from the Deathbird to Kane's actions, snorted in derision. "Imagine that—a Pit boss who doesn't tell the truth. That's a new one."

Kane didn't respond to Grant's sarcasm. Dropping the rocks, he glared toward the other barge. Castigleone, Belevedere and Tashlyn were nowhere in sight. Faintly he heard the cough of an outboard motor coming to life.

"Castigleone wouldn't hand everything he got from Chaffee over to Zakat," he said angrily. "We saw what he brought to Thule. It didn't amount to a quarter of what would have been in the Snakefish armory."

Brigid impatiently brushed a strand of wind-tossed hair out of her face. "Breeze has the rest of it stashed someplace else, obviously. He never had any intention to selling it to us, remember."

She sounded infuriatingly calm about the double-cross, even slightly amused. Kane was not inclined to seek out the humor in the situation. Raggedly, between clenched teeth, he snarled, "We wasted nearly two weeks setting this up! The couriers we used to contact Castigleone could be in custody right now."

"They don't know the location of Cerberus," Brigid replied, not sounding very self-assured. "We used two levels of intermediary."

"Let's argue about it once we're out of here," Grant declared curtly. "I think the Bird finally made up its mind."

The three of them looked to the sky. The Deathbird swooped down over the graveyard of derelicts, its blades chopping through the air. Its landing skids were barely twenty feet above the surface of the sea, the vanes whipping wide ripples in the water.

The gunship zeroed in on the dinghy holding Breeze Castigleone and his two people. Bullets from the helicopter's chain gun sent up miniature water spouts all around the boat, then a missile scorched from the aircraft's portside pod. The air thundered and shook and lit up with a brief flare of red light. The explosion gushed upward, shooting bits of metal and wood in all directions.

"I think Breeze has been paid back for tricking us," Brigid said grimly. "Hope that makes you feel better."

Grant, Kane and Brigid watched as the Deathbird curved back around for another pass. This time the pilot skimmed even lower, the rotors beating up spuming waves across the ocean surface as it swept in to attack.

Grant brought the rifle to his shoulder, but before he squeezed the trigger, a rocket streaked from the Bird's starboard stub swing, seemingly propelled by a wavering ribbon of spark-shot smoke. He and his two friends dropped flat to the deck.

The missile fell a little short, impacting against the side of the barge instead of its deck, but it carried an incendiary warhead. It exploded in a gushing bloom of red and yellow flame. The concussion slammed painfully into their bodies and the intense heat washed over them, as if they had just opened the door to a blast furnace on full capacity.

The three of them climbed to their feet, retreating from the blaze eating hungrily at the hull of the barge. The gunship swerved up, inscribed a short but sharp parabolic curve and dived down again, chain gun hammering.

Bullets snapped all around them, sparking from the deck plates, chunking into canvas-covered cargo. Instinctively the three outlanders scattered, running in different directions. They knew that by separating, the pilot would pause for a couple of seconds while he decided which target to pursue.

Kane reached the far side of the barge and hesitated at the rail long enough to cast a glance over his shoulder. He glimpsed the gunship arrowing directly for him and he growled under his breath, "Figures."

He vaulted overboard, entering the surprisingly cold water feet first. Helped by the weight of his Sin Eater, he sank quickly, his ears registering the muffled, multiple thumps of bullets striking the water. He opened his eyes, the brine stinging them, but he saw bubble-laced streaks of the slugs punching into the sea around him. Highlighted by the jeweled glitter of sunlight, the patterns looked almost pretty.

He swam up close to the sheltering hull of the barge, scraping his shoulders against the barnacles. The Commtact hissed with a squirt of static, and Brigid's breathless voice suddenly sounded inside his head. "Kane, you need to—"

The barge suddenly shuddered brutally, shock

waves travelling through it and into the water around him. He heard the thunderclaps of detonating missiles, and the suffused sunlight acquired a flickering orange hue. The pilot of the Deathbird was apparently taking out his frustration over losing Kane against the barge—or he simply intended to flash-blast Brigid and Grant.

Pushing the fear for his friends from the forefront of his mind, Kane stroked toward the shadow of another derelict, a half-submerged sailboat. He swam under the surface, pushing jetsam and debris aside. When he reached the overhang of the boat's prow, he slowly rose, raking his hair out of his eyes.

Flame washed the deck of the barge, acrid smoke boiling up from it darkened the sky. "Grant," he said. "Baptiste! Are you all right?"

He did not receive a response from the Commtact and cold fingers of dread knotted in his chest. Treading water, he inched out from the sheltering shadow cast by the prow of the boat, scanning the sky for the Deathbird. He couldn't hear the sound of its vanes or the engines over the fierce crackle of the fire aboard the barge.

Staying close to the hulls of the wrecks, Kane swam out into the ship graveyard, working his way warily, cursing the oppressive heat and the brilliant sunlight. He heard the strong thrum of the engines and the chop of whirling blades as the Deathbird hovered over a nearby derelict. It fired a strafing burst, then moved on. He could only hope the pilot was hunting for Brigid and Grant and not just him. If they were being sought, it meant they still lived.

BRIGID RACED across the deck of the barge, the rattling of the chain gun filling her ears. She reached the stern and hazarded a swift look behind her. She saw Kane leaping overboard and realized he had the right idea, since the chopper had evidently chosen to pursue only one of them—him.

She crouched at the side, not able to see Grant because of the canvas-covered crates. Activating her Commtact, she said, "Kane, you need to—"

The ripping whoosh of a missile lancing from the Deathbird's launch tube reminded her she had more immediate concerns and galvanized her into motion. She dived over the side, plunging into the sea, dragged down by the weight of Grant's Sin Eater, her Copperhead and handgun at her belt. She felt and heard the missile barrage impact against the barge.

She stroked deep, opening her eyes despite the salty sting. The water was clear, the sun shone bright and her visibility was unimpaired. The Sin Eater was an encumbrance, so she had no choice but to let it go. She watched it spiral lazily down toward the bottom, a stream of bubbles rising in its wake.

The shadow of the hovering gunship momentarily blotted out the sunlight. She stroked steadily toward a collection of derelicts, squeezing between those positioned closely together. A couple rubbed hull to hull and she swam under those.

Only when her lungs began to ache intolerably did Brigid decide to surface. She came up slowly near a floating cluster of jetsam, parting her hair and pushing it away from her face. She tried raising Kane and Grant on the Commtacts, then she simply shouted their names. She received no response by either means, and she wondered briefly if immersion in seawater had caused the Commtacts to malfunction.

Moving to the clot of debris, she climbed atop a floating timber, carefully stood, then sprang from that to a capsized boat and over more solidly packed jetsam. Although Brigid had spent most of her life as an academic involved in scholarly pursuits, she possessed a natural, inborn agility and surefootedness. She managed to keep her balance on logs that bobbed and rolled, selecting with keen precision which piece of driftage appeared to be the most likely to support her weight.

As she gained a heavy timber, the thrumming of the Deathbird's engines and the whickering of its vanes suddenly increased in volume. Brigid instantly dropped into the water, taking a breath and ducking under the timber. She heard the chopper's minigun strafe the immediate area and could feel the timber tremble as slugs slammed into it.

She dived deep, noting the comet streaks of bubbles marking the trail of .50-caliber bullets plowing beneath the surface. Stroking determinedly for the hulk of a nearby sloop, Brigid's ears registered the sudden cessation of gunfire and engine noise.

When she reached the sloop, she surfaced, pressing against the waterlogged hull timbers. She looked around, but did not see the Deathbird hovering over the graveyard of seagoing vessels. It was a marvel that even a vestige of the marina remained, so it must have been a huge, sprawling place two centuries before.

During the nukecaust, bombs known as "earthshakers" had been triggered, seeded months before by submarines along the fault and fracture lines of the Pacific Ocean. ICBMs had pounded the Cascades from western Canada down to California. The concentrated destructive force had ripped that part of the coastline to pieces.

Tidal waves had swept inward and, pummeled by earthquakes and volcanic activity, millions of square miles of California had sunk beneath the waves. When it was over, the Cific coast was barely twenty miles from the foothills of the Sierra Nevada.

After a century, the sea had retreated somewhat, leaving islands in its wake where most of the land mass had once been. Many of the islands were the high points of old California, or regions that became more elevated with the shifting of the tectonic plates. The islands were now known as the Western Isles.

The term was a catch-all to describe a region in the Cific ocean of old and new land masses. The tectonic shifts triggered by the nukecaust dropped most of California south of the San Andreas Fault into the sea. The New Edo island chain was part of that region.

After waiting nearly a minute without hearing or seeing the Deathbird, Brigid pulled herself out of the water and through a jagged rent in the side of the sloop. She found herself standing thigh-deep inside a stateroom, its floor tilted at a thirty-degree angle. She took the opportunity to catch her breath, drinking in great lungfuls of oxygen.

Suddenly the whine of the gunship's engine penetrated the interior of her shelter like the buzz of a gigantic, furious insect. The shadow it cast floated right beside the schooner. She stepped back from the opening in the hull, but obviously the pilot knew she was inside. She doubted he would waste time raking the ship with machine-gun fire, not when an incendiary missile would turn her bolt-hole into a crematorium.

Brigid sloshed across the cabin to the door, but one glance showed her rust-eaten hinges and a warped frame. It would probably take a missile to open it. She turned to the decaying bulkhead, holding her Copperhead at hip level. Pressing down the trigger, she stitched a human-size oval into the wall. Little gouts of soggy, rotten wood mushroomed up like a series of miniature explosions. Casting a glance over her shoulder, she saw the light peeping in from the outside blotted out by a black shape.

Without decreasing her finger pressure on the trigger, she whipped the flame-blooming bore of her subgun toward it, hearing the clang and whine of ricochets.

Ceasing fire, Brigid tucked her chin against her shoulder and sprang forward, hurling her entire weight against the bulkhead. The bullet perforations broke away and the section burst outward in a scattering of waterlogged fragments.

Before she struck the water, the Deathbird spit out a missile and with an earsplitting, teeth-jarring *crack!* the warhead erupted with a flash of orange flame and black smoke in the cabin she had just occupied. The concussion slapped her sideways and flipped her into midair like a poker chip. She smashed into the water on her back, forcing the air from her lungs. Her mouth reflexively opened as she gagged for breath, and water gushed down her throat, into her nose and trickled through her sinus passages. Dazed, she felt the hellish heat of the incendiary compounds wash over her and she clawed at the water to get away from it.

A distant part of her realized that diving was a mistake since she hadn't taken a breath. She tried to stroke back to the surface. She had no idea in which direction it lay. There seemed to be nothing but blackness all around her, a chill, engulfing blackness. Over two years before she had nearly drowned in the Irish Sea, and since that day, she had developed a morbid fear, almost a phobia, of dying by water.

Brigid kicked furiously, praying she wasn't stroking for the bottom of the graveyard of ships.

Chapter 6

Grant and Kane shared almost as many differences as similarities. However both men possessed one particular personality trait so strongly they were almost twins—they hated being chased.

His heart pumping hard, Grant sprinted across the deck of the barge. He felt a surge of angry revulsion at being forced into the role of prey yet again. His many years as a Magistrate had accustomed him to being the hunter, not the hunted, even if a fellow Mag was hunting him.

As he bounded toward the aft section of the boat, Grant heard the vanes whipping the air and the engine sounds growing louder with every passing instant. He risked a backward glance. The helicopter was barely thirty feet behind him, perhaps only fifteen feet above the deck.

Flickering spear points of yellow flame danced briefly just beneath the chopper's prow. There came a rattling roar and .50-caliber bullets knocked up great gouts of planking behind him. Grant sprinted in a left-to-right zig zag. A rocket exploded against the deck and the concussive force lifted him like a child's toy and sent him cartwheeling over the side.

He plunged headlong into the water, struggling to maintain his grip on the big Barrett. Its thirty-five-pound weight dragged at his arms, threatening to pull him under like a stone. He kicked furiously, wincing at the complaints from the areas of his body where Baron Beausoliel had tortured him with an infrasound wand only a few weeks before. Blinking the stinging brine from his eyes, he watched as the black helicopter whirled, ascended and zoomed away.

Turning onto his back, rifle held crossways across his chest, Grant kicked away from the blazing barge, praying the dancing wall of fire and the corkscrewing clouds of smoke would mask his threshing movements from the Deathbird's pilot. As he kicked furiously, he saw the gunship swoop down some yards away, the multiple barrels of the minigun flickering with fire.

A storm of .50-caliber slugs punched a cross-stitch pattern in the hull of a half-sunken derelict. Grant wondered whom he was shooting at—Brigid or Kane—then the Bird moved on.

He reached a fishing trawler. Despite how clumsy it looked compared to some of the more modern craft, it floated surprisingly high in the water, supported by the wood of its hull. Although pieces had fallen out of it and the wheelhouse lacked a roof, it was a miracle the ship floated at all.

Grant experienced a little trouble boarding the craft, burdened by sodden clothes, water-filled boots and the rifle. As he clambered onto its deck he noticed traces of paint in spots not directly exposed to the sun and guessed an excellent paint and sealer had been applied to the boat right before the nukecaust. That had probably helped it survive so long, relatively intact.

Boots squishing loudly, water streaming from his clothes, Grant crossed the canted deck to the wheelhouse and crouched in the shadow it cast. Within seconds he heard the ominous thump of the gunship's rotor blades.

Grant assumed the pilot was still searching for targets, and his hands tightened around the Barrett at the notion he might be the last one the Bird sought. Carefully he inched his way to the corner of the wheelhouse and peered around. He glimpsed the aircraft bank leisurely to starboard, then a pair of rockets streaked smoking from both stub wings. Before the first two struck, another pair of missiles burst from the pods.

Fiery yellow-red eruptions and mushrooming billows of smoke rose among the collection of derelicts. The thunder of the detonations compressed his eardrums. For a moment the air itself seemed to ignite as columns of flame flashed among the hulks. The minigun started hammering again, the streams of slugs pounding through rotten, water-soaked wood at a thousand rounds per minute.

Clenching his teeth so hard his jaw muscles began to ache, Grant grasped the Deathbird pilot's strategy. He no longer cared about bringing any of the three of them to Baron Snakefish—or any part of them, for that matter. He intended to keep up the barrage on the ruins of the marina until nothing was left but a few bits of charred flotsam.

Grant checked the action of the Barrett, but he knew

the only sure way to ascertain if the rifle had been damaged by its immersion in seawater was to fire off a round. He hazarded a quick glance to fix the position of the black chopper, then he rolled from cover, crab-walking until he reached the point he wanted.

The Deathbird hovered only twenty-five yards away, less than half that in altitude. The cockpit presented only a one-quarter view to Grant, so a clean shot at the pilot wasn't an option. He centered the Barrett's sights on the tail boom assembly and squeezed the trigger.

The report was an ear-knocking boom, and the recoil slammed him backward on the slick, slanted surface of the trawler's deck. He saw flinders of metal fly away from an exhaust cowling and the helicopter sideslipped violently.

The chopper veered to starboard, the overstressed engine whining. It rotated in the air until the foreport faced Grant. He put the scope's crosshairs over the outline of the pilot and growled, "Thanks, asshole."

His finger constricted on the trigger and the firing pin struck with an impotent click on the empty chamber. His belly turning a cold flip-flop, Grant realized a fresh round had not been cycled automatically from the box magazine. He also knew the Deathbird's pilot wouldn't permit him the time to manually recycle the weapon.

The black chopper arrowed toward him, but Grant stood his ground, too angry to run or to jump overboard. The minigun's barrels flickered with fire. The lines of impact scampered across the surface of the sea, intersected with the hull of the trawler and flung wood chips and splinters in all directions.

The chain gun suddenly stopped its jackhammer rhythm. The pilot realized he had fired it dry at the same time Grant did. His course and trajectory were too steep, his altitude too low to safely launch a rocket. He would fly right into the explosion.

The gunship began a whining, straining vertical ascent, and Grant, moving on impulse, cupped the butt of the Barrett rifle in his right hand and lunged forward, right beneath the chopper. He heaved the weapon straight up.

The rifle struck the main rotor blades and the crashing of steel against steel sounded like a ton of machine parts being shaken violently inside a metal drum.

Fragments of the rifle and the vanes flew off in all directions, slicing through the mast of a half-sunken schooner and skimming across the surface of the sea like a stone cast into a pond. The Deathbird's engine faltered, keened and stuttered as the pilot frantically struggled to bring the craft back under control. When the rotor blades slowed their spin, Grant glimpsed ugly notches marring the edges.

The Deathbird inscribed a wobbling course over the trawler. Grant sprinted across the deck. A hoist-and-boom-arm assembly still stood intact. He bounded toward it, leaped, his feet gaining uncertain purchase on the tilting, slick surface of the assembly. He ran up it as if it were a ramp and, using the topmost block as a springboard, launched himself from it, arms extended.

His hands slapped against and closed around the helicopter's port-side landing gear. With a whiplash motion of his body, he swung up onto the metal rail, right arm and leg hooking around the struts. He unsealed the latch and popped it open.

The pilot turned in his seat, uttered a cry of fright and struggled with the controls. He was a relatively young man with Hispanic features. He was not wearing his helmet or even his Sin Eater. The aircraft lurched, then righted itself. The Magistrate drove a fist in a straight-arm punch at Grant. His gloved hand rebounded from the crown of Grant's head. Shots of pain streaked through his skull, but the Mag howled in pain and shook his hand furiously.

"Take us down!" Grant bellowed, reaching across him for the control stick.

"Fuck you!" Snarling in exertion and fury, the Magistrate unlatched his safety harness and half slid out of his seat, punishing Grant with a flurry of punches and kicks. His eyes were wild with rage and a mounting panic. Grant had seen men react like this before— men who, when faced with the possibility of their own deaths, turned into mindless, snarling animals.

Legs hooked around the strut of the landing skid, Grant defended himself instinctively, and the pilot's feet and fists hit only his arms, elbows and shoulders. One penetrated his guard, a side-handed blow that split the corner of his lower lip. At the sudden blaze of pain, the taste of blood, Grant lunged into the cockpit and grabbed the Magistrate around the throat in a stranglehold.

The pilot gagged and clawed at his hand, trying to prise Grant's fingers from his windpipe and larynx. With every iota of his upper body strength, Grant slammed the man's head against the side ob port. Even over the rush of wind and the chopping beat of the blades, he heard the Plexiglas crunch under the force. A small network of cracks spread from the impact point.

The Magistrate didn't lose consciousness. He threw himself from side to side, trying to break Grant's death grip on his throat. His elbow struck the control stick and the helicopter yawed and went into a prolonged, stomach-turning spin. Grant was forced to release the pilot and grasp the edges of the hatch. Beneath him he glimpsed a stretch of blue water, smoke and derelicts, all wheeling crazily.

The aircraft's spiraling descent slowed and finally ceased, a bare twenty feet above the deck of the fishing trawler. The pilot had regained control and the chopper rose again, straight up as if drawn by a celestial magnet. Grant clawed himself back into the cockpit, bracing his feet against the landing skid.

"Take us down, dammit!" he shouted.

The Magistrate's polycarbonate-shod elbow came up, slamming hard into Grant's sternum. Grant lost his balance, his feet slipping from the skid. He teetered on it, trying to tip himself forward, toward the cockpit. His groping hand found the control stick and he shoved it forward.

The chopper's nose pitched down at a sharp angle as the horizontal stabilizers were locked out. The Deathbird plummeted toward the trawler.

Grant kicked himself away from the skid, launching himself into empty air. The blue surface of the Cific sped up toward him. He didn't have the time to slip into a vertical position, and so enter the water in a dive, so he curled himself into a tight ball.

The water smashed at him, the brine stung his cut lip like liquid hellfire, but he fought to stay beneath the surface. He opened his eyes and looked up, seeing the outline of the fishing trawler only a few yards away. Within a second a hell-hued blossom of fire flared as the Deathbird crashed into the ship's deck. Tongues of flame lapped out and leaped in all directions. Pieces of ship and chopper splashed all around him. The vanes snapped from the shaft and pinwheeled away.

The remaining missiles in the pods detonated upon impact. A few of the rockets went screaming away on crazed, corkscrewing trajectories. They splashed down harmlessly in the open ocean or exploded against the hulks of vessels.

When the noisiest and most pyrotechnic aspects of the Deathbird's crash tapered away, Grant slowly rose to the surface and surveyed his surroundings. The burning, ebony hulk of the gunship lay canted at a grotesque angle on the trawler's deck. Its stub wings had been blow off by the missile detonations, and with the rotor blades missing and the tail assembly bent almost double, the chopper's fuselage looked like a giant, maimed grasshopper. Scarlet sheets of flame jumped high all around the derelicts, and a pall of smoke blurred the wrecks.

Treading water, Grant activated his Commtact but received no signal. At the top of his lungs he shouted, "Kane! Brigid!"

After a moment his ears caught a faint reply, but because of the crackle of flames he wasn't sure who had responded. He swam slowly in the direction he thought the voice had come from and yelled again, "Brigid! Kane!"

"Here!" Kane's voice sounded hoarse and breathless, as if he had just been exerting himself. "Over here!"

Breast-stroking around a clot of jetsam, Grant saw Kane and Brigid Baptiste hanging on to a long timber. She was retching, dry-heaving. Her eyes were closed, her mouth sagging open. Her shoulders shuddered, but she didn't seem to be aware of much of anything.

"I saw her go down," Kane said grimly. "I think an explosion dazed her, but I got to her in time. She probably swallowed only a gallon of the Cific."

Brigid gasped and vomited a cupful of water. She struggled to take a deep breath and opened her eyes. She stared around unfocusedly with reddened, glassy eyes and managed to husk out a question. "Status?"

Kane smiled crookedly. "We're safe for the moment. Grant clipped the Bird's wings."

Brigid shifted her clouded green gaze toward Grant. "I had to jettison your Sin Eater," she said, her voice a trifle stronger and less strangulated. "Sorry."

Grant tried to shrug but it wasn't easy while treading water. "Plenty more of them back in Cerberus."

A dozen Sin Eaters and their forearm holsters were in storage in the Cerberus redoubt. Grant and Kane had appropriated the spares a year or so before from a squad of hard-contact Mags dispatched from Cobaltville.

The squad's mission had been to investigate Redoubt Bravo to ascertain if it was inhabited. The Magistrates had been stopped and soundly defeated by Sky Dog's band of Amerindians in the flatlands bordering the foothills. Grant and Kane, instrumental in the victory, had they managed to keep their involvement concealed from the invading Mags.

The survivors of the engagement had been disarmed and allowed to go on their way, believing the Indians alone were responsible for their humiliation. Kane and Grant had taken their discarded Sin Eaters since they were murderous weapons and almost impossible for a novice to manage. Mag Division recruits were never allowed live ammunition until a tedious, six-month-long training period had been successfully completed.

Unaccustomed to blasters of any sort, Grant and Kane had feared the Indian warriors would wreak fatal havoc by experimenting with them and so had appropriated them, adding them to the Cerberus arsenal.

Kane glanced into the sky, at the smoke staining the limitless canopy of azure. It seemed strange that it was barely midmorning after all that had happened since daybreak. "Speaking of home, why don't we start back? We've got a jump on the day at least."

"You feel strong enough to get back to dry land?" Grant asked Brigid.

She smiled wanly. "I've had about all I can stand of water sports for the day."

Brigid clung to the timber while Grant and Kane pushed it ahead of them, propelling it with their kicking legs, maneuvering through the graveyard of ships.

When the shoreline became visible, Kane groused, "This mission was a complete waste of time. Instead of adding to our store of ordnance, we lost some."

"Yeah," Grant agreed gloomily. "But we cost Baron Snakefish some, too...in matériel and manpower."

Brigid coughed, cleared her throat and declared, "I don't think we or the baron lost as much as Breeze Castigleone. We ought to take a little consolation in that."

Kane turned his head and spit out a jet of seawater. His tongue felt like a strip of cured leather, the soft tissues of his throat were as abraded as if he had been gargling with sand, and his eyes stung. He knew if they couldn't find a source of fresh water to bathe in, they would be scratching at their salt-caked bodies all the way back to Montana.

"Oh, I do take it like that," he replied with icy sarcasm. "This is how I look when I'm consoled."

Grant glanced at him and grunted. "You look like shit."

"Now you're getting it," Kane said.

Brigid sighed and rolled her eyes skyward. "There are a lot worse things we could be doing, you know."

"Yeah," Kane retorted. "But they'll have to wait until I change into some dry underwear."

Chapter 7

By the time Domi trotted up the crumbling blacktop, the sun had begun to set. Long shadows lanced from the peak of the mountain towering high above her. The blazing glory of fusing sunset colors filled the sky. They should have been a beautiful sight, but the girl scarcely noticed them. Instead she glanced worriedly at the chron strapped to her wrist and quickened her pace. The full knapsack hanging from her belt bumped against her left hip. The Detonics Combat Master .45 filled a holster on her right hip, but her step was swift and sure.

Born a half-feral child of the Outland, Domi had never fallen into the habit of paying much attention to the passage of time. Her attitude toward it was simple and pragmatic. When the sky was light, it was time to wake and hunt. When it grew dark, she slept. But as dusk began to collect around the plateau, she was thinking of activities other than sleep. At such a high altitude, despite the spring growth far below in the flatlands, the frosty night winds were not kind to creatures of warm blood.

A chill breeze suddenly gusted down from the peaks and Domi shivered. She wasn't dressed for low temperatures—khaki shorts, a white tank top and nothing else. She almost never wore shoes since her feet were thickly callused on the soles. An albino, Domi was barely five feet tall and weighed every ounce of a hundred pounds. Her unruly bone-white hair was cropped close to her head, and her bright red eyes, shining like polished rubies on either side of her thin-bridged nose, lent her a ghostly aspect.

Despite the scars marring the pearly perfection of her white skin, particularly the one shaped like a starburst on her right shoulder, Domi was maverick beautiful. Her body was a liquid, symmetrical flow of curving lines, with small, pert breasts rising to sharp nipples and a flat, hard-muscled stomach extending down to the flared shape of her hips.

The old blacktop she walked was steep and treacherous. It stretched up from the foothills and plunged deeply through the Bitterroot Range before turning into a twisting, rugged hellway. It skirted dizzying abysses on one side and slid along foreboding, overhanging crags on the other. On her left, beyond the tree line, rocky ramparts plunged straight down to a tributary of the Clark Fork River nearly a thousand feet below.

The few people who lived in the region held the Bitterroot Mountain range, colloquially known as the Darks, in superstitious regard. Due to their mysteriously shadowed forests and deep, dangerous ravines, a sinister body of myths had grown up around the range. Enduring folklore about evil spirits lurking in the mountain passes to devour body and soul kept the curious and greedy from exploring too far.

There were other reasons for the sinister body of myths ascribed to the Darks, the least of them legends about ferocious, blood-freezing storms and flesh-eating fogs. Both had their basis in reality, but over the past century they had been blown out of all rational proportion. Neither Domi nor anyone else who lived in Cerberus cared to tear away the veil of frightful fable from the shrouded peaks. All the scare tales were a form of protective coloration that no amount of jack, not even ville scrip, could buy.

Domi stumbled on a loose piece of asphalt and hissed out an obscenity as she stubbed a toe. The road wound and twisted, as if its builders had followed the trail made by a giant broken-backed snake, thrashing and whipping in its death throes. She turned another bend, then topped a rise. The road widened as it entered a broad plateau.

A grim gray peak of granite shouldered the sky on the far side of the plateau. At its base gaped open the vanadium-alloy security door that led into the heart of the Cerberus redoubt.

The mountain peak concealing the Cerberus redoubt was an organized masterpiece of impenetrability and inaccessibility. Two centuries before, trained labor and the most advanced technology available had worked hand in glove to ensure that no one might even suspect it existed. For a handful of years, from the end of one millennium to the beginning of another, it had housed the primary subdivision of the Totality Concept's Overproject Whisper, Project Cerberus. The Totality Concept was the umbrella designation for

American military supersecret researches into many different arcane and eldritch sciences.

The three-level, thirty-acre Cerberus facility had come through the nukecaust more than intact. It, and most of the other Totality Concept-related redoubts, had been built according to specifications for maximum impenetrability, short of a direct hit. With its vanadium radiation shielding still in good condition, and powered by fission nuclear reactors, Cerberus could survive for at least another five hundred years. The multiton vanadium security door was already folded aside accordion-fashion as Domi crossed the tarmac. As she approached, Lakesh stepped out of it.

"I was getting a little worried," he said, a lilting East Indian accent underscoring his cultured voice. "You're overdue by about an hour."

Mohandas Lakesh Singh was a well-built man of medium height, with thick, glossy-black hair, an unlined dark olive complexion and a long, aquiline nose. He looked no older than forty-five, despite a few strands of gray streaking through his temples. In reality, he was just a year or so shy of celebrating his two hundred and fiftieth birthday.

As a youthful genius, Lakesh had been drafted into the web of conspiracy the overseers of the Totality Concept had spun during the last couple of decades of the twentieth century. As a physicist and cyberneticist, he worked for Project Cerberus, which dealt with matter transfer.

"I can take care of myself," Domi replied in her piping, childlike voice.

"With Grant, Brigid and Kane away on a mission," Lakesh said, striving for an admonishing tone, "there are very few here who are capable of finding you, if you became lost."

Domi threw him an impish grin. "You could find me easy enough if you had the right kind of motivation."

"And what might that be, young lady?" Lakesh asked with mock severity.

Domi increased her pace and threw herself into his welcoming arms. He kissed her passionately and she reciprocated, her tongue touching his. Reluctantly breaking the embrace, Lakesh asked, "How went the herb hunt?"

Domi unslung the knapsack and patted it. "Not too badly. I found a lot of useful things."

Lakesh smiled slightly. "I'm not so sure how useful Dr. DeFore will find them."

Domi shrugged as if the matter were of little importance. "It's Quavell's choice."

The sack bulged with roots, plants and herbs Domi had spent most of the day gathering in the woods. Although the infirmary of the redoubt carried a wide assortment of drugs and pharmaceuticals, the outlander girl placed more faith in natural healing agents, particularly when prenatal care was involved.

Quavell's pregnancy had already manifested a few unusual qualities, so Domi figured any and all treatments should be made available to her, not just those approved and dispensed by Reba DeFore. Domi had grown up in a primitive settlement on the banks of the Snake River in Hells Canyon, Idaho. More than once, despite her young age, she had assisted in the birth of children.

"As Quavell's physician," Lakesh said, "Dr. De-Fore might feel she should have some input."

Domi shrugged again. "Let's find out."

Lakesh followed her into the redoubt, smiling as she kissed the forefinger of her right hand and then planted the finger on the illustration of Cerberus on the wall beneath the door control. Although the official designations of all Totality Concept-related redoubts were based on the phonetic alphabet, almost no one who had ever been stationed in the facility referred to it by its official code name of Bravo. The mixture of civilian scientists and military personnel simply called it Cerberus.

One of the enlisted men with artistic aspirations went so far as to illustrate the door next to the entrance with an image of the three-headed hound that had guarded the gateway to Hades. Rather than attempt even a vaguely realistic representation, he used indelible paints to create a slavering black hell-hound with a trio of snarling heads sprouting out of an exaggeratedly muscled neck.

The neck was bound by a spiked collar, and the three jaws gaped wide open, blood and fire gushing between great fangs. In case anyone didn't grasp the meaning, he emblazoned beneath the image the single word Cerberus, wrought in overdone, ornate Gothic script.

Domi had drifted into the habit of giving the illustration, the totem of the redoubt, little greeting and farewell kisses when she passed by. Lakesh found the ritual silly but endearing.

He had found very little endearing in the past fifty years of his life. After the nukecaust, Lakesh had volunteered to be placed in cryogenic stasis in the Anthill, the largest of the Totality Concept-linked installations. Five decades before, he had been revived and drafted to serve the Program of Unification, the agenda to create the nine barons, the nine god-kings to rule the Earth. It was only after his resurrection that he had realized the horrific magnitude of the plan to conquer humanity.

Lakesh had tried many times since his resurrection to arrest the tide of extinction engulfing the human race. First had been his attempts to manipulate the human genetic samples in storage, preserved in vitro since before the nukecaust to provide the hybridization program with a supply of the best DNA. He had hoped to create an underground resistance movement of superior human beings to oppose the barons and their hidden masters, the Archon Directorate.

A revolutionary force needed a headquarters, and the Cerberus redoubt seemed the most serviceable. When Lakesh had reactivated the installation some thirty years before, the repairs he made had been minor, primarily cosmetic in nature. Over a period of time he had added an elaborate system of heat-sensing warning devices, night-vision vid cameras and motion-trigger alarms to the plateau surrounding it. He had been forced to work in secret and completely alone, so the upgrades had taken several years to complete.

The redoubt contained a frightfully well-equipped armory and two dozen self-contained apartments, a cafeteria, a decontamination center, an infirmary, a swimming pool and even detention cells on the bottom level.

The facility also had a limestone filtration system that continually recycled the complex's water supply. In a cleft on the peak, mostly hidden by the granite walls and camouflage netting, was an array of dish antennae, a transmitting tower and even a slowly revolving radar emitter.

Domi padded barefoot down the main corridor, a twenty-foot-wide passageway made of softly gleaming vanadium alloy and shaped like an arched square. Great curving ribs of metal and massive girders supported the high rock roof.

Lakesh walked beside her, noting the curious looks she received from some of the people they passed, but the glances were essentially respectful and even admiring from the men. Although the redoubt had been constructed to provide a comfortable home for well over a hundred people, it had pretty much been deserted for nearly two centuries.

When Domi, Grant, Kane and Brigid had arrived at the installation two years before, there had been only a dozen permanent residents. Like them, all of the personnel were exiles from the villes, but unlike them, the others had been brought here by Lakesh because of their training and abilities. The redoubt had suffered a number of casualties over the past couple of years, and for a long time, the Cerberus personnel were outnumbered by shadowed corridors, empty rooms and sepulchral silences.

Over the past month and a half, the corridors had bustled with life, the empty rooms filled and the silences replaced by conversation and laughter. The immigrants from the Manitius Moon base had been arriving on a fairly regular basis ever since the destination-lock code to the Luna gateway unit had been discovered. Whether the new arrivals intended to remain in the installation or to try to make separate lives for themselves in the Outlands was still an open question.

In any event, as more women arrived from the Moon colony, the redoubt's permanent male population was for the first time in the minority. Bry, Banks, Farrell, Auerbach and even the misanthropic Wegmann acted either like shy schoolboys or Mags in a gaudy house after a long patrol.

Lakesh followed Domi into the infirmary and saw that both Reba DeFore and Quavell were present in the examination room, Quavell lying on her back on one of the beds. When Lakesh realized a pelvic examination was in progress, he murmured a hasty excuse and an apology and performed a quick about-face.

DeFore, standing at the foot of the bed between Quavell's outstretched legs, called after him laughingly, "I thought we were all scientists here."

"I'm an old-fashioned boy first," Lakesh retorted over his shoulder, "and a scientist second."

As he stepped out into the corridor, Domi called after him, "Don't forget our dinner plans!"

DeFore eyed the knapsack and moved away from the bed. "What've you got there?"

A stocky, buxom woman in her early thirties, DeFore always wore her ash-blond hair pulled back from her face, intricately braided at the back of her head. Its color contrasted starkly with the deep bronze of her skin and her dark brown eyes. As usual, she was attired in the one-piece white jumpsuit most Cerberus redoubt personnel wore as duty uniforms.

Domi put the sack on a trestle table and began unpacking its contents, placing little plastic bags full of plant matter in a neat row. "Rhubarb root," she said, "goldenthread, peony root, ginger, limeflower, yarrow, dandelion leaves—"

DeFore barely managed to keep a straight face as she listened to Domi identifying the packages as she removed them. When the girl paused for breath, the medic asked dubiously, "Do you know the *materia medica* of all of those?"

Domi squinted toward her suspiciously. "The what?"

"The pharmacology," said Quavell, pushing herself to a sitting position. Her voice was soft and musical.

"The what?" Domi repeated, this time with an edge in her voice.

DeFore chuckled. "Do you know the uses all those herbs could be put to?"

Domi frowned, as if slightly insulted. "Of course I do. How about you?"

Reba DeFore's smile only widened at the hint of a challenge in Domi's voice. "Actually my knowledge might surprise you. The benefits of herbal medicine were just being rediscovered before skydark. I found a few surviving texts and read up on them."

Quavell said, "The potentials for therapeutic agents

derived from plants are immense. I personally investigated a few."

"But not for yourself, I bet," Domi commented.

Quavell nodded. "No, for the barons, for their use during their annual medical treatments."

Quavell was a hybrid, a blending of human and so-called Archon genetic material. She was small, smaller even than Domi, under five feet in height. She looked almost as young, despite her claim of being sixty-seven years old. Her huge, upslanting eyes of a clear, crystal blue dominated a face that a poetically minded man might have tried to describe as elfin, with its high, angular cheekbones.

Her lips were small, but like those of most hybrids, they curved naturally upward so that she always seemed to be on the point of smiling, even when her face was in repose. White-blond hair the texture of silk threads fell from her domed skull and curled inward at her slender shoulders. Although her beauty had the fascination of being an unhuman loveliness, she was still close enough to humanity's feminine ideal to have aroused a man sufficiently to engage in the sex act with her and impregnate her. A sleeveless white gown swallowed her petite form. It only accentuated the distended condition of her belly and the slenderness of her limbs.

DeFore said, "Did you find any?"

Quavell shook her head. "Not in the kind of quantities wherein a medicine could be distilled."

"Well, there's only one of you," Domi pointed out a little defensively. "I think what I have here will be enough."

Quavell nodded. "Hopefully. If for some reason my physical condition declines, I can be treated with naturally occurring plant remedies. I would prefer them to drugs."

Domi smiled in relief. "Glad to hear it, since drugs could have some bad effects on you and your baby, seeing as you aren't really..." She trailed off, suddenly comprehending what she was about to say, and quickly provided, "Like us. You aren't really like us."

Quavell didn't appear to be offended. "Very true. My presence here has been the cause for a number of different adaptations and adjustments on everyone's part."

"So far," said DeFore, "nothing has arisen good old human ingenuity couldn't deal with. We took care of your nutritional requirements pretty quickly."

As a hybrid, Quavell required food that was easily digestible for her simplified intestinal tract. Although Lakesh had spent a lot of time and trouble to make sure the food lockers and meat freezers of the redoubt were exceptionally well-stocked, there was very little in the way of single-cell protein microorganisms the hybrids normally ingested. Oatmeal and ice cream were improvisations, until a way to manufacture the microorganisms could be perfected. DeFore utilized a synthesization process using equipment recently taken from the Moon base. The process had so far proved successful.

Domi turned toward the door. "If you need any help grinding up the herbs, let me know. I've got to get ready for dinner."

"Are you dressing for dinner or undressing?" De-Fore asked in a silky voice.

Domi threw her an impish over-the-shoulder grin. "That depends on whether Lakesh wants dessert first or last."

After she was gone, Quavell said softly, "I envy her joie de vivre."

"She's young," DeFore said bleakly. "It won't last."

Quavell regarded her gravely. "How can you be so sure?"

DeFore gazed at her steadily for a long moment and answered softly, "Because one of the contributing factors to her joy of life is rapidly losing his. But it's not my place to let her know. That should be Lakesh's responsibility."

"Will he accept it?" Quavell inquired.

Reba DeFore shook her head and moved back to the foot of the bed. "He's the only one who can. It's his life. Or what might be left of it. Now, let's finish up your examination."

Chapter 8

Domi rolled her hips against Lakesh, her knees clasping him tight. She pressed her palms against his chest, raising herself for another deep, downward thrust.

Lakesh looked up at her, entranced by the lust showing on her beautiful, hollow-cheeked face. "Oh," Domi groaned throatily. "Don't stop, don't dare stop!"

Giving himself over to his own lust, Lakesh stroked upward, clutching her narrow waist. Domi whimpered uncontrollably with each of his long, deep lunges. The sound of her passion, her pleasure in heat, nearly drove him out of his mind as his need for his own release hammered at his skull.

Lakesh tried to pace himself, but he started driving harder and allowed his own climax to begin. When he felt Domi trembling violently, he let his body take over from his mind. He sped up the tempo of his thrusts until he was pounding into her furiously and Domi cried out sharply with each one.

A wail of ecstasy escaped Domi's lips. She sucked in her breath noisily as she ground out her final throes of orgasm against him. She shivered, her skin silvery pale in the dim light of his quarters.

"Needed that." She leaned down against Lakesh, sponging up the warmth he gave off.

Her felt her petite body pressed against him like a comfortable blanket. He wrapped his arms around her, enjoying the feeling of repletion that trickled through him.

After the final spasms finished playing through Domi's body, she pushed herself up and looked down into his eyes. He was too winded to speak. She playfully nipped the tip of his nose, then lay beside him, the small nipples of her breasts pressing into his ribs.

"I figured a man your age might already be snoring," she whispered playfully. "Thought I'd better do something to wake you up."

"You make it difficult to sleep," he said quietly, kissing the top of her tousled head. "Regardless of my age."

Her fingertips lightly traced the faint blue pattern of burst capillaries on his chest. "No pain?"

He shook his head. "No, darlingest one. I feel completely healed. Thank you for being so considerate of my rather dissipated physical condition following my encounter with Sam."

Domi's full lips compressed in an angry moue. "He tried to kill you."

Lakesh started to refute her statement, but thought better of it, not wanting to engage the girl in an argument in the aftermath of breaking his doctor-ordered period of celibacy. The fact was, Lakesh knew full well that Sam, the self-professed imperator, had not attempted to murder him during their brief standoff in India.

He still remembered with startling clarity what Sam had said to him, as he writhed in pain across the corridor floor of the Scorpia Prime's fortress: "I will concede my defeat on this occasion, Mohandas, but it's only a small move in a far larger game. But I'm the gamemaster, and it's up to me whether I'll keep you alive to contend against me another day, or kill you at a whim. I have plenty of time to make up my mind."

Months before, upon their initial meeting, Sam had restored Lakesh's physical condition to that of a man in his midforties by what seemed to be a miraculous laying on of hands.

Sam claimed he had increased Lakesh's production of two antioxidant enzymes, catalase and superoxide dismutase, and boosted his alkyglycerol level to the point where the aging process was for all intents and purposes reversed.

Only recently had Lakesh learned the precise methodology—when Sam had laid his hands on Lakesh, he had injected nanomachines into his body. The nanites were programmed to recognize and to destroy the dangerous replicators, whether they were bacteria, cancer cells or viruses. Sam's nanites performed selective destruction on the genes of DNA cells, removing the part that caused aging.

Faced with a damaged protein, a cell-repair machine first had to identify it by examining short amino acid sequences and then look up its correct structure in a database. The machine compared the protein to the blueprint, one amino acid at a time. The nanites stimulated the metabolism by resetting cellular control mechanisms.

"Hope we don't have to deal with Sam again," Domi said grimly, "or that bitch of a mother of his."

Lakesh couldn't help but smile, recalling that Sam's "bitch of a mother" was well over two hundred years old, too, and was as dependent on Sam for her restored youth and vitality as he was. He said, "I doubt we'll contend with either one of them any time in the near future. We knocked the pins out from under Sam's plan to dominate the Asian subcontinent. He'll be reassessing his resources for some time to come."

Domi stifled a yawn. "He still has a toehold in Australia. And what happens if he learns he's really Colonel Thrush?"

"Sam's true identity is still a matter of speculation," Lakesh replied, although he knew otherwise.

Testimony had indicated that Sam's mind was actually a receptacle for the mind of the loathsome Colonel C. W. Thrush. However, even if Sam served as the living storage vessel for the Thrush program, apparently he had yet to fully download all the algorithmic data and realize his true identity. Quavell had been the one to theorize that the complete Thrush entity ID was suspended in a kind of a memory buffer, with the Thrush identity compressed and not fully downloaded.

Domi murmured wordlessly either in agreement or ennui. Lakesh held her in his arms and wondered if she was dozing. Her eyes were closed, the long sweeping lashes reminding him of pine needles dusted with snow. He hoped she slept since he wanted a little time to concoct and rehearse an opening line for the information he needed to impart to her.

The results of a recent medical examination had shown that the nanites in his body were now inert. They no longer worked to maintain his metabolism at its restored levels. If Sam had exerted control over them, he had either relinquished it on his own accord as a way to punish him or the influence had been broken for another reason. Regardless of the reasons, DeFore's prognosis was that he would begin to age, but at an accelerated rate.

He'd had no choice but to agree with her gloomy diagnosis. The worst-case scenario she had offered had him back to his prerestoration physical condition inside of a year. The absolute best-case situation would be one where he simply began to age normally from the point the nanites stopped working. He knew that was an unrealistic hope at best.

Without the help of Sam's nanomachines, his body simply could not maintain its present state. In fact, the possibility existed that his cardiovascular system would not be able to withstand the strain of rapid aging and would shut down. To be fair to Domi, he knew she needed to be apprised of the circumstances, but he had trouble finding both the words and the courage.

He wasn't sure how the little albino girl would react to the prospect that their relationship could conceivably end at any moment. Suppressing a sigh, Lakesh decided to wait until he had more concrete data with which to work before addressing the issue. He would let Domi sleep and catch a nap himself.

When he felt her hand stealing toward his groin, Lakesh realized Domi had only been feigning sleep.

He sucked in a breath sharply. "Darlingest one, I don't know if I'm ready for—"

Domi giggled, her fingers running up and down the shaft of his penis. "I'll get you ready."

To his surprise and slight consternation, he realized her touch was indeed having its desired effect. He felt his organ thickening, hardening. The celibate weeks he and Domi had observed after Sam's attack had apparently had no lasting effect on his enhanced sex drive. For that, at least, he was grateful to Sam.

Domi's white-haired head moved down his torso, her soft lips planting kisses along the way. Lakesh groaned slightly in delicious anticipation of when she reached her final destination.

"Lakesh, are you there?"

Donald Bry's voice blared out of the trans-comm speaker on the wall. The surprise of hearing it, coupled with its strident urgency, was like a bucket of water drawn from a polar sea dashed onto Lakesh's genitals. Both he and Domi sat up straight in bed, voicing startled, angry cries.

"Lakesh!" Bry sounded impatient and even angry.

Turning toward the voice-activated comm, Lakesh demanded, "What is it?" It required a great deal of restraint to prevent him from adding the epithet "asshole" onto the end of his question.

"The mat-trans sensor lock is registering an anomalous signature from the Luna gateway unit." Bry's tone carried an edge of accusation, as if the situation were one of Lakesh's doing.

Lakesh frowned. "Anomalous how?"

"The molecular imaging scanners made a verification lock-on of the incoming matter stream," Bry answered, "but during the reference signal trace, we got some energy readings that the sensors don't recognize."

Domi snorted, impatient with what sounded like technobabble. Lakesh glanced over at her, regarding him petulantly. "Mr. Bry," he said coldly, "either I'm being uncharacteristically obtuse, or you're not expressing the nature of this so-called emergency very clearly."

"I didn't say it was an emergency," Bry's voice responded peevishly, "but an anomaly. Every piece of matter, whether organic or inorganic, that has ever been transported to or from our gateway here has a computer record in the database."

"Yes, yes," Lakesh said, rising from the bed and moving closer to the trans-comm, glad its transmission was audio only. "Our image processor scans for patterns corresponding to those in the record."

"Well, whoever or whatever is gating in here from the Moon colony is carrying something with a completely unrecognizable energy signature."

Interested in spite of himself, Lakesh, asked, "Who from here is on Manitius at the moment?"

"Neukirk gated there yesterday, so I suppose it could be him returning along with a couple of others. But if it is him, he's got something that's never been materialized or dematerialized in this particular unit."

"'Something,'" Lakesh repeated in a growl. "By that, do you mean it's inorganic?"

"Yes, of course," Bry shot back irritably. "I wouldn't bring it to your attention otherwise."

Lakesh, despite the fact he dearly wished to lambaste Bry with a torrent of profane invective, realized the man was only following established security protocols. Although something of an obsessive-compulsive, Bry was not an alarmist by nature.

"I'll be right there," Lakesh said. "Until then, divert the matter stream into the pattern buffer and hold it there."

"That was the first thing I did," Bry snapped. "I'm not a moron, you know."

"No," Domi half shouted, "we didn't." But the man had cut the channel and hadn't heard her.

Lakesh reached for his clothes, giving the girl an abashed smile. She returned it with a stony expression. "I'm sorry, darlingest one. This is an unusual situation so it's best I look into it."

Domi uttered a wordless noise of disgust and flopped backward onto the bed, the nipples of her small breasts pointing impudently toward the ceiling. "What about the situation you have here?"

Zipping up his bodysuit, Lakesh said, "Hopefully it won't spin out of control until I get back. I shouldn't be long."

Domi closed her eyes and said flatly, "You better not be."

Lakesh gave her nude, supine body a lingering, regretful look and left his quarters. The lights in the main corridor were dimmed as they were for eight out of every twenty-four hours to simulate nightfall. He made for the operations center, but he heard a clinking of metal from a side passageway and turned down that way. He stopped in front of an open door bearing a keypad rather than a knob.

He hesitated for just a second before entering, looking warily around the wide, low-ceilinged room. Most of the furnishings consisted of desks and computer terminals. A control console ran the length of the right-hand wall, glass-encased readouts and liquid-crystal displays flickering and flashing. A complicated network of glass tubes, beakers, retorts, Bunsen burners and microscopes covered three black-topped lab tables.

Upright panes of glass formed the left wall. A deeply recessed room stretched on the other side of the glass. Although there was no longer a reason for it, the room was dully lit by an overhead neon strip, glowing a dull red.

Despite the gleaming chromium, glass and electronic consoles, the room exuded the atmosphere of a cobwebby attic in an old abandoned house, holding the accumulated bric-a-brac of lost dreams.

"Is anyone in here?" Lakesh called.

"Just us salvagers," responded Mariah Falk's voice from a glass-walled cell.

He walked to the doorway and saw the woman kneeling in front of an open cabinet, apparently examining its contents. She greeted him with a broad, infectious smile that he couldn't help but return. Dr. Mariah Falk wasn't beautiful or young, but she was attractive. Her short, chestnut-brown hair was threaded with gray at the temples. Deep creases curved out from either side of her nose to the corners of her mouth. Dark-ringed brown eyes gazed up at him from beneath long brows that hadn't been plucked in years, if ever.

"What are you doing here, Mariah?" he asked.

She nodded to the assorted odds and ends in the cabinet. "Just checking on the kinds of materials in storage. We could move them out to a regular supply room, right? There's no reason not to find a use for this facility, now, is there? I mean, your guest is gone for good, right?"

Lakesh hesitated before saying a little sadly, "Yes, I suppose he is."

It had never occurred to him during Balam's three and a half years of imprisonment in the glass-walled cell that he would miss him when he was gone. Of course, it had never occurred to him that he would ever be gone. Lakesh hadn't thought that far ahead.

After a couple of years he had ceased to view the entity as a prisoner or as a source of information about the Archon Directorate. Instead, Balam had become a trophy, a sentient conversation piece, like a one-item freak show.

In hindsight it was fairly apparent that Balam had chosen to remain in the Cerberus redoubt for reasons of his own. He had used his psionic abilities to manipulate Banks, his former warder, into initiating a dialogue when he probably could just as easily have manipulated the man into releasing him.

"Carry on," Lakesh said, turning away.

"Wait," Mariah called after him. "You don't mind me doing this, do you?"

Lakesh smiled at her wryly. "Not at all. This room should be converted into something useful, now that we actually need the space. For a long time it served as a prison for a sentient entity. There's not need to make it a shrine now that he's gone."

Lakesh briefly considered stopping by the cafeteria and brewing a cup of green Bengali tea, but decided to put that task low on the priority list. He walked to the central control complex, the nerve center of the redoubt. The long, high-ceilinged room was filled with comp terminals and stations. The central control complex had five dedicated and eight-shared subprocessors, all linked to the mainframe behind the far wall. Two hundred years ago it had been an advanced model, carrying experimental, error-correcting microchips of such a tiny size that they even reacted to quantum fluctuations. Biochip technology had been employed when it was built, protein molecules sandwiched between microscopic glass-and-metal circuits.

On the opposite side of the operations center, an anteroom held the eight-foot-tall mat-trans chamber, rising from an elevated platform. Upright slabs of translucent, brown-hued armaglass formed six walls around it. Bright flares showed like bursts of distant heat lightning on the other side of the walls of the jump chamber. Armaglass had been manufactured in the last decades of the twentieth century from a special compound that plasticized and combined the properties of steel and glass. It was used as walls in the jump chambers to confine quantum-energy overspills. The emitter array within the platform emitted a low, steady hum as the device cycled through the materialization process.

Lakesh didn't even glance at the indicator lights of the huge Mercator relief map of the world that spanned one entire wall. Pinpoints of light shone steadily in almost every country, connected by a thin, glowing pattern of lines. They represented the Cerberus network, the locations of all functioning gateway units across the planet. The mat-trans unit on Luna wasn't represented on the map.

Half a dozen people were sitting in front of computer stations. Monitor screens flashed incomprehensible images and streams of data in machine talk. In the cool semidarkness the huge room hummed with the quietly efficient chatter of the system operators.

The control center was surprisingly well manned, particularly for the late hour, but inasmuch as the complex was the brain of the redoubt, it naturally attracted personnel from all quarters. Most of the people sitting at the various station were émigrés from the Manitius Moon base—Nora Pennick, Brewster Philboyd and two men he knew only as Marsh and Everson. The only long-term Cerberus staff members he saw were Farrell and Bry.

Marsh, a wiry man of medium height with uncombed ginger hair, manned the biolink-transponder monitor. He greeted Lakesh with a deference that he found almost embarrassing.

"The transponder signals show strong, sir," the man reported.

Lakesh glanced at the monitor screen upon which three white icons throbbed and pulsed. "So I see. And please, don't call me sir."

Everyone in the redoubt had been injected with a subcutaneous transponder that transmitted not just their general locations but heart rate, respiration, blood count and brain-wave patterns. Based on organic nano-technology, the transponder was a nonharmful radioactive chemical that bound itself to an individual's glucose and the middle layers of the epidermis. The signal was relayed to the redoubt by the Comsat, one of the two satellites to which the installation was uplinked.

The telemetry transmitted from Kane's, Brigid's and Grant's transponders scrolled upward across the screen. The computer systems recorded every byte of data sent to the Comsat and directed it to the redoubt's hidden antennae array. Sophisticated scanning filters combed through the telemetry using special human biological encoding.

The digital data stream was then routed to the console on his right, through the locational program, to precisely isolate the team's present position in time and space. The program considered and discarded thousands of possibilities within milliseconds.

"Their current locations?" Lakesh asked.

Marsh's fingers tapped a sequence into the keyboard, calling up the triangulation tracking program. A topographical map flashed onto the monitor screen, superimposing itself over the three icons. The little symbols inched across the computer-generated terrain.

"They're still on the move," Marsh said. "I guess they decided to drive straight through the night. They should be back here by the day after tomorrow if they maintain their present progress."

Lakesh nodded, gratified that Kane, Brigid and Grant were alive and, judging by the lack of spikes in the transponder signals, in good health. "Good work, friend Marsh."

"That's 'Doctor,'" Marsh ventured timidly. "I have a Ph.D. in astrophysics."

"Like just about everyone else who came down from the Moon," put in Philboyd with a dour smile. "If we all start referring to each other by our honorifics, we'll sound like a comedy routine—'calling Dr. Marsh, Dr. Singh, Dr. Philboyd.'"

Lakesh allowed himself a short chuckle and moved on to Bry's station. The slightly built man pushed his chair back from the mat-trans control console on squeaking casters. The eyes he turned toward Lakesh were reproachful beneath his tousled mass of coppery curls.

Staring at Lakesh, he said nothing, but he meaningfully tapped the monitor screen, which displayed a drop-down window. A jagged wave slid back and forth across a CGI scale. Above the window flashed the words No Match Found.

Without preamble, Lakesh declared, "That doesn't necessarily mean anything sinister or even significant has been gated here, Mr. Bry. Perhaps Neukirk is only returning with a piece of Annunaki or Danaan technology."

Before Bry could respond, Brewster Philboyd interjected sternly, "Not bloody likely."

Lakesh turned toward him. The lanky physicist stood a little over six feet tall, appearing to be all protruding elbows, kneecaps and knuckles. His thinning blond hair was swept straight back, which made his high forehead seem very high indeed. He wore a pair of black-rimmed eyeglasses. The right lens showed a spiderweb pattern of cracks.

Philboyd, like all of the scientists who had recently arrived in the Cerberus redoubt from the Manitius Moon colony, was a "freezie," postnuke slang for someone who had been placed in cryogenic stasis following the war.

"Why do you say that?" challenged Lakesh.

"Because if something new had been discovered of extraterrestrial origin," Philboyd said matter-of-factly, "particularly if it were of Annunaki manufacture, George wouldn't just beam back here with it in tow without forewarning. He knows the drill. He'd put it into decam and quarantine first."

Bry scowled up at him. Since the physicist's arrival in the redoubt, a string of tension that Lakesh attributed to professional jealousy had stretched between the two men. "Then how do you explain that?" He tapped the image of the energy signature again.

Philboyd shrugged. "I can't. It could just be a glitch in your scanner module, couldn't it? Your equipment is very old."

"It's never happened before," Bry argued, his voice rising as if he had been personally insulted.

Lakesh repressed a grin. Not too long ago he would

have taken affront at the implication his systems weren't always operating at peak efficiency. "Since the materialization cycle has already begun, we might as well let it cycle through and find out for ourselves."

Bry hesitated, then sighed and returned his attention to the keyboard of his console. He tapped in a numerical code and the steady hum from the mat-trans unit changed pitch. The droning hum climbed to a hurricane wail then dropped to inaudibility.

Lakesh and Philboyd went to the doorway of the gate room. It was unfurnished except for a long wooden table with a highly polished veneer. After a moment they heard the click of the solenoids opening and the heavy armaglass door of the jump chamber swung open on counterbalanced pivots.

George Neukirk stepped down from the platform, his eyes darting back and forth as if he were looking for someone. When they fixed on Lakesh, an expression of relief crossed his face. "Dr. Singh, you're here—good."

"Good?" Lakesh inquired. "Why good?"

Neukirk shifted to one side, away from the open door of the mat-trans unit. He put his right hand behind his back and when he brought it out again, a rail pistol was gripped within his fist. "It's good because we won't have to hunt you down. It'll save us time and just might save the lives of the people here. Would you mind sending someone to fetch your interphaser?"

Chapter 9

Lakesh had been threatened too often over the past couple of years to react with much fear. Facing the hollow bore of the rail pistol, he found himself feeling more insulted than endangered. Rather than complying with Neukirk's order or even responding to it, he instead turned his head and called into the command center, "Friend Farrell, please summon an armed security detail."

Farrell, a shaved-headed man who affected a goatee and gold hoop earring, stared at him in surprise from the enviro-ops station for a handful of seconds. He activated the public address system, half shouting, "Armed security detail to operations, stat! Armed security detail to operations!"

The man's voice echoed hollowly throughout the redoubt. A formal security force didn't exist as such in the installation. All of the personnel, including the recent Moon base émigrés, were required to become reasonably proficient with firearms, primarily the lightweight SA-80 subguns. The armed security detail Farrell summoned would be anyone who grabbed a gun from the armory and reached the control center under his or her own power.

Neukirk's weather-beaten features locked in a hard,

tight mask and he took a threatening step forward. "Do you want to die?"

"No," Lakesh replied calmly. "Do you?"

Before Neukirk could respond, Everson suddenly appeared at Lakesh's shoulder, pushing past him into the gate room. He was a black man about Neukirk's age and Lakesh was surprised by his anger. "What the hell, George! Put down that fucking gun!"

From within the jump chamber came a faint shivery vibration, a single, throbbing note as if the heavy bass string of a giant guitar had just been plucked. Lakesh felt it as a pressure against his eardrums. Everson stared intently into the mist-shrouded interior. A rippling pattern, so swift and brief it was almost subliminal, seemed to pulse from inside the unit. Lakesh was reminded of a stream of water squirting from a hose.

All comparisons to water or anything else vanished from his mind when the ripple fanned out and intersected with Everson's upper body. As if he had been slammed by an invisible locomotive, the man performed a complete somersault, his feet reversing positions with his head. For a crazed instant, he spun end-over-end in midair, making no outcry. He slammed face-first into the wall beside the doorway, a scant few inches from where Lakesh stood. He stared, shocked into immobility as Everson slid headlong down the wall with a moist, sucking sound.

When the crown of Everson's head touched the floor, he toppled limply forward, onto his back. Lakesh caught a glimpse of the man's face and bile rose up his throat in an acidic column.

Everson's mouth gaped open. From between slack, mashed lips drooled a scattering of splintered bone mixed with little scarlet bubbles. The man's teeth and very likely all the bones in his face had been completely pulverized. His eyes were sunken deep in his sockets, as if punched back into the rear of his skull.

Lakesh could only gape in mind-numbed paralysis. While the echoes of the bass note still chased themselves around the gate room, figures began rushing out of the jump chamber. They were garbed identically in drab gray armored exoskeletons. The mechanical joints clicked in a castanet-like rhythm as they swarmed all over the antechamber, taking up positions against facing walls. They appeared to be armed with a variety of hand weapons, from the pulse plasma rifles to conventional autopistols. At a quick count, Lakesh counted a baker's dozen, which comforted him somewhat. Regardless of their weaponry, the invaders were seriously outnumbered by the Cerberus personnel.

Heart thudding fast and frantic within his chest, Lakesh saw another figure shift within the gateway unit, walking through the wreaths of mist still swirling within it.

A tall, lean man stepped down from the platform, sweeping his surroundings with a superior gaze. He walked with a flat-muscled, almost tigerish arrogance that stopped just short a swagger.

He was a warrior—that much was obvious—with the look of the hawk or a great jungle cat secure in his powers. He wore a golden helmet with incurved jaw guards, the forepart inset with jewels and inscribed with cup-and-spiral glyphs.

A molded breastplate, apparently made of the same kind of material as his helmet, encased the upper half of his strangely elongated torso and bore odd, twisting, interlocking Celtic designs known as interlace. Spurs jangled at the heels of his knee-high, black leather boots, an accessory that should have struck Lakesh as absurdly superfluous, but for some reason seemed perfectly in keeping with the man who wore them.

A metal gauntlet of a gleaming silver alloy covered the man's right hand and forearm, reaching almost to the crook of his elbow.

At first, Lakesh didn't recognize him, although his translucently pale face, the blue-white hue of skim milk, struck a distant chord of recognition. Then his wide, slanted eyes flamed up with a molten orange shimmer and Lakesh knew who he was. He didn't have the time or the opportunity to speak his name.

From behind him, he heard Brewster Philboyd blurt in sheer terror, *"Maccan!"*

PHILBOYD'S STRIDENT VOICE broke the chains of shock-induced paralysis weighing down Lakesh's limbs and senses. "Who are you people?" he demanded, glad that his voice didn't quaver. "What do you want?"

The long-armed man Philboyd had identified as Maccan took another step forward, rounding the end of the table. He extended his right hand, palm outward, but not in a gesture of greeting or pacification. He stared imperiously at Lakesh, who tried but failed to return the other's fiery gaze with the same arrogant intensity.

He shifted his gaze to the man's gauntlet and felt the moisture dry in his mouth to the consistency of a dusty film. Made of a segmented metal, it bore the same Celtic labyrinthine designs as Maccan's helmet. Tiny threads of energy sparked from the fingertips, jumping from one to the other, then back again.

Inset into the palm gleamed a round, convex lens. Miniature lightning played within it. A faint pulsing pattern, like a ripple spreading out on the surface of a pond, surrounded the man's hand, apparently exuded by the lens. Despite his mounting fear, only one thing came to Lakesh's mind: the Silver Hand of Nuadhu.

Maccan glanced toward Neukirk. "So this is the scientist Lakesh, the master techsmith?" His voice was soft, melodic, holding a slight burr of an Irish brogue.

Neukirk nodded nervously, the long barrel of the rail gun in his hand trembling slightly. "This is Lakesh."

"Ah." A smile creased the man's thin lips. "Do you know who I am, Lakesh?"

Lakesh managed a nod. "I do."

"Really? Have we met?"

"No. I observed you in stasis on the Manitius colony."

"I see." The fierce molten hue of Maccan's eyes ebbed a bit. Lakesh recalled how Kane described the manner in which his eyes changed color according to his mood of the moment. "You will bring us your interphaser."

Lakesh stared at him in silence, his mind racing and wheeling with conjectures and wild speculations.

"Did you hear me?" Maccan's eyes burned hot orange again.

"Yes," Lakesh answered hastily. "Why do you want it?"

"Obey him!" snapped a sharp female voice. "Don't question him!"

Lakesh cast his eyes to the left and saw a dark-skinned, scar-faced woman with long, tawny hair knotted atop her head. Her gloved hand rested on the square butt of a Gyrojet rocket pistol sheathed in a vacuum-formed holster attached to the right thigh of her space suit.

Forcing a smile to his face, Lakesh wondered what was taking the security detail so long to arrive. Then he heard a scuff of running footfalls from the operations center and he glanced toward George Neukirk, who refused to meet his gaze. Very quietly, but very politely, he said, "You are a treacherous son of a bitch. And I'll bet you weren't much of a physicist, either."

Then he kicked himself backward, away from the doorway, elbowing Philboyd to one side in the process. He shouted, "Clear operations! Evacuate the controls!"

A cluster of people wearing white bodysuits, eight in all, raced down the aisle between computer stations, toward the gate room. He saw only two he recognized, both of them permanent Cerberus exiles—Banks and Auerbach. The other four were Moon base émigrés. All were armed with the little SA-80 subguns.

"Keep them from leaving the gate room!" Lakesh bellowed as he backed toward the main entrance. "Everybody else get out!"

The staff obeyed with surprising alacrity, rising from their stations and rushing in an orderly fashion toward the door. Lakesh noticed Bry hadn't stirred from his console and he shouted stridently, "That means you, as well, Mr. Bry! *Move!*"

Bry regarded Lakesh with a reproachful stare, then rose and did as he was told. Lakesh sighed with relief, knowing that if he himself became a casualty, at least Bry would still function as the resident technical expert. Other than himself, Bry was the only exile who possessed a knowledge of all the operational systems of the installation.

"What the fuck is going on?" Auerbach demanded as he sprinted past Lakesh toward the gate room. He was a tall, burly man with a red buzz cut. His body language telegraphed fear.

"We've got an incursion," Lakesh snapped. "Apparently from the Moon base."

"Who is it?" Banks demanded as he took up position behind a desk. A young black man with a neatly trimmed beard, he usually presented a phlegmatic facade to everyone, but now he seemed as tense as Auerbach.

Maccan appeared in the doorway, his face still creased in a thin smile, his eyes glowing with blood-red luminosity. One of the Moon base personnel, a balding man named Dylan, stumbled to a halt at the sight of him, shrieking, "Maccan!"

The helmeted man nodded his head in his direction

and thrust out his gauntleted hand. With a wave, a whorl of energy sprang from the lens on the palm of his glove and struck Dylan in the center of his chest.

The man threw back his head and screamed, his back arching as if he had received a terrific blow at the base of his spine. He dropped the subgun and clawed at his chest.

With a wet tearing of muscle, a snapping of bone and the crunching of cartilage, Dylan's left pectoral burst open and outward. His quivering heart catapulted from his chest cavity, riding a column of blood. It shot across the intervening two yards as if drawn by a magnet, slapping solidly into Maccan's open hand.

As Dylan fell limply to the floor, his face a cyanotic blue mask of agony, Maccan closed his metal-shod fingers, squeezing the man's still-beating heart as if it were a sponge.

Droplets of crimson sprayed in all directions, splattering walls and speckling monitor screens, even splashing across the slack-jawed faces of Auerbach and Marsh.

The sudden mutilation and brutal death of Dylan occurred in the space of only a few eye blinks. Maccan contemptuously hurled the crushed organ at Auerbach's feet, the gesture breaking his spell of shock. Roaring a curse, Auerbach stood up in plain view and fired his SA-80, holding the trigger down. The weapon shook and stuttered, bright brass arcing out of the ejector port.

A shimmering, hazy aura sprang up around Maccan's gauntleted hand. It seemed as wavery as a reflection distorted by disturbed water. The sharp clangs of impact filled the big room and little sparks jumped from the blurred halo surrounding his hand. The deflected rounds struck the walls and smashed into computer terminals with the keening whine of ricochets.

Auerbach emptied the subgun's clip and stood there, gaping at Maccan, who smiled at him in return, hand still raised. Softly, sorrowfully, he said, "Humans. So brave, so stupid, so easy to kill. I don't know *what* I ever saw in you."

He stabbed his hand toward the dazed Auerbach. The ripple pattern surged toward him. Lakesh bounded forward, catching Auerbach around the waist and bearing him to the floor. He heard the crash of metal and the shattering of glass as the stream of force struck a computer station.

Banks began firing his subgun at Maccan, and the other members of the detail did likewise. Lakesh and Auerbach crawled to cover behind a desk and watched Maccan fend off the full-auto fusillade with the force field projected by his gauntlet.

Sparks flew from the energy shield as the bullets struck it. Ricochets screamed and whined all around, but Lakesh felt a momentary sense of relieved triumph when he saw an expression of angry frustration cross Maccan's face. He couldn't rely on his gauntlet to deflect every round fired at him and he knew it. He backed away, retreating into the gate room.

During the brief respite, Lakesh shouted, "Everyone fall back!" Craning his neck, he saw Farrell hunched over by the interior security station. "Drop the security doors!"

Farrell's hands flew over a series of buttons on the console. A moment later the pneumatic hissing of compressed air, the squeak of gears and a sequence of heavy, booming thuds resounded from the corridor. Heavy vanadium bulkheads dropped from the ceiling and sealed off the living quarters, engineering level and main sec door from the operations center.

Alarm klaxons jangled, echoing all over the redoubt. The entrance to the control complex remained open. Lakesh glanced quizzically toward Farrell who declared, "In case we need a place to retreat to."

Lakesh thought it over, then nodded approvingly. A pair of gray armored figures appeared in the doorway to the gate room. One of them was the scar-faced woman. The Gyrojet pistol in her hand spouted a short tongue of flame and five shots ripped across the operations room in less than three seconds.

One of the tiny, flaming projectiles slammed into Marsh, in the process of running out of the control complex. It struck him in the back of the neck and bowled him off his feet, a little finger of blue fire squirting from the entrance wound as the propellant continued to burn for a second after it penetrated his body.

Another rocket round struck a member of the security detail when he rose from cover, sending him sprawling back into a chair, smoke puffing from the hole in his belly. He rolled backward a score of feet, casters squeaking. The third projectile hit only a vanadium-sheathed wall with a spurt of fire and an eruption of acrid smoke.

The fourth and fifth shots scorched their way out of the control complex and into the corridor where, Lakesh prayed, they found no targets at all. The sweetish, sickening odor of burned flesh clogged his nostrils.

Auerbach, wild-eyed with fear, cried, "We need more people, more blasters, more grens in here!"

Lakesh didn't waste time or breath telling him that he had no intention of raising the security bulkheads now. As the woman with the Gyrojet ducked out of sight, another gray-armored interloper took her place, wielding a pulse-plasma emitter, one of the so-called quartz cremators. A stream of blue-white energy whiplashed from the bell-shaped muzzle of the rifle. Auerbach dropped flat onto the floor, screaming, "Fuck!"

The torrent of incandescence engulfed a computer station and the man using it as a breastwork. He burst into flame, transformed instantly into a capering, fire-wreathed scarecrow. He staggered drunkenly, arms windmilling. Then his body exploded from within and viscera splattered the central control complex for twenty feet all around. Nausea roiled in Lakesh's belly when he heard the slap of body parts rain down around him.

"Fuck!" Auerbach screamed again, clasping his hands at the back of his head.

The big, vault-walled room suddenly shivered with a thunderclap. The invader's forehead erupted in scarlet, gelatinous spray, the top portion of his face vanishing in a bloody smear. He fell backward into the antechamber, dropping the quartz cremator, his fingers snatching futilely at the air, as if to grab handfuls of life.

Lakesh turned his head and saw Domi, a white wraith of red-eyed fury, sidling into the operations center, holding her Detonics Combat Master in a double-fisted grip. His head went momentarily light with relief. Her diminutive frame was swathed in one of Lakesh's T-shirts; and he wasn't sure if she wore anything under it. At the moment he was more interested in the Bushmaster machine pistol hanging from her neck by a lanyard and the contents of the war bag slung over her right shoulder by a strap.

She kicked a fallen SA-80 across the floor to Lakesh, who snatched it up like a beloved pet. Raising himself up behind the desk, he fired a short burst into the gate room, feeling a slight pang when he saw the rounds splat against the armaglass walls of the jump chamber. He knew the bullets wouldn't damage it, but since that particular gateway unit was the first fully debugged and operational model in the Cerberus network, he felt a strong degree of fondness for it.

The man Domi had shot was dragged out of sight and although he experienced a little guilt over the action, Lakesh fired the entire magazine at the people recovering the corpse of their comrade. He knew he hadn't hit anyone.

Domi joined him, panting, her eyes gleaming as bright and as hard as polished rubies. Her respiration came hard and fast, her breasts rising and falling under the shirt. "Damn near got squished by a sec shield. What we up against here? Who?"

"It's a little too complicated to go into now," Lakesh answered brusquely, taking the Bushmaster from her. He wasn't an expert with firearms, so he turned it over in his hands, a little dismayed by how the magazine fit into the shoulder-stock, behind the pistol grip and trigger guard.

Swiftly, Domi demonstrated how to use it, saying grimly, "Brace against forearm. Has 30-round clip. Select rate of fire here. Got it?"

Under stress, she reverted to the abbreviated mode of Outland speech. She thrust the weapon at him. "Got grens, too."

A male voice, hoarse with fury, wafted from the gate room. "Hey, you bastards! Throw down your guns and throw up your hands or we'll kill every fucking bastard in this place! Do it *now!*"

Chapter 10

Lakesh didn't know who shouted the order, but he knew it came from one of the armored interlopers, not Maccan. Dropping the empty subgun, he put the Bushmaster stock against his shoulder and groped for the trigger.

"Answer us!" the man bellowed again.

Auerbach looked over at Lakesh with fearful eyes. "What are you going to tell him?"

Domi regarded Auerbach scornfully, then she and Lakesh rose simultaneously from behind the desk. He brought the machine pistol up, putting his left wrist under the stunted barrel. A dark-haired invader peered around the door frame, swinging a rail pistol in Lakesh's direction.

Before Lakesh could fire, Domi blasted off two rounds, pounding dents in the wall next to the man's head. He pulled back out of sight. At the same time, Banks finished switching magazines on his SA-80, his eyes bright with combat heat. He rose from behind the desk, propped his elbows atop it and fired a short burst into the gate room. Answering fire erupted.

Farrell had recovered Dylan's subgun and placed it against his shoulder, opening up with a full-auto barrage into the antechamber. He ignored the bullets whistling through the air around him. The dark-haired invader showed himself again, an Uzi blazing in his right hand.

Farrell suddenly stutter-stepped as a round cored into his thigh, but he remained standing, bellowing in pain and rage. Domi cursed, shooting into the center mass of the man who had wounded Farrell, putting him down but not penetrating his armor.

Farrell half fell behind a desk, clutching at the wound in his thigh. Lakesh called to him, "Raise a shield and get to the infirmary."

The shaved-headed man glared at him. "No damn way, Lakesh. Besides, I sealed off that section first."

A movement at his peripheral vision caused Lakesh to turn. He saw Philboyd elbow-crawling between the desks, gripping an SA-80. He made his way over to Farrell, gave his leg a quick, cursory examination and said to Lakesh, "The proverbial flesh wound."

"What are you doing here?" Lakesh demanded. "I ordered the operations center evacuated."

Philboyd shrugged. "This is my home, too, now."

"Do you know any of these people?"

Philboyd shook his head. "I don't personally, but I imagine they're what's left of the Saladin's troop of Maccan followers."

"Can you tell me anything about the armor they're wearing?"

"We called them hard suits, designed for excavation out on the Lunar surface. Unless you've got some armor-piercing rounds, I don't think you'll be able to shoot through them."

Lakesh looked away, gritting his teeth in a combination of frustrated fury and fear. His back ached from crouching in such a cramped position for so long and perspiration slicked his body under his clothes, making him feel like he was wearing a bog.

He realized even if the Cerberus personnel kept Maccan and his warriors hemmed within the gate room, they had the superior weapons and their return fire was destroying precious, perhaps irreplaceable equipment. If the mainframe computer was damaged, Lakesh seriously doubted it could ever be repaired.

Domi inched closer to him, her porcelain face tight with tension. She patted the war bag. "Got some gas grens in here, couple of flash-bangs. Might discourage 'em."

Lakesh nodded, but he was dubious such actions would work. However, he knew some kind of offensive action needed to be taken soon to break the standoff. He couldn't even speculate on the uses Maccan intended for the interphaser, but he knew whatever they might be, none of them in Cerberus would benefit.

The only reasonable tactic Lakesh could perceive was to make the situation so desperate for Maccan and his people that they would be anxious to gate back to where they'd come from. However, Lakesh couldn't quite figure out how to do it without incurring more casualties.

He found himself wishing fervently Kane, Grant

and Brigid were present in the redoubt. When they worked in tandem, they seemed to exert an almost supernatural influence on the scales of chance, usually tipping them in their favor.

Almost as soon as the notion registered, like a cue, Maccan's voice floated to him. "Where is the man named Kane? Bring him to me and perhaps we can negotiate a settlement, find an alternative to all this bloodshed."

Domi and Lakesh exchanged nervous, worried glances. After a moment Lakesh called, "There's nothing to negotiate. I won't give you what you want so you might as well leave. That is the most logical option left to you if you wish to avoid more bloodshed."

Maccan's response wasn't what Lakesh had expected to hear. It was a laugh, a rising and falling titter with a hint of a sob. The laugh was full of bitterness and even a touch of contempt, underscored by a note of hysteria.

"Very well," Maccan replied, voice still suffused with laughter, "I won't bother trying to be civilized. Just bring him forward. I'd so enjoy the chance to talk with him again."

Before Lakesh could frame even a noncommittal response, Farrell rose slightly from behind the desk and shouted angrily, "Kane isn't here right now, but he'll be back directly. You could wait for him, I guess, but there won't be a point to it—because you'll be deader than fucking hell by the time he gets here!"

During Farrell's maddened rant, Lakesh waved at him, trying to persuade him to stop talking, to not give away any information. But the man was too consumed by pain and rage to have complied, even if he had paid attention to Lakesh's hand gestures.

"I suppose," came Maccan's voice, unruffled by Farrell's threat, "we'll just have to do this the hard way."

"That may not be necessary," Lakesh interjected hastily. "Perhaps a compromise is possible. What do you need the interphaser for?"

"I doubt you'd understand, my friend."

A strange lilt to Maccan's voice, an almost undetectable change in its timbre, caused Lakesh to peer over the edge of the desk. Domi followed suit, cautiously rising to eye level. At that moment one of the interlopers came charging out of the gate room, a plasma rifle held at waist level, aiming at Domi and Lakesh's position. Philboyd rose to his feet, shouting in accusation, "Lazlo, is that you?"

The man tried to alter his aim in Philboyd's direction, but Lakesh beat him to it. The Bushmaster's line of steel-jacketed death tore into the man's head, ripping bloody chunks out of his face. Staggering backward, his finger pressed convulsively on the firing plate of the quartz cremator and a crackling stream of lethal energy burst from the barrel. Raw energy came scorching out in a blue torrent.

Lakesh dropped behind the desk, pulling Domi with him. Although he had never fired one before, he knew pulse-plasma emitters were designed to operate in rarified atmospheres and so didn't pack much of a kinetic punch. They accelerated and bunched ions into a

stream, stripping the particles of their negative charge.
Since the beam wasn't subject to the effects of wind
or gravity, it cut through anything in its path.

He saw the wild plasma charge slice through one
of the Cerberus security detail, carving him open di-
agonally from right shoulder to his left hip amid a
bright shower of blood.

The invader's finger relaxed on the trigger plate of
the rifle as he dropped. By the time the armored man
hit the floor, another interloper surged out of the antechamber. It was the scar-faced woman. Without hesitation, Lakesh pulled the trigger of his Bushmaster.
The stream of 9 mm subsonic rounds caught the
woman in her armored chest with a sound like a sledge
banging repeatedly against an anvil and knocked her
back into the gate room. Even as she fell, she managed
to retrieve the quartz cremator, snatching it by the barrel.

Her reeling fall seemed to be a signal. The invaders
began a surging charge into the operations center, but
were hampered by their bulky suits and the relative
narrowness of the doorway. Only two could squeeze
through at a time, firing their weapons in a wild frenzy
as they did so. Bullets and tungsten-carbide pellets
ricocheted all over the complex. Fire was directed upward, toward the neon light strips stretched across the
high ceiling. Several of them sputtered with a shower
of sparks and went out, plunging the command center
into semidarkness.

Philboyd raised his SA-80, pulling the trigger and
unleashing 3-round bursts. Farrell lurched upright and

stood shoulder-to-shoulder with him, firing with his own weapon. The blistering full-auto cannonade hammered into the front line of invaders, knocking them off their feet, sending them staggering.

Banks picked off two men, placing shots through their unprotected heads. They flailed and went down. Two other men got their legs tangled with those casualties. Lakesh managed to drill one through the side of one skull, but his companion struggled free and scooted back into the antechamber on the seat of his hard suit.

The other invaders retreated into the gate room. Farrell continued firing, keeping the trigger pressed down, not relaxing the pressure until the magazine cycled dry. Then he howled in fury, "Get out of our house, you stupe bastards!"

When a bullet fired from the gate room came too close to him, Philboyd wrestled the man down behind the desk again, throwing Lakesh a feeble grin. "Hell of a party."

Lakesh felt a swell of pride at the bravery displayed by Farrell and Philboyd. He felt less kindly disposed toward Auerbach, who cowered under a nearby desk, hugging his knees. He heard a commotion from the antechamber. Judging by the profanity, as well as the meaty smack of blows being struck, he guessed that Maccan and his warriors had not expected such fierce resistance. Apparently, George Neukirk had underestimated the resolve of the Cerberus residents and was the target of the vituperation

"Maccan!" Lakesh called.

"Right here," came the smooth reply. "I don't plan on taking my leave anytime soon."

"That's a shame, because you're losing people," Lakesh pointed out, trying to sound reasonable and not gloating. "Far more than is necessary."

"I'm not keeping score," the man retorted breezily. "All I know is that I don't have the interphaser."

Tamping down his anger, Lakesh shouted, "You're not likely to get it, either. The part of the installation where it is kept is completely sealed off from this section. You're basically trapped."

Maccan replied with his peculiar laugh. "I don't see it that way. Besides, I've been basically trapped before. You might have heard of my prison. It's called the Moon."

"I know about your imprisonment. But from what I was told, it was self-imposed captivity."

"Indeed? From where or whom did you hear that?"

Lakesh started to tell him how he had learned of the man's life during his research into Celtic histories, specifically the areas that dealt with the Tuatha de Danaan, but he decided the time wasn't proper for a scholarly discussion.

"It doesn't matter," Lakesh answered. "Tell me why you need my interphaser."

Maccan did not answer for so long, Lakesh was on the verge of repeating the question when he retorted, "I need it to help me take a long, final look in the mirror...to step through the looking glass."

Lakesh felt his eyebrows crawl toward his hairline. "Do you even know what my interphaser is?"

The reply, when it came, was cold and heavy with contempt. "Of course I do. It's a device constructed on the scientific principles my kind gave to your people, millennia ago."

"If that's the case," Lakesh countered sarcastically, "then what do you need mine for? Build one yourself."

"I don't have the time or patience," replied Maccan.

Lakesh replayed Maccan's enigmatic comment about mirrors and looking glasses and despite the situation found himself intrigued. "Mirror symmetry," he blurted. "Is that what you're talking about? The mirror-matter theory?"

Maccan only sighed heavily. "I suggest you give me what I want, Lakesh. I'll answer all your questions then."

"That's not going to happen."

"Oh, dear Dr. Singh," Maccan announced confidently, "I believe it will."

Domi rose to her knees and a single shot fired from the gate room plucked at her hair. She didn't take cover. Her hand dipped into the war bag and brought out an Alsatex concussion grenade, a flash-bang.

Lips peeling back over her teeth in a silent snarl, Domi waited until another target presented itself. For a fleeting second a man peered around the edge of the door. Her finger caressed the trigger of her Combat Master and one round took off the top of the interloper's head in a mist of blood.

Outraged cries came from the gate room as the corpse stumbled back from the doorway. Domi lunged forward, tucking and rolling and coming up under a desk.

Lakesh focused on the doorway to the anteroom. A

tall, lean shadow shifted. "Domi!" he cried. He wasn't sure of her location.

"What!" Domi responded peevishly.

"Don't take unnecessary chances—"

Domi made no reply, but she rose and ran at an oblique angle for the gate room, the flash-bang gripped in her left hand. She slipped the spoon and hurled it through the doorway in one smooth motion. The grenade exploded a heartbeat later with an eardrum-piercing bang and an eruption of dazzling white light.

Lakesh felt the concussion even at the distance that separated him from the anteroom. Hoarse screams of people blinded and deafened interwove with the echoes of the detonation.

Domi sprinted back across the operations center as a barrage of gunfire erupted from the antechamber. The fusillade wasn't aimed at anyone in particular, but was meant only to prevent any of the Cerberus personnel from staging a concerted assault. It worked insofar as keeping Lakesh and the others hunkered down, but Domi was at risk from wild shots.

Bullets peppered the floor and the desks around Domi, ricocheting off steel and vanadium. The gunfire was like a continuous roll of thunder in the enclosed space. Banks and several other people provided the Outland girl with covering fire until she dived to safety under a table.

Wild rounds struck the Mercator projection map spanning the opposite wall, crashing into it with a metallic clangor and a tinkling of glass. The network of lit lines shorted out, the tiny bulbs exploding. A spray of bullets tore gouges in the surface of a desk very close to Lakesh's arm, splinters stinging his hand. He ducked beneath it, biting back swearwords in three languages.

The barrage continued and Lakesh saw Philboyd grimace each time another burst of shots rang out. None of the arrivals from the Moon base had combat experience and Lakesh's was exceptionally limited, as well, restricted to a couple of missions over the past year or so. He knew from the reports made by Philboyd, Nora Pennick and a few others that a paramilitary organization had held the reins of power on the Manitius colony in the years following the nukecaust.

Even before the atomic megacull scorched across the Earth, the Manitius Moon base had been divided into two castes—the support personnel with the military among them, and the scientists. The scientific staff of the base tried to come to terms with the reality that they were forever marooned, that they could not expect any rescue missions. They attempted to convince the other inhabitants of the Moon colony of the same thing, but were never quite successful.

Unsurprisingly, the scientists composed the elite of the new postnuke society and for a few years following the conflagration, the two groups had dwelled in peace, practicing a form of democracy. But over a period of time there were many disagreements, which finally boiled over into dissension. The military and support people reached the conclusion that since scientists had brought on the holocaust, they should have no part of the new lunar society.

After a few months of being essentially isolated from the rest of the colony's population, the main technical staff decided to enter cryostasis, both as a way to spare the base's resources and to hid from the new regime.

When the fire from the gate room tapered off, Lakesh raised his head and voice. "Neukirk! George Neukirk! Are you still alive in there?"

He heard a faint, surprised murmur of voices, then Neukirk shouted, "What do you want, Lakesh?"

"I want you to leave. Get back in the jump chamber and go."

"Back where we came from?" Neukirk's tone held a note of mockery.

"Not necessarily. I don't care where you go, but it's inadvisable to stay here much longer."

"Leaving before we get what we came for isn't part of the plan."

"But getting yourself and your friends killed is?" Lakesh challenged. "You've seen the armory here. We could lob high-explosive grenades in there, or use rocket launchers on you any time we cared to. Did you tell Maccan about that?"

Lakesh spoke the truth about the matériel available in the Cerberus armory. The big room was jammed with glass-fronted cases holding M-16 A-1 assault rifles, SA-80 subguns and Heckler & Koch VP-70 semiautomatic pistols complete with holsters and belts. Bazookas, tripod-mounted M-249 machine guns and LAWs lined the walls, as well as several crates of grenades. Every piece of ordnance and hardware, from the smallest-caliber handblaster to the biggest-bore M-79 grenade launcher, was in perfect condition.

All of the armament was of predark manufacture. Caches of matériel had been laid down in hermetically sealed Continuity of Government installations before the nukecaust. Protected from the ravages of the environment, nearly every piece of munitions and hardware was as pristine as the day it rolled off the assembly line. Over a period of years Lakesh had smuggled out all of the weaponry from the largest COG facility, the Anthill in South Dakota.

Neukirk responded with a derisive laugh. "You could do that, but you won't."

Lakesh tightened his hands on the Bushmaster. "And why not?"

"I don't doubt that if Grant or Kane or even Baptiste were here, they'd agree to a collateral-damage tactic like that. But they're gone and that's why I chose this time to act. Didn't that occur to you?"

Angrily, Lakesh shouted, "Why the hell are you so sure I won't take the same action as they would?"

"A couple of reasons." Neukirk's voice purred with patronizing amusement. "First of all, you're a humanitarian. Secondarily, you'd risk destroying your life's work."

"My jump chamber?" Lakesh demanded incredulously. "Don't be ridiculous."

Despite his tone, Lakesh did take a great deal pride in the Cerberus mat-trans unit, since it was the first one built after the prototypes. It had served as the basic template for all the others that followed.

"Not just that," Neukirk retorted impatiently. "The entire redoubt and everyone in it. By the time you drive us out or kill us, Cerberus will be useless to you, either as a sanctuary or a home. By the time we're done, we'll turn it into a mortuary. I can guarantee that."

"You crazy son of bitch!" an enraged Philboyd yelled. "Why are you doing this? All of us who were trapped on the Moon are finally back on Earth. We have a chance for a future—"

"This isn't the kind of future any of us want!" a sharp female voice shouted. "You destroyed what we had going up on the colony!"

"All you had going for you," Philboyd shot back, "was an insane suicide pact, struck between a couple of insane aliens who thought they were gods!"

Lakesh didn't involve himself in the argument. The situation was definitely a stalemate, but he didn't doubt George Neukirk's conviction. He had also accurately gauged Lakesh's feelings about the Cerberus redoubt and the people in it.

He heard a short, warning hiss from where Domi had taken cover and he peered around the corner of the desk. She had removed a CS gas canister from her war bag and held it up, eyebrows raised toward him meaningfully. He shook his head, indicating she should wait.

The girl scowled at him and shook her head in response, rising to her feet. She sidled along the wall toward the doorway. Lakesh watched her progress, a chill hand of dread stroking the base of his spine. He also felt more than a little angry. He seriously doubted

Domi would have so blatantly disobeyed an order from either Kane or Grant under like circumstances.

Maccan's voice cut through Philboyd's and Neukirk's argument. "Enough of this! Decide on a course of action, Lakesh! My followers and I have nothing to lose, therefore everything to fight for. Give me what I want or prepare to wade in blood—yours *and* mine."

Chapter 11

Lakesh waved frantically to Domi, shaking his head and mouthing, "No!" Domi merely narrowed her eyes, pinched away the gas gren's pin and hurled it with a looping overarm throw. It passed through the doorway, trailing a little stream of acrid vapor. When it struck the floor beyond, it erupted with a loud pop and spewed a billowing plume of white smoke. Almost immediately the gate room was engulfed by clouds of roiling vapor.

Yells and shouted commands became incomprehensible as the gas seared eyes, lungs and nostrils. The interlopers coughed and gagged, groping for whiffs of fresh air. Two of them opened up with their autoblasters at the doorway. One of them raked the ceiling, blowing out more of the light strips. Gloom shrouded almost all of the operations center.

Lakesh could barely see flame wreathing the stuttering muzzles through the blinding smoke, but the bullets smashed into the computer stations, chips of plastic and shards of glass flying in all directions. Slugs bounced from the walls beating a drumroll on the vanadium alloy sheathing. Banks, Farrell, Philboyd and the other defenders didn't return fire. They ducked down behind their shelters.

Dark shapes shifted through the planes of gas, fanning out of the gate room. The chemical vapors wafted into the command center, and Lakesh heard Domi cough then choke as she tried to suppress it.

The result Lakesh feared became a reality when the invaders used the CS gas cloud as a screen to cover their charge into the operations complex. The security detail triggered their weapons, but those nearest to the gate room coughed and gagged as they inhaled the gas, their eyes tearing from the touch of it.

Lakesh rose from behind the desk, but he didn't fire his Bushmaster, fearful of hitting Domi. Squinting against the chemical fog, he saw that the invaders wore rebreathers, transparent respiration masks that covered their nostrils and mouths with goggles to protect their eyes. Slender flexible tubes corkscrewed from the lower edges of the mask and stretched to epaulets on their shoulders. He guessed the epaulets contained small emergency oxygen tanks.

The billowing cloud of vapor dimmed the few overhead lights still shedding illumination, so it was almost impossible to track the invaders. Banks, Philboyd and a few others squeezed off several rounds from their SA-80s, shooting into the cloud at different angles, trying to bring the shifting shadows into target acquisition.

Lakesh glimpsed Domi dropping her Combat Master's sights over one of the armored men lunging out of the gate room. She squeezed the trigger. The bullet slammed through the back of the interloper's head, jerking him forward like a puppet on a string.

The next barrage of rounds from the surviving invaders crashed into a computer station, tearing metal loose and sending sparks cascading high into the air. Cursing, Lakesh shifted his weapon, targeting a man's upper body He squeezed the trigger of his machine pistol, firing it one-handed.

The three bullets hit the man in the shoulder and spun him around like a top. Lakesh missed with his next burst, then fired again, hitting the man above the neckline of his breastplate, crushing the spine and ripping out his throat in a geyser of blood.

A bullet whipped past Lakesh's face, and he felt rather than heard the little slap of displaced air. It had missed him by no more than an inch and it had come from the general direction of the security detail.

"Cease fire!" he shouted. "You'll hit each other! Cease fire—"

Lakesh inhaled a bit of gas and for a handful of seconds he bent over the desk, gagging himself blind. Through the jiggling, burning water in his eyes, he caught glimpses of shapes moving through the billowing chemical vapors, spreading out all over the command center.

Dropping to all fours, Lakesh breathed through his throat. His eyes leaked tears and he felt sick to his stomach. He crawled forward, toward the main entrance. An invader having as much trouble seeing as the defenders stumbled to a stop no more than three feet away. He caught sight of Lakesh and brought his assault rifle to his shoulder. Lakesh lifted the Bushmaster first, firing a 3-round burst, the bullets hammering into his chest and knocking him down, flares sparking from the impact points.

Farrell shouted, trying to organize a flanking maneuver, but his words clogged in his throat as he succumbed to a coughing fit. Autofire drove the defenders back, the rounds tearing through desks and computer terminals. Another invader crossed Lakesh's blurry line of vision and he fired. The armor stopped the rounds and most of the blunt trauma, but the zigzag line of bullets stitched the man from hip to shoulder, sending him staggering out of sight.

A brilliant blue flash pulsed in the room, synchronized with the characteristic crackle of the quartz cremator. Lakesh shouted for everyone to get down. He heard a brief scream, then a mushy explosion. He bit back a cry of horror when he felt something hot and wet slap the back of his neck.

Crawling quickly, he made it to the door, but before going out into the corridor he called Domi's name several times. He received no response. By the sound of it, the battle had resolved itself into a hand-to-hand slugging match. Cries of pain, half-gagged curses, the crash of bodies slamming into furniture and the meaty impact of flesh against flesh replaced gunshots.

Slowly he rose, squinting through the vapors. Shadow shapes shifted all around him, and he drove the butt of the Bushmaster at one. He missed and nearly fell. Then a rush of bodies knocked him sprawling out into the corridor. He lost his grip on his machine gun, hearing it clatter out of reach. Metal-shod knees pressed into his stomach and a pair of large, gloved hands closed around his neck and squeezed.

Lakesh heaved, bucked and twisted, blinking back tears to see a distorted face bobbing over him. The interloper was by far the stronger and he easily resisted each of Lakesh's efforts to throw him off. Lakesh hammered at him with his fists, but he struck only his armored chest.

"I got 'im!" the man crowed in triumph. "I got Lakesh!"

The deep-throated boom of Domi's Combat Master reverberated from the operations complex. A crimson spray erupted from the bridge of the invader's nose. His grip around Lakesh's neck loosened, and he slowly slid to one side. Elbowing the dead weight from his body, Lakesh rolled away and got to his feet.

From what he could see through the gas-shrouded murk, the command center was engulfed by screaming chaos. He couldn't discern who was who. He turned, scanning the floor for his Bushmaster. Two yards from the entrance to operations, the passageway was bisected on both sides by the security bulkheads. Before he could locate his weapon, he heard Domi's voice rising wild and shrill. He caught only a fragmented glimpse of her using her knees and elbows to break free of an invader's grasp. Then a gloved hand chopped at the side of her neck and she dropped out of sight.

Concern for the girl making him reckless, Lakesh bounded back into the operations center. He had taken only a few steps when a hand closed around his neck from behind, squeezing with an agonizing pressure. His nervous system was almost overwhelmed by the sudden pain. He clawed at the wrist but his fingernails scraped futilely on metal segments. He felt a round object pressing against the base of his skull and realized instantly it was the lens on the palm of Maccan's gauntlet.

Panicky images of his skull exploding filled his mind, and he struggled madly to pry Maccan's alloy-shod fingers apart. He back-kicked desperately. Maccan's hand mercilessly crushed tendon, muscle and ligaments against his vertebrae. Distantly, with a detached sense of horror, he heard the dry creak of bone.

Through clenched teeth he forced himself to husk out, "Don't dare kill me—never figure out how to operate interphaser—"

Maccan snorted, either in amusement or disgust, and flung Lakesh aside as if he weighed no more than a dummy filled with straw. He landed on his left side, the impact knocking what little breath he had left out through his nostrils and mouth. He lay where he had been tossed, his face against the littered floor of the operations room, trying to cough, to move, to breathe. He heard and felt glass crunching beneath him. He gasped in lungfuls of the gas-tainted air, choked and gasped again. His head throbbed in cadence with his pulse. The world spun and tilted around him.

Then voices were snarling, shouting and cursing all around him. Rough hands hauled him to his feet.

Lakesh blinked his eyes against the chemical-induced tears swimming in them. All he could see in the smoky murk was the gray armor of the invader's hard suits. He found himself standing in the center of a tight circle of foes.

He couldn't help but smile in grim satisfaction when he noticed the smallness of the circle. He counted only three of the hard-suited invaders. His people had acquitted themselves well—more than well, in exemplary fashion, despite the fact that he saw only Philboyd and Banks standing up. He assumed Auerbach still cowered beneath a desk and hadn't been spied.

"What's so fuckin' funny?" a furious male voice shouted.

Lakesh looked at the man, white with rage and humiliation, and said nothing. But his smile widened. The back of the invader's hand smacked across Lakesh's mouth, his teeth cutting into his lower lip. He reeled backward and spit crimson at the man's feet.

Maccan strode to him, his eyes glowing like red-hot coals. Their crimson intensity put Lakesh in mind of the mouths of furnaces—or apertures to Hell. "Raise the security shields."

Lakesh turned his smile into a smirk, despite the pain it caused him. "Blow it out your ass."

Maccan's eyes widened and Lakesh felt his throat constrict. He suddenly remembered Maccan's psionic assault on Kane and he steeled himself to receive a telepathic attack. Instead, the helmeted man turned away and made a short, sharp gesture with his gauntleted hand. "Bring her, Shayd."

The scar-faced woman stalked forward, dragging a struggling Domi. Her respiration mask was missing and the flesh around her left eye was puffy, fast swelling shut. Judging by her bare-toothed grimace of anger, she held Domi responsible. She twisted both of the girl's arms in painful hammerlocks, holding her hands up between her shoulder blades. The girl refused to cry out or to meet Lakesh's eyes. Tension coiled in the pit of his belly.

"Raise the security shields," Maccan repeated. He sounded almost bored. "Please."

Lakesh refused to answer, keeping his face impassive.

Maccan smiled coldly, then stepped over to Domi, extended his gauntlet-clad right hand, positioning it close to her head, fingers spread wide. Tiny skeins of electricity sizzled along the fingers, and Domi's eyes followed their thready arcs.

"I knew men like you of old," Maccan stated conversationally. "Warriors, noble chieftains of a brave people. You would rather die than betray their trust or bow to torture."

Maccan paused, his smile widening to a wolfish grin, exposing only the edges of his teeth. "But to stand by and watch pain inflicted on one of those who are under your protection—" He made a tsk-tsk sound of pity and shook his head sorrowfully.

With the deliberate swiftness of a striking snake, Maccan's hand darted forward and clasped the upper portion of Domi's head, the round lens pressing against her forehead. Her white face twisted, contorted, lips writhing back over her teeth in a silent shriek. She squeezed her eyes shut as a ripple spread over her piquant features. Her petite form shuddered violently. Lakesh received the distinct impression she was too consumed by agony to even scream. Blood suddenly sprayed from both delicate nostrils.

Lakesh strained against the arms holding him. "Enough, damn you! Stop! I'll do what you want! *Stop!*"

Maccan didn't remove his hand. He continued to grin at Lakesh as Domi's body went into spasms. Her eyes rolled back into her head, showing only the whites. Saliva drooled from her slack lips, mixing with the blood streaming from her nose and over her chin.

Lakesh threw himself against the arms pinioning him but was unable to break their grip. He knew Maccan's device was disrupting Domi's molecular structure, breaking it down, battering every bone, organ and cell in her body. In a matter of seconds, Domi would be dead.

"Stop!" Lakesh roared, his voice hoarse with anguish. "I give you my word—I'll do whatever you say!"

Maccan nodded graciously, as if he had finally heard the words he wanted to hear and pulled his hand away from Domi's head. She slumped forward, sagging limply in Shayd's hands, her head lolling loosely on her neck. Maccan said, "You may let her go now. I think both she and Lakesh have been made more tractable."

Shayd released her hammerlock on Domi and allowed the girl to fall heavily to the floor. She lay unmoving, curled up in a ball. Lakesh stared at her, barely able to form words due to the terror clouding his mind. He could scarcely detect signs of respiration. "Will she be all right?"

"I really couldn't say," Maccan answered dismissively. "Now, for the third and final time—open the security shields."

Lakesh squinted through the thinning clouds of vapor until he saw Banks standing with the bore of a rail pistol pressed against the side of his head. Neukirk held the weapon. "Friend Banks," Lakesh said wearily, "if you will do as Maccan demands, I will be very appreciative."

Banks cut his eyes sideways, glaring at Neukirk. He seemed to be on the verge of arguing, then he wheeled away from the rail gun and marched to an intact computer station. He tapped a numerical sequence into a keyboard, and within a few seconds came the squeak and creak of hydraulics as the bulkheads began to rise.

Maccan cautiously peered around the edge of the doorway, looking both ways. A burst of gunfire filled the corridor with a staccato drumming. A spark jumped from the top of his helmet and he hastily withdrew his head. With a rueful smile creasing his lips, he touched the small dent on his headpiece with his left hand. His eyes acquired a deep yellow hue.

"Some of your people are lying in wait for us," Maccan said softly.

"I'm not surprised," Lakesh retorted.

Gesturing to the woman called Shayd, then over to Neukirk, Maccan snapped, "Once Lakesh and I are out, if you hear anything remotely resembling a gunshot, kill everyone in here, then go through the rest of this place. Kill every person you see—man, woman, child or otherwise."

He swept his gauntleted hand imperiously toward the prone body of Domi. "Starting with her."

Shayd touched the welt around her eye and flashed Lakesh a savage grin. "Be happy to."

Maccan beckoned to Lakesh with a forefinger to join him at the doorway. When he did, Maccan placed his right hand on the back of his neck. The pent-up energies pulsing within the lens felt like a weak static discharge playing up and down his spine. "Instruct your people to let us pass unmolested. Otherwise you will live just long enough to know the hostages here have been put to painful deaths."

Lakesh swallowed hard and nodded in agreement. He allowed Maccan to push him out into the passageway. Almost immediately he heard the metallic clatter of firearms being raised, from his left and right. Looking to the left, he glimpsed Wegmann, the slightly built, balding engineer, positioned at a corner, sighting down a rifle. On his right, he saw at least three other gun barrels protruding from around a bend in the corridor.

"I've made an agreement with our visitors," Lakesh announced loudly. He despised the way the acoustics in the passageway seemed to amplify the tremor in his voice. "I'm taking him to the workroom and then we'll be returning here, whereupon he and his companions will leave."

In a low voice, he inquired, "You *will* leave, right?"

The corners of Maccan's lips quirked in a smile. "Of course."

They began walking down the wide corridor, adopting a casual gait as if they were just two friends out for a stroll. Maccan's spurs made a jingling, somewhat nerve-racking accompaniment to their footfalls. Maccan did not speak and at first Lakesh was just as glad.

They passed a quartet of redoubt personnel. Lakesh was dismayed, but not overly surprised to see DeFore standing among them. She followed their progress with angry eyes and the barrel of a Colt Scamp machine pistol.

"Say the word, Lakesh," she breathed. "Say it and I'll drop him."

Metal-encased fingers tightened on his neck, and Lakesh winced. Between clenched teeth, he said, "This is Maccan. You remember what Brigid, Kane and Grant had to say about him."

The medic's eyes widened, the anger suddenly displaced by fear. She lowered her weapon and stepped back, allowing them to pass. She asked, "Does anyone need medical attention?"

"Too damn many," Lakesh replied bleakly. "Thanks to our visitor."

As they continued down the corridor, Maccan commented, "Ah, this reputation of mine gets out of hand now and then."

"Do you think so?" Lakesh asked with mock innocence. "I'd say it's richly deserved."

Maccan shrugged. "Perhaps. Sometimes it's to my advantage, other times it can be a damn nuisance. But if you'd known me two thousand years ago—"

"I probably would have found you just as intolerably obnoxious as I do now."

Fire seemed to ripple out of the gauntlet lens, a force that streaked along the length of his spine. For a sliver of an instant Lakesh had the impression of being stung simultaneously by a hundred wasps, all up and down the buttons of his backbone. The flaming agony seemed to erupt from the nerve roots outward. The pain vanished immediately, before he could drag enough breath to cry out.

"Understand?" Maccan asked him in a low tone, sibilant with menace.

Lakesh said quietly, "Understood."

The gauntlet patted the back of his head. "Good boy."

They turned a corner and entered the workroom adjacent to the armory. Rows of drafting tables with T-squares hanging from their sides lined one wall.

Maccan removed his hand from the back of Lakesh's neck. "Show me your miraculous device."

Lakesh walked to a long, low trestle table and pointed to an object that resembled a very squat, broad-based pyramid made of smooth, dark metal. Side panels were open and revealed a confusing mass of circuit boards and microprocessors gleaming within. The pyramid was barely one foot in overall width, its height not exceeding ten inches. From the base protruded a small power unit and a keypad.

Maccan eyed it critically, crossing his arms over his chest. "So this is your interphaser."

"Interphaser Version 2.0," Lakesh corrected.

"It's what brought you to the Moon." It was a question rather than a statement. Lakesh didn't feel like responding to it one way or the other. He had spoken the truth.

The interphaser was the second version of a device that evolved from the Totality Concept's Project Cerberus. More than two years before, he had constructed a small device on the same scientific principle as the mat-trans inducers, an interphaser designed to interact with naturally occurring quantum vortices. Theoretically, the interphaser opened dimensional rifts much like the gateways, but instead of the rifts being pathways through linear space, Lakesh had envisioned them as a method to travel through the gaps in normal space time.

The interphaser had not functioned according to its design and was lost on its first mission. Much later, a situation arose that showed him the wisdom of building a second, improved model.

A mission a few months ago had brought Brigid Baptiste, Kane and Grant to a Totality Concept installation, the primary Operation Chronos facility. They assumed the installation had been uninhabited and forgotten since the nukecaust of two centuries before. It was not until much later that they learned the place was inhabited by an old enemy, a brilliant but deranged dwarf named Sindri.

Sindri had told them that during his investigation of the installation, he had discovered a special encoded program that was linked to but separate from Chronos. It was code-named Parallax Points. Sindri had been far more interested in the workings of the temporal dilator than the Parallax Points program, but his tampering with the technology had caused it to overload and reach critical mass, resulting in a violent meltdown of its energy core.

Lakesh learned that the Parallax Points program was actually a map, a geodetic index, of all the vortex points on the planet. This discovery had inspired him to rebuild the interphaser, even though decrypting the program had been laborious and time-consuming. Each newly discovered set of coordinates had to be fed into the interphaser's targeting computer.

With the new data, the interphaser became more than a miniaturized version of a gateway unit, even though it employed much of the same hardware and operating principles. The mat-trans gateways functioned by tapping into the quantum stream, the invisible pathways that crisscrossed outside perceived physical space and terminated in wormholes.

The interphaser interacted with the energy within a naturally occurring vortex and caused a temporary overlapping of two dimensions. The vortex then became an intersection point, a discontinuous quantum jump, beyond relativistic space time.

Evidence had indicated that there were many vortex nodes, centers of intense energy, located in the same proximity on each of the planets of the solar system, and those points correlated to vortex centers on Earth. The power points of the planet—places that naturally generated specific types of energy—possessed both positive and projective frequencies, others were negative and receptive. He referred to the positive energy as *prana,* which was an old Sanskrit term meaning the world soul.

Lakesh had known that some ancient civilizations were aware of these symmetrical geoenergies and had constructed monuments over the vortex points to manipulate them. Once the interphaser was put into use, the Cerberus redoubt reverted to its original purpose— not a sanctuary for exiles or the headquarters of a resistance against the tyranny of the barons, but a facility dedicated to unfathoming the eternal mysteries of space and time.

However, everyone was nonplussed when one set of Parallax Points coordinates led to a location not just above solid ground, but off the planet itself, on the Moon. All of them knew the stories about predark space settlements, even of bases on the Moon, of course. It wasn't until they activated the Parallax Points coordinate that they learned the stories about Moon bases were far more than folklore.

"Fascinating device." Maccan's comment brought Lakesh out of his reverie. "My compliments."

Lakesh nodded. "Thank you."

"But it is more than merely fascinating...perhaps it can serve as the means to my ultimate salvation."

"How so?"

Maccan regarded him gravely. His eyes were now

a pale pewter-gray, but Lakesh wasn't comforted. The helmeted man didn't speak for a long moment, as if he were pondering a weighty problem. Then, musingly, he said, "Perhaps I should take you with me, so you may learn the answer to that question yourself...and in doing so help me attain my objective. I promise you'll find it an astonishing experience."

Lakesh forced himself to stare at Maccan levelly. "I've visited Manitius base. There's not much there you can show me that I'll find particularly astonishing."

Maccan's smiled widened. "Who said anything about going to the Moon?"

Lakesh felt his brow furrowing. "Then where?"

Maccan cast his eyes toward the ceiling and kept his gaze there, as if he could see through vanadium, solid rock and the atmosphere. "The fourth planet from the Sun, Dr. Singh. I called it Lahmu. You call it Mars."

Chapter 12

Grant nearly had all the spark plug leads hooked back up to the distributor cap when Kane leaned down and demanded, right in his ear, "What's holding things up?"

Grant jerked and banged his head on the underside of the jeep's hood. He struggled to keep the wires together and his temper from fraying any further. He speared Kane with angry eyes. "Trying to do engine work when it's damn near dark."

He glanced toward Brigid, who stood at the front of the jeep, the flashlight in her hand trained on the engine block. "Hold that damn light steady," he snapped at her.

"I'm trying to," she retorted peevishly, her shoulders quaking in a shiver. "I'm getting cold."

"We're all getting cold," Kane complained.

"I'm hungry, too," she challenged.

"We're all hungry," he shot back. He sighed wearily. "It might make more sense to leave the jeep here and go the rest of the way on foot."

"I warned you about taking the jeep instead of the Hussar or a Sandcat, didn't I?" Brigid asked, an accusatory edge to her tone.

"Yeah," replied Kane. "But you also agreed it would draw less attention. With what's happened lately, we don't need to make ourselves any more conspicuous in the Outlands."

Grant snorted but said nothing, returning to his work.

Kane stepped away, pulling up the collar of his jacket. All of them wore jackets against the chill creeping down from the mountain peaks.

The clouds had lowered around the Bitterroot Range, bringing veils of mist and a more persistent drizzle. It cut down on visibility, not that there was much to see as twilight deepened, a sea of russet and indigo flowing down from the western sky. The last few minutes of sunset were strikingly beautiful.

Sunsets always were spectacular in the Outland, due to the pollutants and lingering radiation still in the upper atmosphere. Full night would fall swiftly, like the dropping of a curtain, and the crags above them would be swathed in deep shadow. A deep, thickly wooded gully yawned below the crest of the hill on which the jeep had stalled. The forest blazed with orange, red and gold late-autumn colors. The tall trees were fir and pine and aspen. The shadows between them were very dark and ominous.

On their left, beyond the tree line, rocky ramparts plunged straight down to a tributary of the Clark Fork River almost five hundred feet below. The ancient two-lane highway wended its way up toward the chain of mountain peaks that comprised the Continental Divide and formed the natural boundary between Idaho and Montana.

Standing at the front of the jeep, Kane looked up in the general direction of the distant mountain peak that sheltered Cerberus and sniffed the wind. His pointman's sixth sense reacted unpleasantly to its chill, moist touch. Something was in it, a faint scent of fear. He couldn't pin down the reason for his apprehension, since he and his friends were pretty much back on their home turf.

The three of them were two and a half long, hard days from Crescent City. Other than a skirmish with a group of scavengers who coveted their vehicle, the return trip had been relatively quiet. Now Kane almost wished they had given the jeep over to them, since about an hour had elapsed since it had sputtered, shuddered and finally died altogether.

Well over two hundred years ago, before the world had died in a nuclear inferno, the vehicle had started life as a mil-spec Army jeep. Since then it had been pieced back together at least a half dozen times by people with various degrees of skills and limited access to parts.

Metal patches welded over the body showed signs of rust, ripped open in places by dents and dings. Kane and Grant had captured it from a band of Roamers who'd been traveling too close to the Bitterroot Range a few months back. The encounter had resulted in some of the new bullet holes decorating the wag's body.

But the vehicle provided good cover for the overland journey, not quite as attention-getting as a Sandcat or the Hussar Hotspur available in the redoubt. The downside of traveling in a less conspicuous vehicle like the jeep was the exposure to the often lethal elements around hellzones, the least of which were the showers of acid rain.

Fortunately the weather had held on the return trip,

and when they skirted hellzones, their instruments showed tolerable levels of ambient radiation. Only twice did they come near orange or warm regions. The far western inland states had, for the most part, been spared multiple direct strikes.

For a day, the jeep rolled steadily along old Interstate 199 through lower Oregon, before cutting over to Route 12, which carried them through part of Idaho and then into Montana. They passed piles of overgrown rubble that had once been towns. A few old buildings still rose at the skyline, then broke with ragged abruptness. Other than the scavengers with whom they had exchanged shots and insults, they saw no people and fewer animals.

The had stopped briefly at the permanent encampment of the Lakota/Cheyenne where they were welcomed as friends and heroes, before continuing on to a road that cut through the foothills of the Bitterroot Range and then began a steady incline.

The old, two-lane blacktop wasn't simply steep, it was treacherous; the greater the elevation, the more painstaking the drive became. The road stretched up from the foothills and when it plunged into the Bitterroot Range proper, it turned into a twisting, inhumanly rugged hellway. It skirted dizzying abysses on one side and foreboding, overhanging bluffs on the other. The jeep's engine strained and labored not just to climb the path, but to stay on it.

Ascending through the foothills, they kept the ridgelines between them and the flatlands, although even Grant, the most pessimistic of the team, doubted anyone was trying to track them. The past year, particularly the battle of Area 51 and the siege of Cobaltville, had taken its toll on most of the baron's resources. Where the Magistrate Divisions had once been able to fill their ranks with generation after generation of warriors, they were now in the position of badging new blood far too soon. In the wake of the Imperator War, the Mags were too concerned with putting down sporadic rebellions in ville territories to engage in a concerted search for three renegades.

The journey to the mountain plateau was always nerve-racking, so much so that Grant insisted he be the one to drive, not wanting to trust his life to Kane's sometimes impatient piloting. Brigid sat in the back seat apparently not in the least disturbed by the violent jolts or the whine of the overstressed V-8. She resolutely stared at her lap.

After leaving the Indian camp, they had lost a little time down below, clearing away, then re-camoflauging the narrow track cut through the rockfall that blocked the highway as it entered the foothills. Two years before, they had used an explosive charge to trigger an avalanche and thus make the road impassable to all but the most foolhardy of intruders, and then only those who cared to make the trek on foot.

In the interim, an alliance had been struck with Sky Dog and his band of Sioux and Cheyenne living out on the flatlands. With their help, a narrow and easily disguised path had been forged through the fall. The undertaking had required a week of hard labor and the judicious use of demolition charges, but the warriors had been eager to help. If it hadn't been for Grant, Kane and Domi, a squad of Magistrates would have slaughtered the entire settlement. The Amerindians also received a fully operable war wag in the bargain.

As always, Kane felt strangely regretful about leaving the band of Lakota and Cheyenne whereas Grant and Brigid were only too happy to continue the trip to Cerberus. Brigid was ville-bred and the rough life on the plains didn't appeal to her. In that, she was much like most of the other redoubt personnel, particularly the Moon base émigrés. They were accustomed to an artificial environment and rarely did any of them stray more than ten yards from the edge of the plateau.

Grant, though accustomed to hardship during his Mag days and after, made no bones about his preference for a bed over a fur robe spread on the hard ground. He also didn't find herb-and-bark tea much of a substitute for coffee.

Kane felt a strong affinity for the wild and free people and their unfettered way of life and he wasn't sure why. Perhaps it had something to do with the vision he had glimpsed a couple of years before during a bad mat-trans jump. At the time he had dismissed it as a hallucination caused by an out-of-phase transit feed connection. Lakesh had explained that when the modulation frequencies between two gateway units weren't in perfect sync, jump sickness would result, a symptom of which was startlingly vivid hallucinations.

The hallucinations Kane had suffered weren't dreams—they were more like glimpses of past lives, vignettes from his soul's journey over the long track of time. In one of the visions he had seen himself astride a pony, feathers in his long, streaming hair as he galloped down on the bluecoat soldiers in a place called the Greasy Grass. The soldier's chief had been named Pahaska.

It wasn't until much later, delving secretly into the redoubt's database, that he learned Greasy Grass was what the Lakota called the Little Bighorn and Pahaska's *wasicun* name was Custer.

Kane wondered how such obscure historical details, which weren't in his conscious storehouse of knowledge, could bubble to the surface during a bout of jump sickness.

Regardless of whether he'd really lived a past incarnation as a Plains Indian, Kane would occasionally suffer from redoubt fever. Then he would requisition one of the vehicles to drive down the treacherous mountain road to the foothills to Sky Dog's encampment.

No one had ever asked what he did down there among the Amerindians, where he was known and admired as Unktomi Shunkaha, which meant Trickster Wolf. It was a name the band of Sioux and Cheyenne had bestowed upon him, first conceived as something of an insult. It became synonymous with cunning and courage after he orchestrated the Indians' victory over a Magistrate assault force.

Kane knew Brigid and the others wondered if he had a willing harem of Indian maidens who always looked forward to a visit from Unktomi Shunkaha, but everyone knew better than to inquire about it. That restraint didn't keep Brigid from scrutinizing the babies in the encampment to see if there were any with blue eyes among them.

The loud bang of Grant slamming down the jeep hood caused Kane to jump and spin around, biting back a startled curse. Grant met his irritated gaze with one of mild amusement. "If it was only a plug, then it should be fixed."

They all climbed back aboard. Once settled in behind the wheel, Grant turned the ignition key. The jeep engine roared to life, running smoothly and without a single stutter or stammer. Grant experimentally pressed down on the accelerator a time or two to race the engine. When it continued to run without hesitation, he engaged the gears and set off up the road again.

"With luck," Brigid said, speaking loudly to be heard over the engine, "we should be home before the Moon rises."

"Almost be better if we didn't," Grant responded over a shoulder. "Then our visibility would improve."

Grant turned on the headlights, the jeep skirting the crumbling edge of the road. The ground looked solid but it was deceptive. Even the vehicle's four-wheel drive might not be enough to get them free if the road began to collapse under its weight. Twisting the wheel in one direction then turning it the other, Grant rode the brakes, all the while watching for familiar landmarks.

Grant guided the jeep expertly with gravel rattling beneath the wheels and chassis, traveling along the high, far side of the road to avoid the crumbling edges. When the highway swung in a wide curve along the backside of a ridge, Brigid, Kane and Grant released their pent-up breath in a long exhalation of relief.

"About the worst is behind us now," Grant commented. "We should be in comm range. Give 'em a holler."

Kane picked up the trans-comm from the seat. Thumbing up the cover of the palm-size radiophone, he pressed a key, held it up to his ear and spoke into it. "This is Rover. Do you read me, Cerberus? Acknowledge."

Kane repeated the request, but only static filtered out through the unit. He spoke twice more, but received only a hash of crackles and pops. Irritably he folded down the unit cover. "Could be the cloud cover blocking the signal."

Brigid leaned forward. "Try again when we're closer. You'd think they'd be expecting us."

"Lakesh didn't seem too enthusiastic about this mission in the first place," said Kane.

"That's probably because he didn't come up with it," replied Grant. "He still wants the final say on all ops."

Brigid interjected, "He had a point about this particular mission. It wasn't a strike against either the barons or the imperator. We hurt Baron Snakefish by accident, not by design. And since he's an ally of Sam, he'll more than likely resupply Snakefish's ville with anything he lost."

"It's a new war," Kane argued. "We have to come up with new strategies."

"It's a new phase of the same old war," Grant corrected him dourly. "We may have more allies to go along with more enemies, but the war is the same."

Kane nodded reflectively, remembering all the times he had told Lakesh that a war that was already lost could not be fought. A new one had to be waged. It wasn't until they learned that the Archon Directorate didn't exist that they devoted much thought to the means of waging the new war.

Before then, the missions Lakesh concocted never dealt with head-on confrontations. Always they involved finding some way to strike covertly at the Archon Directorate, not at the barons, their plenipotentiaries who actually held the reins of power.

After Balam's revelation that the Directorate was but a diversionary smoke screen created two centuries ago by corrupt government officials and military men to mask their own ruthless ambitions, an entirely new set of strategies had to be drafted.

The earlier tactics had been hampered by their own belief that they contended with a vast, omnipotent opponent, and by Kane's way of thinking they wasted a lot of time and energy searching for ways to fight an enemy that didn't exist.

He couldn't really blame Lakesh, particularly in lieu of the fact that he was the man who came to the pivotal conclusion that the Directorate was but a cunningly crafted illusion. Even so, he seemed reluctant to accept the findings of his own detective work, despite Balam's essentially confirming his suspicions.

Not that it really mattered at this point. Lakesh's

self-assumed position as the final authority in the re-doubt was no longer absolute. A smile tugged at the corners of Kane's mouth. It wasn't as if he, Grant and Brigid had ever obeyed him unquestioningly in the first place, but now any proposals for action had to be agreed upon by a majority vote.

Kane knew Lakesh bitterly resented this change in procedure, but to hell with him. His plans had nearly gotten them all killed—worse than killed—on a number of occasions. Lakesh often gave them just enough information to plunge them into serious trouble. That was all over now. Lakesh was a changed man.

At least Kane hoped so.

The jeep, all four tires gripping the cracked asphalt, topped another rise, turned another curve, and Grant exhaled a deep sigh of relief as the road widened to the huge plateau.

Kane tried raising the redoubt on the trans-comm again, but once more received only static. "They have to be receiving us," Grant said flatly.

Kane nodded, but folded the cover down over the comm and put it in his pocket. He didn't voice the anx-iety that had crept over him like a shroud since their breakdown. His pointman's sixth sense howled an alarm. The skin between his shoulder blades seemed to tighten, and the short hairs at the back of his neck tingled.

Grant steered the jeep in a semicircle around the plateau and braked to a halt only a few yards away from the sec door. It was completely closed. Normally one of the panels was left open until midnight, until the security watch closed it. As it was, the security watch should have been alerted to their arrival by the motion detectors planted around the perimeter and the night-vision vid system.

"I don't like the looks of this," Brigid murmured, her voice barely audible over the idling engine.

"That makes two of us," Grant concurred, unconsciously lowering his voice. He glanced over at Kane. "How about you?"

"I'm with Brigid," he answered, eyeing the wide, heavy door inset into the base of the peak. "I don't like the looks of this, either. Not one damn bit."

Grant keyed off the engine, and the abrupt silence set their flesh to crawling. They heard nothing, no trill of a night bird or chirp of a cricket, not even the sigh of the wind stirring the boughs of the evergreen trees. The three people climbed out of the jeep, Kane wincing at the grate of his boot soles against the tarmac.

"Maybe everybody is waiting to jump out and yell 'surprise,'" Brigid whispered.

A line of confusion creased Grant's forehead. "Why the hell would they do that?"

She smiled wanly and shook her head. "An old predark custom, a way to celebrate birthdays. It was called a surprise party."

"That makes sense," Kane muttered dismissively, approaching the door. "Or it might under other circumstances."

Since Brigid's forced exile, she had taken full advantage of the Cerberus redoubt's vast database, and as an intellectual omnivore she grazed in all fields. Coupled with her eidetic memory, her profound knowledge of an extensive and eclectic number of topics made her something of an ambulatory encyclopedia. This trait often irritated Kane, but just as often it had tipped the scales between life and death, so he couldn't in good conscience become too annoyed with her.

Grant's eyes narrowed. "I'm not even sure I remember how to get into this place from the outside when the front door is locked."

Kane threw him a startled glance, then raised an eyebrow. "I'm not sure if I do, either. Have we ever had to do it before?"

Brigid sighed in mock exasperation and stepped to the thick metal frame. She ran her hands across its dull surface, then popped open the lid to a small, square panel set at shoulder level. Reaching into it, her fingers found a small keypad, then tapped in three-five-two.

A prolonged grating sound came from the top and bottom of the huge sec door. Her hand grasped a lever beneath the keypad and she forced it down, holding it in position. For a few seconds nothing seemed to happen, but they heard the faint groan of buried gears and the hiss of hydraulics. A slit of pale light appeared on the right edge.

"Oh," remarked Kane blandly. "So that's how you do it."

"Code," Brigid said. "You enter three-five-two to enter and two-five-three to seal the door again. You were briefed on it the same time I was."

"I forgot," Kane said. "Something you don't have to worry about."

"It has more to do with mental discipline than a photographic memory, Kane," she retorted. "But you know that."

Brigid was a trained historian, spending over half of her life as an archivist in the Cobaltville Historical Division, but there was more to her storehouse of knowledge than simple training.

Almost everyone who worked in the ville divisions kept secrets, whether they were infractions of the law, unrealized ambitions or deviant sexual predilections. Brigid Baptiste's secret was more arcane than petty crimes or manipulating the system for personal aggrandizement.

Her secret was the ability to produce eidetic images. Centuries ago, it had been called a photographic memory. She could, after viewing an object or scanning a document, retain exceptionally vivid and detailed visual memories. When she was growing up, she feared she was a psi-mutie, but she later learned that the ability was relatively common among children, and usually disappeared by adolescence. It was supposedly very rare among adults. Brigid was one of the exceptions.

The massive door began folding aside, opening like an accordion. It was so heavy, it took nearly half a minute for one panel to open just enough to allow them to enter. Seeing the twenty-foot-wide, vanadium-sheathed corridor gleaming beyond it, Kane felt a quick spurt of anxiety.

In the half light of approaching dusk, the open door looked like a maw, the mouth of some gigantic predator. After spending the past few days in the open, with no walls or ceiling except the trees and sky, returning to the windowless confines of Cerberus made him feel instantly claustrophobic.

Brigid released the lever and stepped up to the opening, peering around the flat slab of vanadium. "See anything?" Kane asked, stepping up behind her.

Brigid's reply, if she had one, was drowned out by the deep-throated boom of a heavy-caliber gun.

Chapter 13

Despite its caliber, the gun that fired the shot had been poorly aimed. The round whipped past Brigid's right hip, missing it by over a foot. The bullet didn't miss the jeep, slamming into the front grille and puncturing the hot radiator. Scalding water and steam spewed out, swiftly forming a cloud in the chilly mountain air.

A cursing Grant jumped first in one direction and then another, trying to decide whether he wanted to risk being shot or parboiled. He decided to brave the steam, shoulder-rolling through it and crouching on the far side of the sec door.

Kane and Brigid threw themselves against the exterior of the door, using the massive vanadium slabs as cover. Nothing less than an antitank shell could even dent it. Kane's Sin Eater sprang from its holster and slapped solidly into the palm of his hand. "Did you see anybody?" he asked Brigid.

Short of breath due to astonishment, she could only shake her head.

Holding his pistol in a double-handed grip, his left cupping his right, Kane inched toward the opening, back pressed against the metal. The jeep radiator continued to hiss and spray out steam, which he hoped might obscure his movements.

Reaching the edge of the opening, Kane crouched,

inhaled a deep breath, then fell over the threshold, half in and half out of the redoubt. Index finger hovering over the Sin Eater's trigger stud, his eyes scanned the semidarkness of the corridor for a target. He caught the faint whiff of cordite.

A white blur of movement in a doorway a score of yards down the passageway caught his attention. Raising the barrel of his pistol a fraction, he fired a single shot. The report was muted by the sound-absorbing properties of the vanadium-sheathed walls and floors.

The bullet struck the wall above the doorway, right at the juncture point where a heavy support beam stretched up toward the rock roof. A spark flared and the round bounced back and forth from wall to wall with the keening whine of ricochets and the hammering clang of multiple impacts.

"Freeze!" Kane roared, using the Mag voice, a sharp, commanding tone at a volume that in the past intimidated malefactors and broke violent momentum. "Drop your weapon or I'll drop you!"

While the echoes of his bellowed "you!" still chased each other down the passageway, a big revolver sailed from the doorway and struck the floor with a metallic clatter. It slid to the opposite wall.

"Come out with your hands on your head!" Kane shouted.

A small figure in a white bodysuit stepped timidly into the corridor, hands clasped obediently atop her black-haired head. Surprised into speechlessness, Kane stared at Nora Pennick. After what seemed like a full minute, he finally regained his composure to demand angrily, "What the hell are you doing, Nora?"

The woman stared toward him, then leaned against the wall, apparently going weak with relief. Lowering her arms, she asked in a quavering voice but with an unmistakable British accent, "Kane, it's you, isn't it? Are Grant and Baptiste with you?"

"Of course," he growled, swiftly climbing to his feet. Glancing behind him, he saw Grant and Brigid peering around the edge of the door panel. With an icy irony he told them, "Don't worry, it was only sweet little Nora trying to blow our heads off. Welcome home, kids."

"Nora?" Grant exploded, stomping into the redoubt and down the corridor toward the woman. He paused only long enough to pick up the big Colt Python revolver from the floor.

"I'm so sorry," the woman said, a sob catching at the back of her throat. "I'm new at this and I overreacted."

"That's for damn sure," Grant half snarled. He started to say more, then cocked his head at her inquisitively. "New to what? Overreacted why?"

The woman's eyes darted from Grant to Brigid to Kane. They were wet, red and puffy, either from weeping or lack of sleep or both.

Despite her haggard appearance, Nora Pennick looked nothing like the woman the three of them had first met on the Manitius Moon base a month or so before. Then, she was dirty, undernourished-looking and her long dark hair was a tangle of uncombed Medusa snarls. Since her arrival in the Cerberus redoubt, she had been dipping into the supply of cosmetics left there by the female personnel of the installation before it had been abandoned in the days preceding the nukecaust.

The white bodysuit she wore clung tightly to her trim, small-waisted figure. Her hair was coifed, neatly trimmed and the makeup she had applied to her face was evidently in fashion before the nukecaust. But now the mascara and eyeliner were smeared across her cheeks.

In a thin, aspirated whisper Nora said, "Bry said not to expect you until tomorrow morning, so he ordered the door to be sealed. I was walking guard when you—"

"Hold on," Brigid broke in impatiently. "You're telling us the end, not the beginning. Why did he order the door sealed?"

Nodding distractedly, Nora dabbed at her eyes. They could tell the woman teetered on the verge of hysterics, brought on by overwrought nerves and too many hours without sleep. She began to speak, her lips trembling, when a group of four people in white bodysuits emerged at a trot from around a corner. They held SA-80 subguns across their chests and took up positions in a half circle facing Kane and company.

Two of them were recent Moon base immigrants, neither of whom Kane, Grant or Brigid knew. The other two were Banks and Wegmann. The people gusted out noisy exhalations of relief and lowered their weapons.

"When we heard the shots," Wegmann said in his characteristically clipped, waspish manner, "we thought—"

He broke off, glancing away in embarrassment. In his midthirties, Wegmann was no more than five and half feet tall and weighed in the general vicinity of one hundred and fifty pounds. As such he was the only man in Cerberus shorter and slighter of frame than Bry, but he always seemed to possess the self-confidence of a someone twice his height and weight.

"Thought what?" Kane snapped.

Banks stepped forward. He looked almost as exhausted and stressed out as Nora Pennick. "We thought it might be another incursion."

"*Another* incursion?" echoed Grant incredulously. "What do you mean by that?"

Banks sighed. "I mean, that about twenty-two hours ago, Cerberus was invaded by a hostile force."

For a handful of seconds Kane, Brigid and Grant were too stunned to speak. Brigid recovered her emotional equilibrium first. "A hostile force from where? Who sent it? Sam? One of the barons?"

Nora shook her head, lips compressed in a tight, grim line. "A lot worse. It was Maccan and what was left of his followers. George Neukirk resurrected him and brought him here through the gateway. When Maccan left, he took Lakesh's interphaser and Lakesh himself."

ON THE WAY to the infirmary Banks provided a terse overview of the events of the night before. Kane wasn't too interested in the finer details, but Brigid seemed both shaken and enthralled by his description of Maccan's energy gauntlet. "The Silver Hand of Nuadhu? It can't be," she murmured.

Banks left them at the entrance, returning to cleanup-and-repair detail in the operations center with Wegmann.

Grant, Brigid and Kane took two steps into the infirmary and came to an unsteady halt, staring with disbelieving eyes at the number of injured people lying in the beds. Kane counted six injured people, all of them bandaged and receiving IV drips. He glimpsed Quavell flit past the doorway of the adjoining room, bearing a tray.

Farrell occupied the far bed of the infirmary. He, too, had an IV drip, but he was awake, staring at the ceiling as though it were a window. He looked terribly haggard, but he forced a smile when he saw them.

"You guys missed the big game," he croaked. "We damn near brought the mountain down."

"Almighty God," Grant husked out in a gravelly whisper. "How many casualties?"

"Seven dead," came DeFore's voice from behind them. "Six wounded."

They turned as the medic strode into the infirmary from the corridor, pushing a wheeled cart filled with medical supplies ahead of her. "We probably wouldn't have had any wounded at all if Farrell here hadn't tried a last-minute rescue of Lakesh."

She spoke without heat or accusation, only a bone-deep weariness.

"Domi," Grant blurted. "Where is she?"

DeFore pushed the cart toward the adjoining room. "In here."

Grant rushed ahead of her, Brigid and Kane on his heels.

For a couple of seconds they had difficulty locating Domi. The girl's marble whiteness blended in with the stark bedsheets. An IV bag hung upside down to the left of the bed, dripping slowly into a shunt on her arm. Diagnostic scanners hummed purposefully, monitoring her heartbeat and respiration. Lividly outlined in blue and red against the bone-whiteness of her skin, a network of ruptured capillaries and blood vessels spread across her forehead. Domi's sleep was fitful and she murmured and twitched.

Leaning over the bed, gazing into her face, Grant demanded, "Who did this to her?"

"I was told Maccan himself," DeFore replied. "With that glove of his. To get Lakesh to cooperate, he tortured her."

"Looks like Lakesh cooperated a little too late." Grant turned toward the medic, his eyes shadowed by his heavy brows. "What's wrong with her?"

DeFore shook her head, crossing her arms under her breasts. "I wish I knew. She's suffering from ruptured capillaries and some intercranial swelling. From what I was told, my guess is that Maccan's glove emitted infrasound waves. So I can only speculate she was subjected to a point-blank dose of it."

"That fits in with what we know of Danaan technology," Brigid said, sounding so calm as to be detached. "We've all faced their infrasound weapons before."

Kane thought back to the harplike instrument played by Aifa in Ireland and a similar device Sindri had claimed had been found on Mars, a relic of the Tuatha de Danaan. The infrasound wands wielded by the hybrids in the Archuleta Mesa installation and in Area 51 converted electricity to ultrahigh sound frequencies by a miniature maser.

The Danaan harp had been described as producing energy forms with balanced gaps between the upper and lower energy frequencies. He'd explained that if the radiation within particular frequencies fell on an energized atom—like living matter—it stimulated it the same way a gong vibrated when its note was struck on a piano. Harmony and disharmony, healing and death.

Sindri had gone on to describe scientific precedents cloaked by myth and legend such as the Ark of the Covenant bringing down the walls of Jericho when the Israelites gave a great shout. He'd claimed the walls were bombarded and weakened by amplified sound waves of the right frequency transmitted from the Ark. Sindri also cited Merlin, who was reputed to be of half-Danaan blood, and had "danced" the megaliths of Stonehenge into place by his music.

"The frequency between seven and eight Hertz can rupture internal organs," Brigid continued. "Seven Hertz is the average frequency of the brain's alpha rhythms, so it can trigger epileptic seizures."

Both Kane and Grant knew Brigid's clinical attitude masked a sharp anxiety about Domi's welfare. They knew her mind could function in a balanced matrix between horror and analysis.

"What treatment are you giving her?" Grant demanded.

DeFore shrugged helplessly. "What you see. An IV drip to keep her hydrated. I'm monitoring her heart rate and blood pressure. I haven't given her an EEG yet, so I don't know about the extent of brain damage, if there is any."

Grant glowered at her. "Why haven't you?"

DeFore met his glower with an angry scowl of her own. Sweeping her arms toward the casualty ward, she exclaimed, "I'm a little overworked and a lot understaffed, if you haven't noticed! Domi may be comatose, but she can breathe on her own and doesn't require constant care, which is more than I can say for some of our gunshot victims and burn-trauma patients out there."

Grant blinked and his stern expression softened, some of his confrontational energy ebbing. "I'm sorry. You're doing the best you can—you always do. We should have been here. Maybe it wouldn't have happened."

"Or," Quavell spoke up as she sidled up to the opposite side of Domi's bed, "you could have only been additions to the casualty list. None of you has any reason to feel guilt."

"I don't," Kane bit out. "But I'm feeling an awful lot like I should finish the job I started with Maccan."

He spun on a heel, stalking out of the room. "I'll be in operations."

None of them was surprised by Kane's abrupt departure. Kane never stayed in Quavell's presence longer than he absolutely had to and he made it a priority to make sure even that time period never exceeded a minute, if possible.

His statement to the contrary, Brigid knew Kane did indeed feel responsible for not ending the threat of Maccan when the opportunity had presented itself. He had suggested it, but had been overruled by Lakesh and Brigid, who'd felt Maccan might serve as a valuable source of information about the Annunaki and the Tuatha de Danaan.

Addressing Quavell, Brigid asked, "Are you sure you should be exerting yourself in your condition?"

The masklike placidity of Quavell's face didn't alter. "I can only know that by the level of exertion. So far, despite a nagging pain in my lower back, I'm experiencing no ill effects."

DeFore smiled at her gratefully. "You've been a great help, Quavell. I couldn't have done this without you."

Quavell acknowledged DeFore's complimentary words with a diffident hand gesture, the hybrid equivalent of a shrug. "It was a task that needed doing and so I welcomed the chance, as some of you have phrased it, 'to pull my freight around here.' Besides, I have a little experience in such matters."

They realized Quavell was making an oblique reference to the incident when Kane, Brigid, Domi and Grant had inadvertently destroyed the baronial medical facility beneath the Archuleta Mesa in New Mexico. The barons depended on the facility to bolster their immune systems. Once a year, the oligarchy traveled to the installation for medical treatments.

They received fresh transfusions of blood and a regimen of biochemical genetic therapy designed to strengthen their autoimmune systems, thus granting them another year of life and power. Grant knew the six-leveled facility in New Mexico had originally been constructed to house two main divisions of the Totality Concept, Overproject Whisper and Overproject

Excalibur. One dealt with finding new pathways across space and time, the other was exclusively involved in creating new forms of life. According to Lakesh, after the institution of the unification program, only Excalibur's biological section was revived to maintain the lives of the barons and to grow new hybrids.

Although all the hybrids were extremely long-lived, cellular and metabolic deterioration was part and parcel of what they were—hybrids of human and Archon DNA. The treatments involved infusions of human genetic material, and the barons relied upon an aircraft to locate sources of raw material in the Outlands, kill the donors, harvest their organs and tissues, and return with the "merchandise," as they referred to it, to the mesa to be processed.

Quavell, who'd been stationed there at the time, had reported that the destruction of the Archuleta Mesa had done more than smash the baron's ability to sustain their lives. It had also taken away their future by destroying the incubation chambers. Only twenty-three infants remained out of two thousand. The war between old and new human, Quavell had declared, was over. The old humans had won simply by killing the babies of the new humans.

"Where's Auerbach?" Grant demanded, not wanting to be reminded of the mission. "I thought he was your assistant."

DeFore's lips pursed as if she tasted something sour. "From what I hear, he didn't exactly comport himself in a way that would earn him medals for bravery. So he was assigned to burial detail, attending to the dead."

Brigid glanced toward Quavell. "Did you see the weapon Maccan used on Domi?"

She shook her head. "No, I was in a section of the redoubt sealed off from the command center."

"From the description of the effects," Grant stated, "it sounds like an infrasound weapon, like the wands you people used in the Archuleta Mesa."

Quavell's small mouth twitched at the mention of the Mesa, but she calmly replied, "It does indeed. But I have never heard of an acoustic weapon in the form of a fashion accessory. Directing infrasound is difficult because of the long wavelength produced. If the weapon is activated by the person holding it, protecting them from the sonic backsplash would be very chancy undertaking."

Grant waved away Quavell's observations. "I just want an idea of what we're dealing with here."

He took a long, final look at Domi and turned away. Half to himself, he asked, "What the hell did Maccan want with the interphaser?"

" 'MIRROR SYMMETRY'?" Kane echoed incredulously. "What the hell does that mean?"

Philboyd straightened from beneath the master ops console and snapped in exasperation, "How the hell do I know? You asked me what I heard and I'm telling you. For what it's worth, it seemed to mean something to Maccan."

Kane put his hands on his hips and slowly surveyed the shambles of the command center. He hadn't allowed the shock he felt upon first sight of the ruins to show on his face. He struggled to control the feelings of disorientation and the overwhelming sense of being violated. It hadn't occurred to him until he saw the extent of the damage to the redoubt and its personnel how deeply he had come to regard Cerberus as his home.

The master operations console was one of the very few control stations still intact. The flat, four-foot VGA monitor screen had miraculously managed to come through the battle without incurring so much as a scratch.

The rest of the big room hadn't been so fortunate. Only a few status lights flickered on the instrument boards, and the center itself was unsatisfactorily illuminated by a tangled netting of extension cords and naked light bulbs. People scurried to and fro, broken glass crunching underfoot, carting away destroyed consoles and computers or trying to jury-rig the ones that had only been damaged.

Many of the panels were just empty squares or rectangular holes in the console casings. Philboyd, Bry and a couple of other tech-heads labored to replace the unsalvageable boards with wired-together switch boxes and automated controls. Wegmann stood atop a ladder, spot-welding a piece of the Mercator projection map back into place. Although the ventilation system still functioned, the odor of burned metal, cordite and even scorched human flesh hung in the air, coating Kane's tongue with a foul tang.

"Any other witnesses?" Kane asked. "What about Maccan's people?"

Philboyd paused in the splicing of wires to a hastily

constructed switch box. "They took their own casualties with them, their dead and wounded."

"Did you know any of them?"

"By name, only one, a jerk named Lazlo. A couple of others I'd seen around from time to time. A scarfaced bull dyke by the name of Shayd seemed to be acting as Mac's lieutenant, though I could be mistaken."

Kane narrowed his eyes. "Bull dyke?"

"Twentieth-century slang for a macho-acting lesbo." Philboyd's voice acquired a patronizing tone. "You know, a female homosexual."

Kane gestured to a video camera bracketed high in a corner. "What about spy-eyes?"

Philboyd shook his head. "They went on the fritz as soon as Maccan made his first power glove blast, almost like they were hit by an EMP."

Dry-scubbing his hair in frustration, Kane asked, "So the whole crew all went back to the Moon—Mac, Lakesh and the bull dyke?"

Bry, overhearing the question called from the mat-trans control console, "I've just about finished rebooting the main gateway CPU. Once it's back online, I'll try the transit-line-trace program to see if we can't locate where they jumped to."

Philboyd returned his attention to his wire-splicing task. "If they were going back to the Moon, couldn't they have used the interphaser?"

Kane nodded. "Yes. That's how we first got there, with the interphaser. The mat-trans unit on the base was down at the time."

"So," intoned Philboyd musingly, "the vortex node coordinate on the Moon is encoded in the interphaser's targeting computer and memory?"

"Yes," Kane said again, a little irritably. "Lakesh explained all of that to you weeks ago—" Then he comprehended and declared, "So if they were just going back to the Moon, they wouldn't have needed the mattrans. The fact they needed the gateway unit indicates their destination was..." He trailed off, eyeing Philboyd expectantly.

Philboyd met his gaze and ventured, "Someplace else?"

Kane barely checked the angry impulse to backhand the supercilious astrophysicist across the face. "I'm not in the mood for your wit, Brewster."

"Neither am I," Philboyd countered, just as angrily. "We've got a lot of good people dead here, some of whom were my friends and all of whom were my colleagues."

"Due," Kane shot back, "to the actions of one of your friends or colleagues. I was told George Neukirk set Maccan free."

"Neukirk was never my friend," Philboyd argued. "He hardly qualified as a colleague. But he probably did kill one of my friends when he let Mac loose. It was Eduardo's week to stand watch on Mac."

Kane glared at Philboyd, who to his consternation didn't flinch. After a moment of taking deep, calming breaths, he realized the man probably hadn't slept or even eaten since the invaders left. He was simply too tired and his nerves too frayed to be intimidated by

Kane, as he might have been under normal circumstances.

Forcing a note of patience into his voice he didn't feel, Kane said matter-of-factly, "Brewster, I need to know everything you saw and heard so we can come up with a strategy to recover both Lakesh and the interphaser. Anything, no matter how trivial, could be of enormous help."

Philboyd frowned, but in concentration. "I know that, Kane. I'm trying. But I'm so tired—"

"Got it!" Bry's triumphant cry cut through the command center.

Kane turned his head toward him. "Got what?"

Bry's fingers tapped the keyboard of the computer station. "The transit-line trace. I'm pulling up the program now. If they jumped to a gateway that we have indexed, I'll be able to get a lock on them."

"If not?"

Bry shook his head somberly. "Then we're screwed." He jerked his thumb over a shoulder toward the Mercator map. "We won't be able to access the master index until the main data infeed is repaired."

Kane walked over to stand beside the slightly built tech. He watched silently as the program came online, machine language blurring over the screen, the drive units humming purposefully. "Is the system itself working?"

"I've completed a level-four diagnostic. Everything from the autosequence scanner to the coordinate lock shows green. It's operational."

The bright outlines of computer-generated images flashed on the screen. Three-dimensional geometric shapes, circles, spirals and squares appeared and disappeared. The graphics were, of course, simplified representations of a hyperdimensional pathway. Actual reproductions were impossible, beyond the capabilities of either human or electronic eyes to see.

A broken, glowing line raced across the screen, brilliant orange against depthless black, piercing the floating shapes. It scrolled back and forth until it literally filled the monitor.

"Oh, no," Bry said in a stunned whisper.

"What?" Kane demanded impatiently.

As soon as he said it, the lines faded from the screen, replaced by bright green words "Destination lock achieved." In the lower left-hand corner, a rectangular window flipped through a dozen sets of numeric sequences. The words "Cydonia Compound One" flashed in the window.

Kane kept his expression and voice studiedly neutral. "Does the intercom still work?"

Bry nodded. "Yeah, I guess so."

"Have Baptiste and Grant meet me in the cafeteria in ten minutes." He glanced over at Philboyd. "Brewster, have you eaten this evening?"

Philboyd shook his head. "I had some toast this morning, nothing since. Why do you ask?"

"I want you to join us, too."

Philboyd narrowed his eyes in consternation. "I'm busy, Kane. If I don't get our uplinks back online, we'll be deaf and dumb to anyone else who might come calling."

Kane knew Philboyd referred to the eavesdropping system Bry had established through the communications linkup with the Comsat satellite. It was the same system and same satellite used to track the subcutaneous transponder signals implanted within the Cerberus personnel.

Bry had worked on the system for a long time and had managed to develop an undetectable method of patching into the wireless communications channels of all the baronies in one form or another. The success rate wasn't one hundred percent, but he had been able to eavesdrop on a number of the villes to learn about baron-sanctioned operations in the Outlands. The different frequencies were monitored on a daily basis. Without being able to tap into the channels, the combined Magistrate Divisions of three villes could march up the road to the redoubt and they wouldn't realize it until they knocked at the sec door.

"It's going to have to wait," Kane said, a steel edge slipping into his tone.

Philboyd opened his mouth to voice an objection, but Kane lifted a peremptory hand. "I wasn't inviting you, Brewster. This is mandatory."

"What's so damn important?" Philboyd demanded impatiently.

"You're going to help us plan our next field trip."

"To where?"

Kane turned on his heel. "To Mars."

Chapter 14

The Cerberus redoubt had an officially designated briefing room on the third level. Big and blue-walled, it was equipped with ten rows of theater-type chairs facing a raised speaking dais and a rear-projection screen. It was built to accommodate the majority of the installation's personnel, back before the nukecaust when military and scientific advisers visited.

Since Kane's arrival in the redoubt, it had only been used once, when the entire staff had been addressed. Generally briefings rarely involved more than a handful of people, so they were convened in the more intimate dining hall. This time Kane chose the cafeteria for the meeting primarily because he was hungry. He knew his friends would welcome the chance to eat something other than the MREs they had subsisted on for the past five days.

As usual when anticipating the end of an away mission, Kane had promised to treat his gullet and palate to a real man-size meal upon returning to the installation. And as usual, although he felt on the verge of starvation, his stomach had shrunk from eating the concentrated rations for the past few days.

There was a variety of meals ready to eat available

in the prepackaged rations, but as far as he was concerned, they all tasted the same—like shit. They may have contained all the minerals, vitamins, proteins and whatever else the dietitians said humans need to keep healthy, and since they were concentrated they didn't weigh much or take up much storage room. But all of them still had the same repulsive flavor.

Now he made four sandwiches thick with ham and cheese wrapped in homemade bread, with a side dish of pickles, and a pot of coffee. It was a simple meal for what he knew in advance would not be a simple briefing.

Kane would have preferred a full-course dinner, but the selection of foodstuffs in the galley was limited at that hour. The personnel usually assigned to food preparation were busy with cleanup duties elsewhere in the installation. However, the cafeteria contained a secondary kitchen where people could prepare small, individual meals as Kane did now.

Most of the people who lived in the Cerberus redoubt, regardless of their specialized skills, acted in the capacity of support personnel. They worked rotating shifts, eight hours a day, seven days a week. For the most part, their work was the routine maintenance and monitoring of the installation's environmental systems, the satellite data feed, the security network.

However, everyone was given at least a superficial understanding of all the redoubt's systems so they could pinch-hit in times of emergency. Fortunately such a time had never arrived, but still and all, the installation was woefully understaffed. Their small numbers had been a source of constant worry to Lakesh, but with the arrival of the Moon base personnel, there was a larger pool of talent from which to draw.

Grant and Kane were exempt from crosstraining inasmuch as they served as the enforcement arm of Cerberus and undertook far and away the lion's share of the risks. On their downtime between missions they made sure all the ordnance in the armory was in good condition and occasionally tuned up the vehicles in the depot.

Brigid Baptiste, due to her eidetic memory, was the most exemplary member of the redoubt's permanent staff since she could step into any vacancy. However, her gifts were a two-edged sword inasmuch as those self-same polymathic skills made her an indispensable addition to away missions.

Kane carried the tray of sandwiches and the pot of coffee over to a corner table just as Grant, Brigid and Philboyd arrived. Philboyd regarded Brigid with a look bordering on adoration. Kane understood his devotion but he had little patience with it.

. Philboyd viewed Brigid as something of an anchor in his new life on Earth. Together they had faced the utter terror of contending with Enki, the last of the Dragon Kings, so he tended to look upon her as something of a security blanket.

The four people sat and for the first few minutes concentrated only on sating their hunger and gratefully drinking their cups of coffee. Access to genuine coffee was one of the inarguable benefits of living as an exile in the redoubt. Real coffee had virtually vanished after skydark, since all of the plantations in South and Central America had been destroyed.

An unsatisfactory, synthetic gruel known as "sub" replaced it. Cerberus literally had tons of freeze-dried packages of the authentic article in storage, as well as sugar and powdered milk.

After Kane washed down his last bite of sandwich with a sip of the coffee, he announced, "Brewster here was an eyewitness to the entire assault."

"An active participant, I was told," Brigid said, smiling at the lanky astrophysicist warmly.

Philboyd cast his eyes down self-consciously, and Kane grunted, "On our side, I hope."

"Farrell was there, too," Philboyd retorted, not responding to Kane's gibe.

"Yeah," Grant mumbled around a mouthful of ham, "but he's not ambulatory and you are. Besides, Reba has him zoned out on painkillers."

In an encouraging tone, Brigid said, "Tell us everything you remember, Brewster. Step by step, minute by minute, shot by shot."

Philboyd took off his glasses and cleaned the lenses with a paper napkin. "I'll try, but I don't have your gift for total recall."

Philboyd began to talk. Except for inserting a question here and there, Kane, Brigid and Grant allowed him to speak uninterrupted for the better part of five minutes. In conclusion he said, "It's obvious now the anomalous energy signature Bry reported was Maccan's power glove. If he'd kept the matter stream confined to the gateway's pattern buffer, none of this would have happened."

"One thing I've learned over the last couple of years," Brigid commented, sipping at her coffee, "is that trying to ascribe blame after the fact doesn't accomplish anything except to further hurt people who are already suffering because of a decision they made or didn't make."

Dabbing at drops of coffee on the ends of his mustache, Grant glanced over at Brigid. "You called that power glove the what? The Silver Hand of somebody?"

Brigid smiled wryly. "I was thinking out loud, saying the first thing that popped into my head. But inasmuch as we already know that some mythological artifacts have their basis in reality, I might not be too far offbase."

"Explain," Kane requested.

"It's tied in with Maccan's people, the Tuatha de Danaan," she stated. "Nuadhu was their first king when they arrived in Ireland. In fact, some traditions have it that all of the Irish are descended from him."

"I think I remember some of this," Philboyd said. "Back on the Moon, you told us when the Danaan landed in Ireland they brought with them four great treasures—Nuadhu's sword, Lugh's terrible spear, the Dagda's cauldron and the Stone of Fal, the Stone of Destiny."

Brigid nodded approvingly. "A couple of years ago we encountered a man who had stolen all of those artifacts and kept them in an underground vault in New London."

Philboyd beamed as if he had just received a gold

star from his beloved third-grade teacher. Kane tried to keep the annoyance he felt from being heard in his voice when he said, "I think I remember what you said now. The Formorians ruled Ireland when the Tuatha de Danaan showed up and they had a damn big battle someplace."

"Right," Brigid said. "The Danaan first bargained for peace and the division of Ireland with the Formorians, but they were refused. So they met the army of the Formorians on the Plain of the Sea near Leinster. For four days, groups of single combatants fought. The Danaan chief, Nuadhu, lost his hand in battle, but the Formorian king, Bochaid, was killed and Prince Bress took his place. In a peace gesture, the Danaan offered the surviving Formorians one-fifth of Ireland and they chose Connaught."

Kane and Grant exchanged surreptitious weary glances, but neither man decided to break into Brigid's dissertation.

"After losing his arm," Brigid continued, "Nuadhu resigned his kingship. But Diancecht, physician of the Danaan, made him a marvelous silver hand. It could move like a real one, so it's apparent the Danaan had expertise in prosthetics. As a result, he was restored to kingship. When he used his so-called terrible sword in tandem with his silver hand, Nuadhu was invincible."

"What was so special about his sword?" Philboyd wanted to know.

"Allegedly no opponent could escape from it and no wound inflicted by the blade could be healed. It was reputedly so dangerous that even if Nuadhu pointed it at an opponent, serious injuries and sometimes death resulted."

Brigid paused and a vertical line of concentration appeared at the bridge of her nose. "Which, now that I think about it, closely fits the description of what an infrasound weapon can do. It's possible the legend and lore of the sword and the silver hand were confused over the centuries."

"Assuming the Silver Hand of Nuadhu was also an infrasonic weapon," Kane said, "how did Maccan end up with it?"

Brigid smiled ruefully. "That's easy. He probably stole it from Nuadhu at the same time he tricked him out of his lands in the Boyne Valley, the tumulus of Newgrange."

"That still doesn't tell us a whole lot," Philboyd observed sourly.

Kane's thoughts flew back to what Brigid had said about Maccan when they were trapped in the DEVIL control nexus on the Moon. She had described Maccan as a chieftain among the Tuatha de Danaan, a name that meant "true vigor" or "young son." Maccan corresponded to the Welsh mythical figure Mabon and to the British Celtic Maponos, who was identified in inscriptions with the Greek god Apollo. He was also associated with a golden harp that made irresistibly sweet music that turned enemies into allies. As such he was the symbol of youth that denied the process of aging.

Those were the legends. Kane had dealt with the vicious reality of the man. His neck muscles were still slightly sore from Maccan's enthusiastic effort to choke the life out of him. Still, he knew little more about Maccan's people than he had before encountering him. The historical and mythological record was more complete regarding the Danaan's age-old rivals, the Annunaki. Both races were responsible for—or guilty of— influencing most human cultures since before the dawn of recorded history.

The Annunaki were the Serpent Kings, the Dragon Lords of Mesopotamian legend. They provided the basis of much culturally diverse ancient folklore in which a godlike reptilian race figured prominently. The Annunaki had come to Earth nearly half a million years ago from the planet Nibiru, a world in the solar system, but one that orbited a considerable astronomical distance away from the Sun, returning to the vicinity of Earth only once every thirty-six hundred years.

Like the Danaan, the Annunaki were a highly developed race with a natural gift for organization. They viewed Earth as a vast treasure trove of natural resources upon which their technology depended. As labor was their scarcest commodity, the Annunaki's chief scientist, Enki, set about redesigning the Earth's primitive inhabitants into models of maximized potentials.

The Annunaki remolded the indigenous protohumans, grading them at rough intellectual levels and classifying them by physique, agility and dexterity. After much trial and error, a perfect specimen was attained and served as the template for succeeding generations. But during the creation process a myriad of monstrosities was also birthed, which gave rise to the legends of the Cyclops, the centaur, the giant.

The early generations of slave labor were encouraged to breed, so each successive descendant would be superior to the first. The human brain improved and technical skills grew, along with cogent thoughts and the ability to deal with abstract concepts.

After thousands of years, the human slave-race rebelled against the Annunaki, who failed to notice the expansion of cognition on the part of their servants. By the time they did, Earth had become an unprofitable enterprise. Although the Annunaki were essentially a peaceful people, Enki's half brother, Enlil, arranged for a catastrophe to destroy their labor force. The catastrophe was recorded in ancient texts, and even cultural memories as the Flood. The Annunaki departed to their home world of Nibiru, determining to wait for another three and a half millennia before venturing forth to Earth again.

As the waters slowly receded, the handful of human survivors bred and multiplied. Over the ensuing centuries, nations and empires rose and fell. It was during the Annunaki's absence that the Tuatha de Danaan arrived. A humanoid race of aristocrats, scientists, warriors and poets, they settled in isolated Ireland. Although preferring their privacy, they taught the Gaelic tribes art, architecture and science. The essence of Danaan science stemmed from music—the controlled manipulation of sound waves—and this became recorded in legend as the "music of the spheres."

But much of their science was interpreted as magic

by the untutored clanspeople of ancient Ireland. But both the Annunkai and the Danaan understood and to some extent manipulated the indivisibility of space and time. They eventually discovered that matter and energy could be interchangeable—the deeper the Danaan probed into the minutiae of matter the more they found energy and complexities of energy at the bottom of everything. These realizations became not only the building blocks of their technology, but also millennia later, the entire template for Project Cerberus.

After a several-thousand-year-long reign by the Tuatha de Danaan, a task force of Annunaki returned to reclaim their world and their slaves. By this time, the Dragon Kings were few in number and used guile instead of force to achieve their objectives. They worked to turn humans against the Danaan, by filling them with jealousy and fear. Mankind became embroiled in the conflict between the two races, a conflagration that extended even to the outer planets of the solar system, and became immortalized and disguised in human legends as a war in heaven.

Finally, when it appeared that Earth was threatened with devastation, the war abated under terms. A pact was struck, whereby the two adversaries intermingled genetic material with that of humanity's to create a new race that was to serve as a bridge between the Danaan and the Annunaki. From this pact sprang the entities later known as the Grays, the First Folk and the Archons.

The First Folk were charged by the Annunaki and

the Danaan to act as custodians of humanity and to restrict their technological and cultural evolution. The Folk's forebears feared humankind's intellect would far outstrip its emotional development and lead to its destruction.

The First Folk established many settlements all over Earth, spreading out from the primary center deep in the heart of Asia. The people were cast in the mold of humanity, but they were not human as later generations would define the term. They were a branch on the mysterious tree of evolution, yet the twigs of humanity sprouted from their bough. They were a bridge, not only between two races, but flowing within them, mixing with the blood of their nonhuman forebears, was the blood of humanity.

The First Folk were mortal, though exceptionally long-lived. Like the humanity to which they were genetically connected, they loved and experienced joy and sadness. Their cities were centers of learning and the citizens didn't suffer from want. They knew no enemies; they had no need to fight for survival. Their duty was to keep the ancient secrets of the Annunaki and the Tuatha de Danaan alive, yet not propagate the same errors as their forebears, especially in their dealings with humankind, to whom they were inextricably bound.

Humanity was still struggling to overcome a global cataclysm, the Deluge brought about by Enlil, striving again for civilization. The First Folk insinuated themselves into schools, into political circles, prompting and assisting men into making the right decisions.

They sought out humans of vision, humans with superior traits. They mingled their blood with them, initiated them into their secrets, advised them. During this thousand-year period, the Golden Age of myth, the First Folk began to feel it was blasphemous to restrict the growth of humanity. After all, they carried the blood of Homo sapiens, as well. They felt it was a crime to curtail Humankind's wisdom, to hide new sciences from him, to direct him away from new inventions, particularly those that would enrich the planet as a whole.

The First Folk knew their forebears possessed too many weapons in their arsenals, stolen and adapted from other worlds they visited and exploited to be able to defend Earth. They didn't have the resources to fight an all-out war, but now that they had aroused Danaan and Annunaki suspicions, they had to take action.

They employed an energy field called "protoplanic force" and it demolished the lunar settlement. Enki and Maccan, the Annunaki and Danaan envoys, took refuge in suspended animation canisters, stasis units. Unfortunately there was a blow-back effect, a reverse reaction the First Folk hadn't foreseen. It nearly destroyed the Earth—and certainly decimated their civilization.

Shortly after the nukecaust, both Maccan and Enki were revived by one of the first Manitius base colonists, who for reasons no one ever discovered, decided Enki was a god and Maccan a devil. The division between the two entities was passed down over the generations of the people living on the Moon and two factions arose—one following Enki and the other swearing fealty to Maccan.

Philboyd laid the blame on one of his own fellow scientists, a woman named Seramis. In the years preceding the nukecaust, she served as a Manitius's chief geologist and historian. She made the initial discoveries that a highly developed race had, in ages past, planted a colony on the Moon. She continued her work even after the nukecaust. She had already uncovered the clues that indicated the existence of a hidden city.

Seramis and a group of followers performed excavations in the so-called Wild Lands and she discovered secrets about the Moon she never told anyone. She found tunnels and passages that led to the crypts of the Serpent Kings, the Annunaki. She plundered the tombs of their dead and stole much of their technology. Seramis claimed that a vast, lost knowledge was hidden in those catacombs, that on the Moon were secrets that were old when Sumeria was new, that were ancient when the pyramids were built in Egypt. The woman lost herself completely in the ancient culture of the Annunaki and became the sworn enemy of the Tuatha de Danaan, claiming they were a race of devils, the fallen angels referred to in Genesis.

Judging by his behavior, classifying Maccan as demonic was not too far from the truth, despite the Danaan's history of helping Humankind. All the evidence indicated the Danaan were a very old race, even when they established a colony on Earth, at least ten thousand years ago, perhaps even before that. Even

Maccan claimed the Tuatha de Danaan had four million years of accumulated history to look back on, but he had declined to expand on that history for Kane's benefit. He'd been too busy trying to kill him at the time.

"One thing we do know," declared Grant grimly, "is that the Danaan established a base on Mars."

They had learned over the past couple of years that the Danaan used Mars as an outpost that was decimated over a period of centuries, first during the war with the Annunaki and by raids staged by the Archons. In the twentieth century, the remaining ruins of the base became known collectively as the Monuments of Mars, which included the Great Stone Face and the gigantic pyramid.

"The question," Grant went on, "is to find out where on Mars Maccan might have taken Lakesh. Then we might understand why he abducted him in the first place and took the interphaser."

Brigid suddenly sat up straight in her chair, eyes narrowed to slits. She inhaled a sharp breath. Kane had seen her react in a similar fashion before when a new thought or concept occurred to her. Turning her intense jade gaze on Philboyd, she said sternly, "Repeat what you overheard about mirrors and symmetry."

Philboyd's eyebrows rose. "Essentially, all I heard was Mac talking about the interphaser helping him to take a look in the mirror and some crap about stepping through the looking glass. Does that mean anything to you?"

Brigid lifted her shoulder in a shrug. "Lewis Carroll wrote a book in the nineteenth century called *Through the Looking Glass*. Maccan could have been making a literary allusion. Is that all he said?"

Philboyd's high forehead furrowed as he tried to call up more memories. "He claimed the interphaser was built by following scientific principles his kind gave to humanity a long time ago. Then Lakesh asked him about mirror symmetry, the mirror-matter theory."

Brigid nodded as if she had expected the answer and it satisfied her. "I'm starting to get this now."

Kane growled impatiently, "I wish you'd give the rest of us an idea of what you're getting...and if it's contagious."

She regarded him with a wry, almost apologetic smile. "An idea, and a very generalized one, is about all I can give you. But I think we'd be safe if we look for Lakesh and Maccan in the vicinity of the Great Pyramid of Mars."

Grant eyed her speculatively, completely mystified. "Why?"

Using the forefingers of both hands, Brigid drew a triangle in the air. "This is the shape of the interphaser, right?"

Both Grant and Kane nodded, but said nothing.

"And what's the shape of a pyramid?" she pressed.

"Ah," Kane said as if he understood totally, drawing his own triangle in the air, but much, much larger.

"Do *you* get it?" Grant demanded of him skeptically.

Kane shook his head. "Not one bit. But at least we're on to something, even if it's only rudimentary geometry."

Chapter 15

"Well," Philboyd said wearily, "that's a lot more than I can say. I know you three have been to Mars already—it's where you first met Sindri—but what does a planet have to do with interphaser, geometry and mirror matter? And just what the hell *is* mirror matter?"

Brigid poured herself another cup of coffee. "It's a theory that garnered some attention among quantum physicists at the very tail end of the twentieth century. I'm surprised you didn't hear of it."

Defensively, Philboyd retorted, "I was on the Moon at the very tail end of the twentieth century, remember? I missed a lot of things...except for the nukecaust. I didn't even have a pager."

Brigid chose not to respond to his complaint. "Surely you've heard of dark matter?" she inquired,

Without hesitation, the astrophysicist crisply responded, "Nonluminious matter whose exact nature is unknown, but whose presence is inferred from observing the motion of the stars and interstellar gas clouds." His lips curved in a superior smirk. "Strictly theoretical, more in the nature of metaphysics."

Brigid shrugged. "Could be. But one thing that was learned over the years is how the interactions of elementary subatomic particles display a variety of symmetries. Some of these symmetries are familiar, such as rotational symmetry and translation symmetry. That's known as parity, which basically means the laws of physics remain the same whether we're in Montana or Moscow."

"And the mirror-matter theory postulates that might not be the case?" Philboyd asked.

"Who knows? Natural symmetries are known as left-right or mirror-reflection symmetry."

"Meaning?" Kane inquired, a dangerous edge to his voice.

"It means," Brigid replied, unruffled, "that for every fundamental microscopic process that occurs, the mirror image process should also occur. Mirror symmetry states that the mirror-image process can occur and should occur with equal probability."

"What the hell has this got to do with anything?" Grant demanded in an impatient growl.

"Essentially," Brigid said, "it has to do with a universal connectedness. Any two particles that have once been in contact continue to influence each other, no matter how far apart they move. Therefore the entire fabric of space time and sidereal space is multiply connected by faster-than-light interaction, like a cosmic glue."

Kane massaged his temples. "I remember some of this now. You and Lakesh had a field day with your quantum hypothesizing and speculating after we visited the parallel casements through the Shining Trapezohedron."

Brewster Philboyd shifted uncomfortably in his chair. "I read your reports. They were pretty tough pills for a tried-and-true Einsteinian like me to swallow."

Brigid favored him with a smile that was almost condescending. "Theories like those are among the most intellectually challenging in science, but Balam's people, the Archons, the First Folk, successfully reconciled quantum and relativistic physics ages ago. The primary subdivisions of the Totality Concept were built on their discoveries."

Kane said nothing, trying to dredge up the chaotic memories of the images Balam had imparted of his people's history and its interaction with the Shining Trapezohedron. The survivors of the cataclysm that had decimated Balam's people consulted the Shining Trapezohedron, desperate to find a solution to their tragedy within its black facets. It had showed them how to build thresholds to parallel casements.

To Philboyd he said, "A long time ago, both the Annunaki and the Tuatha de Danaan used such interdimensional thresholds created by the Shining Trapezohedron, because Earth was the end of a parallel axis of casements. They were still using basic principles of the mat-trans units, but expanded way beyond linear travel from place to place."

"Did any of you ever come to a conclusion about what the Shining Trapezohedron actually was?" asked Philboyd. "That is, before Kane threw the facets of the thing off the plateau?"

Brigid shook her head, frowning slightly. "The tests

we performed on the pieces of the stone were inconclusive. In fact, the tests yielded no results, period. Lakesh suggested that the artifact was a probability-wave packet, a mathematical equation in physical form that formed an interface between our universe and others. Balam described it as a piece of 'pure' matter, which doesn't necessarily mean it's *our* universe's matter."

"Which, of course," Philboyd interjected, "could make it a piece of dark matter."

"That's very possible," Brigid admitted. "Conventional wisdom had it that the fundamental laws of physics are not invariant under parity, but a few quantum physicists took a different view. Their theory of parity predicted the existence of mirror matter. Each particle is postulated to have a mirror partner with similar properties that behaves exactly as the mirror image of its partner, only it exists slightly out of phase with our dimension. This is similar to antimatter, except the mirror particles and ordinary particles only have very weak interactions. They wouldn't annihilate each other on contact."

"And that would explain why they weren't detected," Philboyd said, warming to the topic. "I think I see where you're going with this. Mirror particles could act as dark matter, and since it has the similar properties as ordinary matter, you could conceivably have mirror stars, planets, theoretically even entire galaxies. Mirror stars would be invisible because they would emit mirror photons, which wouldn't interact with ordinary electrons."

"Exactly," Brigid declared.

"That's all very *not* fascinating," Grant growled, "but what does any of that have to do with Mars and Maccan's need for the interphaser?"

The corner of Brigid's mouth quirked in an enigmatic smile. "I haven't worked it all out yet."

"But you will," Kane told her dourly.

She nodded. "I'll do my best."

Inhaling a deep breath, Brigid placed the palms of her hands flat on the table. "So, what's our plan?"

"Since we're making a jump into dark territory," Grant said peevishly, "we don't have many options available to us. The plan should be simple."

"I agree," Kane put in, "but that doesn't mean it should be simple-minded."

Brigid glanced up at the clock on the wall. "Let's get some rest, decide what kind of equipment we'll be taking with us and embark in eight hours."

"Eight hours?" Philboyd echoed plaintively. "Lakesh has already been gone for nearly twenty-four and—"

"And if Maccan decided to tear his head off," Kane interrupted curtly, "he would have done it long before now."

"The mission is to retrieve both Lakesh and the interphaser," Grant rumbled. "Or one or the other. We'll be making a mat-trans jump to Mars...not to another unit in a redoubt across the country, so we need to take a few more precautions than usual. And that means going in as alert and as prepared as we can possibly be."

"Besides," Kane commented, "for all we know, Maccan deactivated the gateway in the Cydonia Compound and we either won't be going anywhere at all, or we'll just bounce around the entire Cerberus network as digital information for eternity."

"What about the Mantas?" Philboyd asked anxiously. "Couldn't we fly one or two of them to Mars if all else fails?"

Brewster Philboyd was an accomplished pilot of the small fleet of transatmospheric craft found on the Manitius Moon base. Of Annunaki manufacture, they were in pristine condition, despite their great age. Powered by two different kinds of engines, a ramjet and solid-fuel, pulse- detonation air spikes, the Manta ships could fly in both a vacuum and in an atmosphere. The Manta transatmospheric plane was not an experimental craft, but an example of a technology that was mastered by a race when humanity still cowered in trees from saber-toothed tigers.

Grant and Kane had easily learned to fly the ships, since they handled superficially like the Deathbirds the two men had flown when they were Cobaltville Magistrates. But when Kane and Grant recently flew two of the transatmospheric vehicles down from the Moon, they reached the unsettling realization that, while in space, the ships couldn't be piloted like winged aircraft within an atmosphere.

A pilot could select velocity, angle, attitude and other complex factors dictated by standard avionics, but space flight relied on a completely different set of principles. It called for the maximum manipulation of gravity, trajectory, relative velocities and plain old luck. Despite all the computer-calculated course programming, both men learned quickly that successfully piloting the TAV through space was more by God than by grace. Skill had almost nothing to do with it.

Brigid, Grant and Kane all regarded Philboyd with expressions of incredulity stamped on their faces. After a lengthy, awkward silence, Brigid demanded, "Have you calculated how long it would take to get to Mars by Manta, even at its maximum speed?"

Philboyd shook his head contritely. "No, I haven't," he admitted. "But it shouldn't be hard to figure out if you—"

Brigid cut him off by announcing, "I already figured it out, Brewster, several weeks ago. First of all, the best time to travel to Mars from Earth is when the two planets are in conjunction, at their maximum distance from each other on opposite sides of the Sun. That makes Earth about six hundred million kilometers away from Mars at the best of times and another conjunction isn't due for several months.

"At the optimum launch window, with the Mantas using maximum thrust when they're out beyond the gravity well of Earth, the minimum transit time to Mars could be accomplished in about one hundred and ninety-five days. Six and a half months trapped in an area not much bigger than this table is asking a little much of anybody, wouldn't you say?"

"And even if Lakesh was still alive when we finally got there," Grant pointed out, "I imagine our muscles would be too atrophied to be much good in staging a rescue attempt."

"And God only knows what the cockpits would smell like," said Kane. When Brigid cast him a cold look he added lowly, "But I guess that's of a secondary concern."

Philboyd smiled nevertheless. "Tell me what you need from me, and I'll see what I can get together."

"You're not going," Kane said in a tone that brooked no debate.

Blinking at him owlishly in a way reminiscent of Lakesh before his restoration, Philboyd stammered, "But I thought—why did you want me to—? I mean, this is a great opportunity for me."

"To get yourself killed, maybe," Grant declared. "No, you're staying put. You've already been a big help getting the systems back up and running and that's of equal priority."

"But to actually visit Mars," Philboyd protested. "It was one of the great unrealized dreams of scientists like myself."

"And it became a realized nightmare for a lot of other people," Kane said darkly. "We can't afford to act as your tour guide, Brewster. The three of us have been there before, we have an idea of the lay of the land and what to expect."

"Sindri and his transadapts?" Philboyd asked.

"I'm pretty certain Sindri is still the guest of Baron Sharpe," answered Brigid. "As for the transadapts..." She trailed off, glancing toward Kane and Grant with quizzical eyes. They could only shrug, indicating her guess would be as good as theirs.

When construction of the secret Cydonia One Compound on Mars began in late 1990, Earth-normal gravity was maintained in the colony by using a network of synthetic-gravity generators that created a field using a controlled stream of gravitons. At first the intention was to terraform the Red Planet, but as time passed, it was found to be more convenient and expeditious to adapt the descendants of the first Martian colonists to the planet's environment. Thus was born the first generation of the gnomelike transadapts.

Capable of existing in very cold temperatures and drawing oxygen from a thinner atmosphere, the load-bearing function of the spine and legs was altered, with the legs becoming a second pair of arms. The transadapts were engineered to have a relatively short life span, with few living past thirty years of age. The transadapts were developed in secret in the Cydonia Compound. The raw genetic material used to create the first generation was provided by people taken forcibly from Earth—an ugly twist on the UFO abduction myths.

"Could be that Mac and his people took care of them for you," Philboyd ventured.

"Wouldn't that be nice," Grant commented wistfully, pushing back his chair and standing up. "Let's meet in the operations center at 1600 hours."

Grant left the dining hall, but he didn't go to his quarters. He knew he should have been exhausted, both from the long trip and the tension born of learning about Lakesh's abduction, but he realized he wouldn't be able to force himself to sleep. Although he had trained himself to catch sleep whenever he could so as to build up a backlog in case he had to go for long periods without it, tonight he knew he could barely nap, much less drift off into deep slumber.

Entering the dispensary, he looked around for De-Fore. When he didn't see her, he soft-footed into the adjoining room to Domi's bedside. Taking her tiny hand in his, he studied the girl's blank, pale face.

His mind raced like an out-of-control engine, thoughts, memories and images colliding within the walls of his skull. He had no trouble mentally conjuring up his first glimpse of her on a muddy street in Cobaltville's Tartarus Pits. Her hair was held away from her piquant, hollow-cheeked face by a length of satiny cloth. She wore a T-shirt and a pair of red, high-cut shorts that showed off her pale, gamin-slim legs.

Grant easily recalled how a minute after his first sight of her, she had led him, Kane and a Magistrate named Boon into an ambush. Domi had been acting under duress, put in fear of her life by the Pit boss, Guana Teague. At her first opportunity, she redeemed her treachery by cutting Teague's throat.

Grant was having the life crushed out of him beneath Teague's three-hundred-plus pounds of flab when Domi expertly slit his throat. After that, Domi attached herself to Grant, viewing him as a gallant black knight who had rescued her from the shackles of Guana Teague's slavery, even though in reality, quite the reverse was true. She always carried the hunting knife with the nine-inch serrated blade, which had done the deed, as something of a memento.

For more than a year Domi had made it fiercely clear that Grant was hers and hers alone, despite the fact he fought hard to make sure there was nothing but friendship between him and the girl, but he feared it was a fight he would eventually lose. He had no idea of Domi's true age; he was pushing forty and felt twice as old. Still, he could never deny he was attracted to her youthfulness, her high spirits and her uninhibited sexuality.

But more than that, Domi had proved herself to be a tough and resourceful, if not altogether stable partner. At one point she had saved his, Brigid's and Kane's lives when the Cerberus mat-trans unit was sabotaged.

Even being in her debt didn't make him more understanding of her, or appreciate her uniqueness. He realized he had never really known her. It hadn't occurred to him they had forged a relationship deeper than he knew or cared to admit.

Always before, he had tried to make the gap in their ages the reason he didn't want to get involved with her, sexually or otherwise. Domi had been patient and understanding for a year until she'd grown tired of waiting. In truth, Grant had deliberately maintained a distance between himself and Domi, so if either she or he died, or simply went away, the vacuum wouldn't be so difficult to endure. He recalled with crystal clarity what she had said to him a month or so ago when she'd confronted him. "If you can't do it, if you're impotent, then let me know right now, so I can make plans."

When he angrily denied a physical disability was the reason, she snarled, "Then it is me, you lying sack of shit." Then, with contempt dripping from every syllable, she said, "Big man, big chest, big shoulders, legs like trees. Guess they don't tell the story, huh?"

That was the last private conversation they'd had. Her angry outburst cut him like the knife she'd turned on Guana Teague. When he remembered the recrimination in her voice, he knew he couldn't make up for anything he had done to hurt her. And he knew he had hurt Domi dreadfully when she'd spied him and Shizuka locked in a passionate embrace.

Until just a couple of weeks ago, it had been Grant's intent to leave Cerberus and to live in the little island monarchy of New Edo with Shizuka, commander of the Tigers of Heaven, particularly after the arrival of the Manitius base personnel and the hybrid woman Quavell. If Quavell really did carry Kane's child, then the entire dynamic of the struggle against the tyranny of the barons had changed.

But after being captured and tortured by the sadistic Baron Beausoliel, Grant realized the struggle remained essentially the same; there were just new players on the field. The war itself would go on and would never end, unless he took an active hand in it, regardless of his love for Shizuka and Domi's apparent devotion to Lakesh—a concept he still found a little disconcerting. However, he was in no position to make judgments, or even to comment on it.

"I just checked on her," DeFore's voice suddenly said from behind him. He covered his startlement by asking, more harshly than intended, "And? What are you doing for her?"

She stepped to his side, apparently not offended by his tone of voice. "All I can, which is very little."

"What did you do for Brigid when she was comatose a few months ago?" Grant demanded tersely.

DeFore reached out and brushed a lock of hair away from Domi's forehead. "About what I'm doing for her. The main difference is that I induced the coma in Brigid because of the head trauma she suffered. I'm still not sure what happened to Domi."

Grant grunted softly. "I see."

"What are your plans?" DeFore asked.

"Plans?"

"To rescue Lakesh."

"We leave in the morning, so I'd—" He broke off, leaning forward, gazing into Domi's face. "Something's happening."

Domi's eyelids fluttered and her eyes moved back and forth beneath the lids. Her lips parted and allowed a groaning sigh to escape.

"We've got rapid eye movement," DeFore exclaimed excitedly.

"Is that good or bad?" asked Grant.

"Good—it means there's some higher brain activity going on. Stay here."

DeFore whirled away and rushed into the next room. Grant started to pull his hand away, but Domi's fingers suddenly closed tightly around it with a surprising strength.

Simultaneously her eyes flew open, wide and wild. Convulsions shook her petite form, racked her violently from head to toe. Domi dragged in a great shuddery breath as if her lungs had been deprived of oxygen for a long time. She clawed out with her right hand, finding Grant's wrist and closing her fingers around it as if it were an anchor to life. Her crimson, glassy eyes asked a silent, beseeching question.

"It's me," Grant told her. "You're in the infirmary."

Air rasped in and out of Domi's throat as she tried to sit up. She managed only a flailing spasm of arms and legs. Grant held her down against the bed, shouting, "DeFore! She's conscious! She's trying to get up!"

"Don't let her!" came DeFore's urgent response. "Put her in restraints if you have to!"

Domi shivered, inhaling and exhaling with deep gasps. She relaxed on the bed, no longer struggling to rise. Finally she managed to say, in an aspirated whisper, "God...mad god."

Chapter 16

Reba DeFore didn't allow Domi to be questioned, but inasmuch as the girl's speech was slurred and her cognitive functions severely impaired, Grant, Brigid and Kane figured she couldn't offer intel any more helpful than that conveyed by Philboyd and the others.

The three of them waited out in the infirmary proper while DeFore examined Domi. Within a few minutes she brought them her provisional diagnosis, saying Domi was suffering from shock and nerve trauma. Although her prognosis was guarded, she couldn't foresee any reasons why Domi wouldn't make a complete recovery in time.

Grant and Kane had both been on the receiving end of infrasound jolts in the past and they knew the effects, although painful in the extreme, were transitory.

"I've given her a sedative," DeFore said in a low voice. "She's not up to eating solid food yet. She's very agitated and keeps asking for Lakesh."

"What did you tell her?" asked Grant.

DeFore shook her head, her dark eyes troubled. "I lied to her. I said he was just fine and would be in to see her tomorrow morning. Once she wakes up from a normal sleep pattern, she ought to be able to think more clearly and understand what really happened. Right now she's still out of it."

"When you tell her the truth," Brigid murmured dolefully, "we'll be gone. And she might be so angry she'll try to follow us."

DeFore's full lips compressed in a tight, determined line. "None of my patients will be taking walks. Besides, she'll be suffering from vertigo and blurred vision for days to come. Even if she could see, she won't have the coordination to whistle and walk at the same time. No matter how mad she gets, she won't be going anywhere." With that, she returned to the adjoining room.

"Mad," Grant echoed quietly. "The first thing she said was 'mad god.'"

"She was obviously referring to Maccan," Brigid interjected.

"You think?" Grant snapped sarcastically. "I just wonder if she meant mad as in pissed, or mad as in fused-out."

Kane snorted. "You saw the pointy-eared son of a bitch decapitate Megaera and then play dodge-ball with her head. What do you think?"

Grant bared his teeth angrily. "He's not a god."

"No," Brigid agreed. "He only thinks he is. And that makes him more dangerous than a real one, in my opinion. He's got that much more to prove."

She turned and left the infirmary. After a moment Grant trailed after her. Kane felt too keyed-up to go to his quarters and sleep, so he checked in on Farrell. He knew the man had never liked him much, due in the main to his background as a Magistrate and a misunderstanding a couple of years ago in which Kane had thrown him headfirst into a wall.

Now Farrell seemed genuinely happy to see him, but Kane figured he was probably glad to have any visitors, just so he could talk about his heroic actions during the incursion. He had already heard Philboyd's version of it, but he listened politely to Farrell's, a little surprised to find not much variation between the two tales.

"I wish you'd been here," Farrell said in conclusion. "It might've gone down a little different. But we still gave as good as we got."

Sourly, Kane reflected that unless Maccan's home was shot to pieces and an object of great value stolen from it, then Farrell was living in an optimist's dream, but he decided not to tell him that.

"We've debriefed Philboyd," Kane said, "and it sounds like you and he saw pretty much everything the other one saw in the firefight. Do you think Auerbach witnessed anything you two didn't?"

Farrell's goateed face twisted in a grimace of disgust. "Unless it was the puddle of his own piss he was squatting in, no way. The bastard hid under a desk after he ran out of bullets."

Kane smiled wryly. "Some people just aren't cut out to be warriors. Good thing we are, right?"

Farrell gingerly touched his thickly bandaged and elevated leg, wincing a little as he did so. "Yeah," he said bleakly. "Good thing."

Kane patted him encouragingly on the shoulder and

left him. He started for the exit, then remembered he intended to ask DeFore to put together a first-aid kit for them by the next morning.

Peering into the adjoining room, he expected to see the medic at Domi's bedside. To his surprise and unease, he saw Quavell there, apparently standing vigil. The hybrid woman dabbed at Domi's discolored forehead with a moist cloth. The albino girl, now under the comforting influence of sedatives, murmured to her in wordless gratitude.

Kane watched the two women for a moment, struck again by their resemblance to one another and how their vast differences had actually brought them together, as if completing a circle that began at opposite poles.

Unlike himself, Grant and Brigid, the only life path Domi abandoned when she'd joined Cerberus was the marginal existence of an outlander, and later, as Guana Teague's sex slave.

Born into a raw, wild world, outlanders were accustomed to living on the edge of death. Grim necessity had taught them the skills to survive, even thrive in the postnuke environment. They may have been the great-great-great- grandchildren of civilized men and women, but they had no choice but to embrace lives of semibarbarism. They were tough and vicious and quite possibly the last genuine human beings on the planet.

Sneered at by the elite of the villes, viewed as little more than expendable dray animals, outlanders were an endangered species. As a Magistrate, Kane had chilled dozens of them in the performance of his duty, but he had murdered more than their bodies. He had destroyed their spirits, as well.

He had killed them, body and soul, because he was carrying out the will of the barons—the hybridized god-kings who had inherited the Earth from their human cousins whom they scorned as "apekin." The hybrids, at least by their way of thinking, represented the final phase of human evolution. They referred to themselves as "new humans" and empowered themselves to control not only their immediate environment, but also the evolution of other species.

The barons did so by planning and creating wholesale alterations in living organisms, changing evolutionary patterns to suit themselves. They considered themselves the pinnacle of evolutionary achievement, as high above ordinary hybrids as the hybrids were above mere humans.

As unaware as Kane was of their existence until she joined Cerberus, Domi learned to hate the barons with the same zeal that he did. Despite how mad the entire tale of Archon-human hybrids seemed initially, they grew comfortable with it and eased into hating the hybrid dynasty and the baronial oligarchy. They woke up hating the hybrids and the barons and they went to bed hating the hybrids and barons.

Domi had had difficulty grasping the new concepts or quenching the fires of her hatred. Although she despised the breed of so-called new human on general principles, she reserved her most unregenerate hatred for the breed of old human that willingly served them. As far as she was concerned, they were worse than traitors to their own kind; they were groveling, submissive lap dogs and deserved no mercy. When she encountered them, she offered none. Waiflike in appearance she might be, but Domi had proved time and again that she was anything but a child.

Then both Kane and Domi had been apprehended while penetrating Area 51. Whereas he was imprisoned by the forces of Baron Cobalt, Domi had actually been rescued by an insurrectionist fifth column made up of humans and hybrids, led by Quavell—whom Domi had been restrained from killing some months before during the Archuleta Mesa mission.

Over a period of time Domi realized that her hatred of the hybrids and barons was derived primarily from what Quavell referred to as "negative conditioning." To end the war between human and hybrid, Quavell explained, the conditioning had to be faced and overcome by both factions.

Domi had remembered conversations between Lakesh and Brigid Baptiste about how the similarity between Balam's folk and the hybrids and the traditional myth-images of demons accounted for the instant enmity that sprang up between humans and the so-called Archon.

Lakesh opined that since ancient depictions of imps, elves and jinn were more than likely based on early encounters between Balam's people and primitive man, humans weren't capable of reaching an accord with creatures who resembled archetypal figures of evil.

Even by crossbreeding with humans, the hybrids were still markedly different from humankind. But as

Quavell pointed out, different was not the same as alien. She herself confessed that her own race viewed humans as savages, little more than bloodthirsty apes who were incapable of transcending their roots as killers. She had other experiences with humans, as well, specifically with Kane. While Quavell's group of insurgents had found Domi, Baron Cobalt sentenced Kane to what amounted to stud service.

The mission that destroyed Archuleta Mesa had also virtually wiped out the genetic-engineering division of the vast facility. What remained of the place, both in personnel and machinery, was transferred to the much larger Area 51 facility. The necessary equipment and raw material to implement procreation had yet to be installed. Baron Cobalt had unilaterally decided that the conventional means of conception was the only option to keep the hybrid race alive.

Since the baron held Kane responsible for pushing the hybrid race to the brink of extinction, he made it his task to repopulate it, as well. Kane wasn't the first human male to be pressed into service. There had been other men before him, but they had performed unsatisfactorily, due to their terror of the hybrids.

Kane's sense of surprise was still fresh when he recollected how Quavell, during one of their scheduled periods of copulation had confided to him that not every hybrid agreed with the baronial policy toward humanity. He was even more surprised when she'd helped him and Domi escape. Both of them were forced to reassess everything they'd thought they'd known about the barons, about the hybrids.

Quavell suddenly sensed his presence in the doorway and lifted her eyes, her crystal-blue, penetrating gaze fixed on his face. Her expression remained the same, one of a calm, almost serene detachment. Resisting the impulse to withdraw, he nodded to her instead. She didn't react for a long moment, then she returned the nod with just a hint of the arrogant hybrid superiority he had learned to despise.

In a soft yet firm voice, Kane said, "Quavell, you and I need to talk."

"Indeed."

She started to move toward him, but he checked the movement by hastily interposing, "When I get back."

Kane turned and left, hoping he didn't appear to be in a hurry. His mind wheeled with memories, fears and conjectures. He recalled how Quavell had reacted when he'd questioned her in Area 51, as if it were truly possible for humans and hybrids to procreate. Although she claimed they were chromosomally compatible, she had admitted the procedure was still experimental.

Then Quavell had smiled at him in a way he could only interpret as coquettish. One of her long fingers traced the faint scar on his left cheek and she whispered, "But some of us here—me, at least—find the process of trial and error very enjoyable."

The most recent memory of Quavell was not hazy in the least, though he wished it were. He still recalled with shocking vividness his first sight of her, nearly two months before, sitting in Lakesh's office when he had entered to brief him about the events that had occurred on the Moon. Kane would have imbibed battery acid before admitting that it was the closest he had ever come to fainting dead away. As it was, his knees had almost buckled, but he was able to attribute his weakness to the injuries inflicted upon him by Maccan.

According to Quavell, she had made the long overland trip from Area 51 in a stolen Sandcat, all alone. She'd traveled as far as the foothills of the Bitterroot Range to the encampment of Sky Dog. The shaman brought her the rest of the way to the mountain peak on horseback. Both Kane and Lakesh were still skeptical of certain details of her story, particularly how she knew the location of the redoubt. She offered only a vague explanation about learning of it from either Kane or Domi during their period of imprisonment in Dreamland.

She had refused to name which one of them actually made the revelation. Neither Kane nor Domi admitted to telling her or anyone else about Cerberus. Still and all, Quavell had provided them with information about the current state of the baronies following the Imperator War, although little of it could be confirmed.

Quavell's presence in the redoubt made Kane distinctly uncomfortable, since the entire situation evoked unpleasant memories of Lakesh's abortive plan to turn Cerberus from a sanctuary to a colony. To that end, babies needed to be born, ones with superior genes. Making a unilateral decision, Lakesh had arranged for a woman named Beth-Li Rouch to be brought into the redoubt from one of the baronies to mate with Kane, to ensure that his superior abilities were passed on to offspring.

Without access to the techniques of fetal development outside the womb that were practiced in the villes, the conventional means of procreation was the only option. And that meant sex and passion and the fury of a woman scorned.

Kane had refused to cooperate for a variety of reasons, primarily because he felt the plan was a continuation of sinister elements that had brought about the nukecaust and the tyranny of the villes. His refusal had had tragic consequences. Only a thirst for revenge and a conspiracy to murder had been birthed within the walls of the redoubt, not children.

And now Beth-Li was dead, killed by Domi and buried in a simple grave out on the hillside. Kane could only pray Quavell's involvement in the lives of the Cerberus residents didn't have similarly tragic consequences.

AT 0600, they convened in the ready room, which held the jump chamber. Brigid, Kane and Grant had made their preparations the night before, filling flat cases with special equipment, rations and water. All three of them wore the hard suits they had brought down from the Moon. The one-piece garments were fairly tight-fitting and relatively lightweight, barely thirty pounds apiece.

The hard suits consisted of ten layers of aluminized Mylar insulation interlaced with six layers of Dacron and tough outer facings of a bronze-colored Kevlar, to blunt impacts that might penetrate the microenvironment provided by the suits. They carried the helmets under their arms. Dark bronze in color like the suits, the helmets were made of a lightweight, ceramic-alloy compound. The treated Plexiglas faceplates polarized when exposed to light levels above a certain candlepower.

Equipped with sealed water dispensers and sipping tubes attached into the interior walls, the helmets allowed freedom of movement for their heads, even though they did limit peripheral vision. They could communicate with each other over UTEL radio systems. Small, secondary oxygen tanks were attached to the back of the headpieces. The design allowed for the venting of exhaled air directly into the environment, much like Scuba gear. Venting from the helmet reduced the collection of moisture on the inner faceplate.

The only modifications Kane and Grant had made to the space suits were the adjustment of the seals between sleeves and gloves to permit the addition of their Sin Eaters. The fingers of the gloves were flexible enough to pick up coins from a carpeted floor. Their combat daggers hung in scabbards from web belts.

Brigid carried one of the tungsten-carbide rail pistols brought from the Moon base and added to the Cerberus arsenal. She tucked the weapon into a holster on her belt. The EVA suits were hot and they each wore formfitting shadow suits beneath them, as well. They were climate-controlled for environments up to highs of 150 degrees and as low as -10 degrees Fahrenheit. Microfilaments controlled the internal temperature.

An extremely nervous Philboyd checked the seals of the EVA suits and made sure the oxygen tanks worked. "I admit I don't understand everything about the gateways," he said, "but Mars seems a damn long way for a gateway jump. If it would take nearly half a year to get there by Manta—"

"Distance is relative when you're dealing with quantum physics," Bry said diffidently from the doorway. "There's no relativistic range limitation on hyperdimensions. The gateways form interstices and interfaces between linear points, regardless of the distance between them. Utilizing hyperdimensional space, there is little difference between jumping from a mat-trans unit in Cuba and one in Australia. The same principle applies to the gateway here and the one on Mars."

No one spoke for a long moment after Bry's pronouncement. Then Grant said, "Hell, why are we bothering with this trip at all? We don't need Lakesh back, not with that dead-on imitation Bry can perform."

Everyone laughed, including, after a moment of annoyed glowering, Bry. "I've got all the coordinates encoded...all you have to do is shut the door."

No one mentioned that once Project Cerberus began mass producing the mat-trans gateways as modular units, conventional spacecraft were rendered virtually obsolete since the gateways permitted swift and relatively easy movement of personnel and matériel back and forth from Earth. A mat-trans gateway was installed on the space station Parallax Red, and experiments were conducted regarding the teleportation of gateway components through space along carrier-wave guides placed at equidistant intervals to the projected destination.

This method allowed travel to the inner planets of the solar system without using conventional spacecraft. The wave guides launched from Parallax Red provided an almost instantaneous method of reaching Mars.

Gusting out a long, weary sigh, Philboyd said, "I don't know if I should envy you or feel sorry for you."

"We've been there already," said Kane brusquely. "Feel sorry for us."

Philboyd gestured toward the helmets under their arms. "You won't need to put those on?"

Brigid shook her head. "The Cydonia gateway unit is located in a habitat with synthetic gravity and an Earth-normal atmosphere. We won't even need the EVA suits unless we go out on the surface. We're wearing them just in case."

Philboyd smiled crookedly. "Good luck, all."

The three people trooped into the jump chamber. Above the keypad encoding panel hung an imprinted notice, dating back to predark days. In faded maroon lettering, it read Entry Absolutely Forbidden To All But B-12 Cleared Personnel.

Kane used to wonder why Lakesh hadn't removed the sign, but he figured the man probably applied the same reasons to keeping the illustration of the three-headed hound intact. Nostalgia could manifest itself in very curious ways.

They took their places on the hexagonal floor plates, and Kane pulled the door closed, initiating the automatic jump circuits. He noted that breathing rates increased, including his own.

Kane glanced over toward Grant. "You know, you haven't said it in a long time."

"Said what?" Grant's tone of voice, like his expression, was flinty.

"You know," said Brigid teasingly. "What you always used to say before we made a gateway jump. Your mantra."

Grant tried to shrug, but it wasn't easy in the EVA suit. "I only said it before I got used to making the jumps. They don't bother me now."

"Oh, really?" Kane arched a challenging, mocking eyebrow toward him.

"Really," Grant grunted.

The familiar yet still slightly unnerving hum arose, muted due to the helmets. The hum climbed in pitch to a whine, then to a cyclonic howl. The hexagonal floor and ceiling plates shimmered silver. A fine, faint mist gathered at their feet and drifted down from the ceiling. Thready static discharges, like tiny lightning strokes, arced through the vapor.

The mist thickened, blotting out everything. Shadows seemed to creep into Kane's vision from all corners. The sound of breathing faded, ebbing away into silence. Right before Kane's hearing shut down altogether, Grant's strained, faraway whisper filtered into his helmet. "I *hate* these fucking things."

Chapter 17

Stepping into a mat-trans chamber, losing consciousness, then awakening in another always felt like dying violently and then being born again—violently.

First the entire universe seemed to explode in a blaze of force. From the hyperdimensional nonspace through which they had been traveling, they seemed to fall through bottomless abysses. There was a microinstant of nonexistence, then a sharp, wrenching shock and their senses returned.

Kane stared up at the pattern of silver disks on the ceiling and realized they were diamond-shaped rather the familiar hexagonal configuration, which meant the phase transit had been successful.

Trying to focus through the last of the mist wisping over his eyes, Kane silently endured the nausea churning and rolling in his stomach. He knew if he waited it out, he wouldn't vomit, but it would take another couple of minutes to regain his emotional equilibrium. No human being, no matter how thoroughly briefed in advance, could be expected to remain unflappable on a hyperdimensional trip through the gateway.

By stepping into the armaglass-enclosed chamber,

one second a person was in the relativistic *here,* surrounded by glowing mist, and in the next second, all eternity seemed to cave in. Perceptions changed, time jumped and for a heart-stopping instant, the cosmos at large seemed to stand still. Then the traveler was wherever the transmitter had been programmed to send him. Whatever else, a trip through the gateway was unsettling to the mind, to the nerves and to the soul itself, as Kane had personal reason to know.

In a hoarse, strained whisper, he heard Brigid say, "It looks like we made it."

"Yeah," rumbled Grant sarcastically. "I guessed that when I noticed we weren't puking our guts out. This unit wasn't made by Russians, after all."

Grant always held up their jump to a malfunctioning Russian gateway as the standard by which all mat-trans journeys should be measured. The Cerberus gateway link had been unable to establish a lock on the Russian unit's autosequence initiators. The matter-stream carrier-wave modulations couldn't be synchronized, which resulted in a severe bout of jump sickness, symptoms of which included, but were not limited to, vomiting, a near crippling lethargy and even hallucinations.

Kane turned his head, squeezing his eyes shut against the momentary wave of vertigo that blurred his vision. When he opened them, he saw Grant and Brigid carefully hiking themselves up to sitting positions. Fading tendrils of vapor wreathed their bodies, a plasma byproduct of what Lakesh referred to as the "quincunx effect."

The floor-plate pattern duplicated that of the ceiling. The jump chamber was small, about half the size of standard. The dark blue color of the armaglass walls allowed only the dimmest light to penetrate from outside.

"Yeah," Grant concurred, rising first to a knee, then standing. "It looks like the same one I remember."

He sounded so phlegmatic about it, Kane couldn't help but chuckle briefly. Grant eyed him challengingly. "I say something funny?"

Kane shook his head and sat up. "Do you ever?"

He reflected how he and his friends now accepted the reality of almost-instantaneous travel across the solar system as routine, when only a couple of years before all of their minds had been completely boggled by their first mat-trans jump—a distance of a few hundred miles, from Colorado to Montana.

After helping Brigid to her feet, Kane sniffed the air experimentally and found it cold, even a little stale, but still breathable. Grant didn't bother, since his sense of smell was seriously impaired due to suffering a broken nose more than once.

Brigid rocked experimentally on the balls of her feet. "The grav-stators are still working."

"I guess the transadapts are still pulling pay," Grant rumbled.

"Let's find out." Gripping the wedge-shaped handle of the door, Kane heaved up on it. With a click, the door of dense, semitranslucent material swung outward on counterbalanced hinges. His Sin Eater popped into his waiting palm. He heard Grant unleathering his own sidearm.

By half inches, Kane nudged the door open with a boot, pausing to listen. Stepping up beside him, Brigid lifted her left wrist. Strapped around it was a small device made of molded black plastic and stamped metal. A liquid crystal display window exuded a faint glow. The motion detector registered no movement within the radius of its invisible sensor beams.

He heard nothing, so he pushed the door wide and saw what he expected to see—a small room with cream-colored walls, a cabinet with shattered glass doors and dark bloodstains on the floor. The last time he'd seen the room, Sindri's chief lieutenant, the venomous transadapt David, lay bleeding to death at the base of the jump chamber. Apparently a few of his brethren had attended to his body and done what they could to scrub away the mess.

Kane took the point as he usually did, carrying his helmet under his arm. He walked carefully, heel-to-toe, leading with his Sin Eater until he reached the open doorway. The room beyond was small and dimly lit, more of a foyer. A turnstile security checkpoint occupied most of the opposite wall.

Brigid came to his side, performed another motion-detector sweep and, one at a time, they pushed through the prongs of the checkpoint and into a narrow tube-tunnel. The passageway was very quiet, as if upon entering they had stepped into a vault that hoarded only silence. Kane eased out into the shaft, walking heel-to-toe in the characteristic way of a Mag penetrating a potential kill zone.

The right-hand walls were perforated at regular in-

tervals with large, round iris hatches. The first hatch
they came to opened into a partitioned office suite
filled with desks and computer terminals. Tacked onto
a bulletin board near the door were dozens of memos,
each one bearing the legend By Order Of The Committee Of One Hundred.

The second hatch opened up into a big room, that
contained a raised dais supporting a lectern that looked
out over ten rows of chairs. They knew it was the
council chamber of the ruling committee of the colony.
All three of them recalled what Sindri had told them
about the governmental setup of the Cydonia colony,
which had actually gotten its start on *Parallax Red.*

In the late twentieth century, shortly after the photographic discoveries of the Monuments of Mars by
the *Viking Mars* probe, construction had began in secret on a space habitat located in LaGrange Region 2
on the far side of the Moon. Originally the project had
been a covert joint undertaking between America and
Russia, under the authority of the Totality Concept's
Overproject Majestic. *Parallax Red,* envisioned as an
elite community with a maximum population of five
thousand, was intended as a utopia for the best of
Earth transported into space. The station provided a
jumping-off point for the colonists building the permanent outpost on the Cydonia plains of Mars.

However, because of the chaos engendered by the
nukecaust and the damage the space station sustained
by Russian killer satellites, both the fledgling Martian
colony and *Parallax Red* were forgotten. The personnel of the station had had no choice but to move per-

manently to Mars. They'd formed a caste-based society built on the labor of the transadapts.

They'd also explored their new home world, particularly the mile-high D&M Pyramid, named after DiPetro and Molenar, the two NASA photoanalysts who'd discovered it on the *Viking* transmissions. The massive pyramid served the Tuatha de Danaan as the cornerstone of their ancient culture, and within it the colonists came across the leavings of their once-mighty science, all of it based on sound and vibration. They'd found a small harplike device, which was a microscopic version of a truly gargantuan instrument occupying the uppermost level of the structure.

The pyramid was more than a monument—it was a gigantic broadcasting tower, transmitting a frequency too subtle for human ears but deadly to the Archons. Sindri had referred to it as a song that played eternally, blanketing the entire planet, penetrating every nook and cranny of Mars and forming an invisible sonic wall that forever barred Archon entry.

Sindri had theorized the true purpose behind the Cydonia colony in the twentieth century was to locate the source of the song and stop it. He'd believed the Archons supported and abetted a Terran colony on Mars, so by proxy, they would still conquer Mars, reclaiming it from the Tuatha de Danaan. Brigid, Kane and Grant had learned much later that Sindri's overall theory was wrong, although close to the truth in some particulars.

In any event, as the twenty-first century became the twenty-second and edged toward the twenty-third, the transadapt population of the Cydonia Compound had continued to grow, eventually outnumbering the human population by at least three to one. Only their much shorter life spans had prevented them from completely controlling the colony.

One of the descendants of the original human colonists devoted his life to divining the purpose of the Danaan infrasound emitter in the pyramid. Micah Harwin postulated that the device transmitted not a signal, but a frequency that blanketed the entire planet. As it turned out, solving that mystery became Harwin's only reason for living.

When Sindri was born, genetic testing determined that he was the offspring of a transadapt mother and Harwin. He possessed far more Earth-human characteristics than transadapt, except for his short though perfectly proportioned stature. Sindri's mother died shortly after his birth and his father was exiled from the Cydonia Compound for the crime of miscegenation.

Making the D&M Pyramid his home, Harwin experimented with the frequencies of the Danaan transmitter and accidentally—or intentionally, no one really knew—altered the harmonics so that the human colonists became infertile over a period of time. It was Sindri himself, as an adult, who had discovered this and brought it to the ruling committee, urging an exodus back to Earth before the entire human population of the colony became extinct.

Rather than accept Sindri's proposal, the dwindling number of human colonists had devised a plan to ensure they would not eventually be outnumbered or outlived by the transadapts. Having already instituted a form of apartheid by segregating the transadapts into their own habitats, the humans used a medical treatment disguised as necessary vaccinations to make the transadapts barren. Since the transadapts had been engineered to have shorter life spans than humans, it was conceivable that they could all be dead within a single generation.

Sindri had led an open, bloody revolution against the human population of Cydonia. At the end of a month, all of the human colonists and three-quarters of the transadapts had perished by violence.

The oppressive silence made the passageways feel haunted by the ghosts of all the people who had died during the Cydonia struggle.

Brigid, Grant and Kane followed corridors lit by luminous neon bands that ran along the curved ceiling. When they reached an intersection Grant asked, unconsciously lowering his voice, "Where do we go from here?"

Brigid said, "If I recall correctly—"

"And there's no reason why you shouldn't," Kane broke in.

She ignored the interruption, gesturing to their right. "This way leads to the residential habitats."

The three walked for a score of yards in silence. When they reached a wide, outward bulging niche in the tunnel wall, Brigid stopped and touched a button. A shutter slid up, affording them a exterior view of the compound. The midmorning light came through the transparent port, the sun hovering a hands breadth over the rust-red horizon in a salmon-pink sky.

Beyond a fenced-in perimeter spread a seemingly endless desert of orange-red sand. Low ridges rose naked from the desolate landscape and grew into a distant, barren mountain range. Many miles to the west rose a vast bulk of stone, a smoothly contoured formation that resembled a slightly squashed mesa.

Windblown sand had piled high in drifts all around the perimeter of the colony. Windmills, water towers, trenches and solar reflectors were placed in functional patterns. Clusters of domes made of dull metal humped up from the sand like half-buried balls connected by tubes. Each one was connected to the others by tubes composed of the same material. Domes with translucent plastic roofs covered blurry green areas, which they guessed were vegetable gardens.

In the far distance they saw a range of stone shouldering up from rock-strewed and barren ground. Lowering his gaze, Kane saw a small object squatting on the ground between two of the tube-tunnels. Flat-topped and suspended by an assembly of tread-enclosed rollers, it looked vaguely like a toy version of a Sandcat.

The machine rested in exactly the same position as he had last seen it, when Sindri had identified it as the Mars *Pathfinder,* landed by NASA in the late 1990s. According to him, the mission had been a cover story to help to quell rumors they were deliberately concealing facts from the American citizenry about the discovery of ancient Martian artifacts.

Within the perimeter of the fence, rust-hued sand spread, piling up in dunes at the bases of the domes. A few of the habitats were larger than others, their exteriors faintly etched with window lines. They contained barracks, manufacturing facilities and even nurseries for transadapt children.

A rusty patina of granules covered every surface. At least once every Martian year, hurricane-force winds whipped up vast dust storms all over the surface of the planet. When Mars was closest to the sun, the storms developed in the southern hemisphere and the winds roared across the desert at three hundred miles per hour.

"Place looks about as inviting as the last time we visited," Grant said darkly.

Kane pointed out through the portal. "Those look new. They're not covered by dust, anyway."

Resting on the ground, on the opposite side of the fence, about one hundred yards away, they saw an array of long, open, flat-decked craft with low sidewalls. They resembled pix of bobsleds Kane had seen, but were about twice as long.

Brigid squinted toward them. "What are they?"

Grant gave them a brief visual examination and grunted. "Who cares. I'm more interested in where the transadapts might've gotten to."

"On *Parallax Red,* maybe?" Kane ventured.

"Maybe," Brigid said doubtfully. "But after the damage we caused the last time we were there, I don't think there are enough transadapts to manage major repairs. The station wouldn't have been able to sustain the entire colony."

Kane nodded in reluctant agreement. "They've got to be someplace. Either here or..."

He trailed off and Grant shot him an inquisitive, impatient look. "Here or where? The pyramid?"

"That would be my guess."

The three people began walking again, their feet almost soundless on the rubbery composition of the floor. Grant remarked tersely, "I'm a lot less interested in the whereabouts of the transadapts than Maccan and his crew."

"I have a feeling that if we find the one, we'll find the other," Kane replied offhandedly. Addressing Brigid, he asked, "Have you given any more thought to a connection between the interphaser and the pyramid?"

She hesitated before answering, "I have. But I want to take a look at the structure first and refresh my memory before I put my theory into words and leave myself open to ridicule."

Kane regarded her with a wide-eyed look of hurt innocence. "Now, who would do that, Baptiste?"

"I can't imagine," she retorted sarcastically. "You've always proved yourself so four-square supportive of all my flights of fancy."

"Please," he said stolidly. "My modesty—"

"Doesn't lend itself to close inspection, Kane."

She smiled wryly to let him know she was only joking. When she and Kane were first thrown together, their relationship had been volatile, marked by frequent quarrels, jealousies and resentments. The world in which she came of age was primarily quiet, focused on scholarly pursuits. Kane's world, wherein he'd become accustomed to daily violence, was supported by a belief system that demanded a ruthless single-mindedness to enforce baronial authority.

Both people had their gifts. Most of what was important to people in the twenty-second century came easily to Kane—survival skills, prevailing in the face of adversity and cunning against enemies. But he could also be reckless, high-strung to the point of instability and given to fits of rage.

Brigid on the other hand, was compulsively tidy and ordered, with a brilliant analytical mind. However her clinical nature, the cool scientific detachment upon which she prided herself, sometimes blocked an understanding of the obvious human factor in any given situation.

Regardless of their contrasting personalities, Kane and Brigid worked very well as a team, playing on each other's strengths rather than contributing to their individual weaknesses. Despite their differences, or perhaps because of them, the two people managed to forge the chains of partnership, which linked them together through mutual respect and trust.

Only once had the links of that chain been stretched to a breaking point. More than a year before Kane had shot and killed a woman, a distant relative of Brigid's, whom he'd perceived as a threat to her life. It had taken her some time to realize that under the confusing circumstances, Kane had had no choice but to make a snap judgment call. Making split-second, life-and-death decisions was part of his conditioning and

training in the Magistrate Division, as deeply in-
grained as breathing.

What conflicted her during that time was not the
slow process of forgiving him, but coming to terms
with what he really was and accepting the reality rather
than an illusion. He was a soldier, not an explorer, an
academic or an intellectual.

When she'd finally understood that about him, the
two had achieved a synthesis of attitudes and styles
where they functioned as colleagues and parts of a
team, extending to the other professional courtesies
and respect.

As they followed a bend in the tube-tunnel, the motion detector on Brigid's wrist suddenly emitted a dis-
cordant, warning beep. They came to immediate halts,
Sin Eaters snapping up and questing for targets.

Brigid stretched out her left arm and the motion
sensor's screen lit up with a wavery green line. She
swept the device slowly back and forth. The line slid
from one side of the screen to the other, formed a dot
and froze in a central position. The dot shifted position and the device emitted a second electronic beep.

"Definitely a moving contact," Brigid breathed.
"Coming this way."

They waited in tense postures, fingers lightly touching the trigger studs of their pistols. They heard a
steady, shuffling scuff and scutter as of leather sliding
over stone. Then the troll shambled around the bend,
his spraddle-legged gait causing him to list slightly
from side to side.

He wasn't much more than three and a half feet tall,

his heavy-jawed face sunk between the broad yoke of his shoulders. His beady, black eyes glittered from the shadows of deep sockets. Coarse, straight black hair fell over his retreating forehead. It bore streaks of gray. He wore a frayed coverall garment of drab olive-green.

Brigid inhaled sharply in startlement when she recognized him. His round gnome's head was still too large for his pipe-stem neck, and his tiny bare feet were still calloused an inch thick on the soles, with nine long, undercurving toes on each one.

The tenth toe was exceptionally long, nearly the length of the foot itself, projecting out at a forty-five-degree angle near the heel. It looked like a double-jointed thumb, topped by a yellow horny nail, caked with dirt to the cuticle.

But the last time they had seen David, his abnormally long arms hadn't terminated in a pair of steel hooks that curved up from metal cups over the stumps of his wrists.

Chapter 18

If Kane had expected to encounter any of the transadapts, he certainly hadn't anticipated it would be David. The troll's blunt face reflected Kane's own surprise and he recoiled, more from caution than fear of the three humans looming over him. The cold glitter in his black eyes betrayed the real hatred boiling away in the little man.

"Well, well," Kane said with a calm he didn't feel. "Little David, Sindri's chief hench-dwarf and personal chef. I didn't expect to see you alive."

"I bet you didn't," David countered in his high-pitched voice, sibilant with spite. He held up his hooks. "I almost wish you hadn't."

"I don't know what you're complaining about," Grant said, gesturing with his Sin Eater to the little man's feet. "You've got a whole extra sct."

David's swart face screwed up as if he intended to spit at Grant, but he contented himself by balancing on one splayed foot and performing a passable imitation of giving Grant the finger with the middle toe of the other one.

Kane repressed a smile, reflecting that the bodies of the transadapts were designed to be superior to that of the normal human physique—at least on Mars. The fact that human beings stood erect against Earth's gravity posed problems that were solved by skeletal and body-mass modifications by Overproject Excalibur's genetic engineers.

They changed the image of humanity to fit the environment of Mars—shrinking its stature, giving it a permanent hunched-over posture, increasing the length of the arms while shortening the legs. They rearranged the foot bones, moving the big toe toward the heel and extending it outward, transforming the digit into a double-jointed opposable thumb.

The legs had been modified to become a second pair of arms to provide extra anchorage in a near-weightless environment. The geneticists enclosed the major organs of the transadapts within their own independent shielding of dense tissue and protected the genitalia within a convenient pouch.

As efficient as the bodies of the transadapts might have been, they were still freaks of nature and couldn't live comfortably on Earth with its increased atmospheric pressure and higher oxygen content. Sindri had lied to them about leading them on an exodus to the planet that had birthed their ancestors.

Dreams of empire consumed Sindri. After living his entire life under the heel of a minority human ruling committee, he was fixated on establishing his own kingdom, regardless of the cost. To that end, he planned a double strike, which would not only unseat the barons on Earth but also literally destroy Mars, his birthplace and the world he despised.

That was only one element of Sindri's plan. Even if he and his transadapts migrated to Earth, the males were still sterile, the women barren and utter extinction was less than thirty years away. He realized their only chance for survival was to successfully hybridize their genetic structure with those of native Terrans, so the women at least could reproduce. When Kane, Grant and Brigid had arrived on *Parallax Red* via the gateway, Sindri saw them as both fonts of information about Earth and the salvation of the transadapts.

Captured and taken to the Cydonia compound, Sindri saw to the removal of sperm from Grant and Kane, and ovum from Brigid. He intended to create recombinant gametes, new combinations of chromosomes, which could be implanted into the females. What he didn't know, nor did Kane at the time, was that like the women transadapts, Brigid was barren due to radiation exposure some months before.

Kane indicated David's pair of hooks with the barrel of his Sin Eater. "Who fixed you up like that?"

David raised his wrists, the light glinting dully from the cups. "Sindri, who else?"

"Right," Grant muttered. "Who else."

David had lost his hands when he'd tried to prevent the three of them from gating out of the compound. He'd fired Brigid's appropriated Uzi at them, and Kane had had no choice but to return the fire with a blast of infrasound from an equally appropriated harp weapon. When the rounds in the subgun exploded, so had the transadapt's hands.

"I thought for sure you'd have bled to death," said

Kane, trying not to make too obvious a show of staring past David into the passageway beyond him.

Brigid took it upon herself to respond to Kane's remark. "I imagine all the transadapts were bred with the ability to seal off epidermal punctures to protect the internal organs and tissues from the effects of zero pressure."

David ignored her observation. "What are you big 'uns doing back here? Sindri is long, long gone."

"We're not looking for Sindri," Grant said. "We know just where the little pissant is. We're looking for a friend."

"A friend?" David's tone was skeptical.

"He was brought here against his will," Brigid put in. "I don't suppose you've seen him, have you?"

David's lips writhed back over his stumpy, discolored teeth in a fair imitation of a mocking smirk. "And if I did, you think I'd tell you?"

Kane matched his smirk, taking a menacing step toward him. "Not without a little persuasion, which we're highly motivated to do."

David glared up at him with eyes like wet pieces of obsidian. Then, with a burst of scuttling motion, he spun around and vanished down the passageway. Kane gaped in astonishment for a couple of seconds, nonplussed by the troll's speed, even though he had seen demonstrations of it from his kind in the past.

Kane sprinted down the passageway, his helmet bumping with an annoying rhythm against his back. Brigid and Grant ran close behind him. Kane saw no sign of David, but he heard the rapid slap-slap of the troll's bare feet on the floor ahead of him.

Once again he was impressed by the speed of the transadapts. Although one of his strides equaled three made by David, the little man still eluded him. He decided when next he caught so much as a glimpse of David's shadow, he would open up with his Sin Eater.

The passageway opened up into an intersection, where the tube-tunnels extended into four directions. As he ran to the hub, he heard Brigid blurt breathlessly, "Be careful! He could be leading us into a—"

Brigid's voice was overwhelmed by the sudden rush of feet and labored breathing, lunging from both sides. Kane caught glimpses of two small figures darting out of the mouths of the shafts.

In his eagerness to strike the first blow, David leaped at Kane with both arms extended. The sharpened points of his hooks could have hamstrung the much larger man, if Kane hadn't pivoted at the waist. He caught David by the left wrist and yanked him forward on his own momentum. He kicked him hard in the rear, sending him sprawling almost under the feet of Grant.

As the troll tried to bound back to his feet, Grant drove the toe of a boot into his face. The sound of teeth splintering under the impact was loud and grisly in the confined space. David fell flat onto his back, uttering a gargling cry, blood spraying from his mouth.

At the same instant another transadapt, this one just as small but with a white-blond mop of shaggy hair, sprang at Kane. He struck savagely at his face with a long-handled instrument that resembled a three-clawed gardening tool. The prongs missed cutting furrows in Kane's eyes by a fractional margin and the down-stroke buried the points in the floor.

As he struggled to wrench it free, Kane brought up his right knee and slammed the little man in the chest, knocking him backward. He staggered into the wall. The way was clear for Kane and Grant to open up with full-auto fire, but the risk of puncturing the tube-tunnel walls was very high. Besides, Kane wanted live sources of information, not dead gnomes.

The blond transadapt made a move to grasp the handle of his weapon and Kane kicked at it. While he was still off balance, he heard Brigid cry out in wordless alarm and he felt steel-muscled arms encircle his knees. He went down heavily, snarling out a profanity.

David released Kane's legs and swung wildly with his hooks at Kane's face, squealing in fury, spitting a mixture of blood and broken teeth. Kane tried to fend the troll off, trying to catch him by the forearms to restrain him. The effort reminded him anew of just how deceptively strong the transadapts were.

Brigid kneed David in the kidneys, slamming him over Kane's body and slapping him face-first against a curved tunnel wall. Brigid pinned him there, knee against the small of his back, hands gripping his shoulders.

"Stay there," she commanded.

David's companion dropped into a crouch, his gleaming eyes darting back and forth uncertainly from Brigid to Grant to his weapon. Grant didn't wait for him to make up his mind. He leaped forward and kicked him hard in the belly. The little man folded up, a keening wail escaping his lips, his hair falling like a curtain over his face.

Stepping around the pinioned David and prone Kane, Grant picked up the three-pronged tool, examined it with a critical eye and tossed it contemptuously behind him, the way they had just come.

Kane climbed to his feet, dragging a deep breath. "All right, enough of this ambush shit. You guys aren't any good at it."

Brigid released David and he sagged to the floor. Reaching down, Kane pulled the little man half erect by his hair. His bloody face twisted in anguish and he half gasped, "Fuck you, big 'un."

"One day," Kane said, "I'm going to get sick of being called that."

"As far as I'm concerned," Grant rumbled, "today is that day."

Kane released the transadapt, but David stayed on his feet, swaying unsteadily. "Where is Lakesh?" Kane asked.

David shook his head. "Don't know...we hid when they came."

"'They'?" Kane repeated. "How many were there?"

The transadapt wiped his bloody mouth with a sleeve. "Don't know. Not too many. All I know."

Kane stared down at the little man for a few thoughtful seconds and decided David wasn't lying to him—too much. Stepping back, gesturing to his blond companion, who showed signs of reviving, he said, "Take your pal and get the hell out of my sight. I see you again before we leave, I'll kill you."

David pulled his comrade up and both of them backed away down a tube-tunnel. By way of a farewell, David growled, "You'll die if you stay here."

Grant lifted his Sin Eater. "So will you."

The pair of transadapts scrambled out of sight. Watching them go, Brigid announced with a forced breeziness, "My, that was easy."

Kane looked toward her questioningly. "What do you mean by that? He didn't tell us much of anything."

She shook her head ruefully. "No, he didn't tell us much of anything. But what he didn't say is more helpful than what he did."

The three people began walking down the tunnel shaft again. "Explain," Grant said.

"Firstly, David didn't seem too interested when we told him we knew where Sindri was. That indicates he no longer follows him."

"Which might mean," Kane suggested, "he follows a new leader. Like Maccan."

Brigid nodded. "David could've been coached to say what he did. But if Maccan and his people aren't here in the compound, then it stands to reason they're somewhere else on Mars."

"The pyramid?" Grant inquired.

"That's the only other place we know of on the planet that can sustain humanoid life," Brigid answered.

Grant gestured in frustration. "Hell, we knew we'd be going there before we left Cerberus. So let's get on with it."

"Do you remember the way to the train station?" Kane asked Brigid.

She smiled wanly. "We'll see."

Brigid turned her head very slowly, trying to reconcile their surroundings with the memory of their last visit to the installation. She led them into the mouth of a tube-tunnel opposite the one David and his fellow transadapt had entered. She walked carefully, Grant and Kane following her. She opened one of the iris hatches and stepped through it into another branch of passageways, then to another hatch. This one was not in the wall but in the floor. When its segments irised open, they saw a metal-runged ladder extending into a poorly lit semi-murk.

"This is the place," Brigid announced, swinging her body into the round opening and climbing down.

Kane and Grant followed her. The climb was short, less than twelve feet, and they found themselves standing on a low-ceilinged platform. A dim yellow bulb cast its feeble rays on a dark, bullet-shaped vehicle resting upon a single raised rail. It was about eight feet long, six in overall diameter. Hooked to it were two empty flatcars of about the same length. The track stretched out of sight down a long round chute.

Brigid touched an almost-invisible button on its side, and a man-size section of the hull slid open, revealing a hollow interior. The door panel lowered to form a short ramp. The interior of the bullet car held nothing but four padded seats. They entered and strapped themselves into the chairs, Kane and Brigid taking the first two.

Sindri had told them that the vehicle was automated, built by the Cydonia colonists to ferry them back and forth in relative safety across the Martian surface. There was nothing one could do once under way. Within a moment of buckling their seat harnesses, the hull panel slid silently shut. Their eardrums registered the car pressurizing, and they heard a faint hiss of oxygen filtering in. Then they felt a shock of acceleration, which pressed them against the padded chair backs.

A curving section of the forewall became transparent, stretching out to the sides. They saw the metal walls of a chute racing past and around them at a rate of speed none of them could estimate, but which was obviously very high. Overhead light fixtures flicked by so fast that they combined with the intervals of darkness between them to acquire a strobing pattern. There was no sound of motors or rush of wind.

The bullet car burst out of the tunnel into the full, pink-hued daylight of Mars, and they all felt the lifting sensation in their bellies as they left the synthetic gravity field of the Cydonia compound. The track stretched out far ahead in a straight line, leading to the base of a mountain in the shape of a pyramid.

All of them had seen the colossal structure before, but they gaped at it again, rendered speechless by awe. It loomed astonishingly high, its gigantic red walls climbing sheer toward the sky. They had to tilt their heads back to glimpse the apex, even though the pyramid was at least a mile away.

The monolith was gargantuan, immensely broad at the base and narrow at the top. The bottom covered a square mile and a half and the top rose to over five thousand feet. The enormous structure was only

vaguely Egyptian in configuration, but so phenome-
nally huge that the Great Pyramid of Giza could have
fit inside it. Unlike the classic Egyptian pentahedron
design, the so-called D&M Pyramid was a tetrahe-
dron.

The sheer size of the monument was almost too
awesome to comprehend and Kane had to consciously
resist the impulse to pinch himself. It exuded antiquity,
a history so incalculably ancient that the Pyramid of
Giza had been built yesterday in comparison.

Sunlight glinted faintly from a metal spire stretching from the pyramid's apex. It looked tiny and thread-
like in relation to the structure supporting it, but he
figured it had to be a minimum of five hundred feet
long, perhaps closer to a thousand.

The side facing them bore a deep V-shaped symmetrical depression, extending the entire length of the
pyramid from bottom to the conical top. Between the
arms of the V great flights of steps led up from the
desert floor.

The rail wound among bleak dunes that at times
towered over the bullet car like giant ocean waves
about to break above their heads. Still transfixed by the
pyramid, Kane murmured, "This is so hard to believe."

"That's for damn sure." Grant's flinty tone held an
undercurrent of apprehension, not awe. "But what are
we going to do about them?"

It required several seconds for the strangeness of
Grant's query to penetrate the shock clouding their
minds. Hitching around in their seats, they saw that
Grant wasn't gaping at the enormous monument as

they were. Instead his attention was focused on what lay beyond the left side panel. Kane looked out onto the desolation of the Cydonia Plains. Far in the distance he saw the squat, mesa-shaped rock formation, and on the horizon sharp-pointed peaks arose, far too regular in shape to be mountains. Then a dark flitting movement caught his eye.

He leaned forward, over Brigid. Through the unearthly, pumpkin-tinted light they saw long, slim craft swooping from the sky. Kane counted three of them as they skimmed with eye-blurring speed over the desert surface, sucking up plumes of grit in their wake. He recognized the craft as the bobsled-like objects he had seen in the compound.

"Now we know what they are," Grant declared grimly. "And we can make our own guesses about the pilots."

They glimpsed helmeted and EVA-suited figures kneeling inside the flying sleds. One of the craft paced the bullet car and the bulky figure within pointed an arm at them as if trying to wave them down. Little specks of light flashed and flickered from the end of the arm. Flares danced like lightning along the track ahead of them.

"I get the feeling," Brigid said with her characteristic blitheness, "they don't think our trip is necessary."

Chapter 19

A storm of shots struck the hull of the bullet car, banging like hailstones. They glimpsed the release of explosive energy, fiery flares bursting up at the impact points of the projectiles.

"What kind of rounds are those?" Grant demanded, fisting his Sin Eater and leaning away from the portal.

"Gyrojet rocket rounds probably," Kane replied, grimacing at the rattling cacophony. "Both Farrell and Philboyd claimed Maccan's forces used rocket pistols."

Through the transparent panels, they watched the three air sleds swoop headlong in a reckless swarm around the bullet car, englobing it. The appearance of the attackers became clear—the armored EVA suits covering them from head to toe gleamed dully like polished pewter. The visors of the helmets were completely opaque.

"What they hell do they want?" Grant snarled. "We can't stop this damn thing or even slow it down!"

More explosive rounds hammered against the exterior of the conveyance, punching dents in the tough substance of the hull. "We should put on our helmets,"

Brigid said uneasily. "If the cabin is breached, we'll depressurize fast."

All three of them did as she said, helping one another slip on the headpieces. Since the surface gravity of Mars was less than half that of Earth and its atmospheric pressure only about 8 millibars, if the bullet car depressurized, they would die within minutes. Brigid, Kane and Grant zipped up each other's collar attachments securely. Oxygen hissed into the headpieces and it required a few moments to regulate the flow and to adjust their respiration patterns. They heard not only their own, but each other's breathing over the UTEL comms built into the helmets.

While they were so occupied, the flying attackers loosed a hot barrage of fire at the rail on which they traveled. The bullet car zoomed over the notches and nicks, shuddering and rocking. Gazing at one of the sleds, Kane noted that its motive power appeared to be produced by a boxlike machine at the stern.

"If they derail us out here," Grant stated warningly, "we're deader than skinned scalies."

Kane and Brigid knew he spoke the truth. Although the outside temperature at noon could reach as high as fifty degrees Fahrenheit, it would plunge to around two hundred degrees below zero at midnight. Neither the temperature controls of their EVA suits nor the shadow suits could handle that kind of extreme low temperature.

Unbuckling the seat harness, Kane rose to his feet, stumbling slightly in the low gravity. "Baptiste, do you know how to open the hatch?"

Brigid swept her gaze over the simplified control board and pointed to a pair of keys. "Here, I think. What do you plan on doing?"

"I don't have a plan, exactly," Kane said. "Just the intention to stay alive." Turning to Grant, he said, "Grab hold of my belt and don't let go."

"Why?" Grant demanded skeptically.

"Because even in this gravity, you weigh a lot more than me and that makes you a perfect anchor."

Grant narrowed his eyes, pondering if he had been insulted or not, but then decided it made little difference. Still seated, he reached out and secured a tight grip on Kane's web belt with his left hand, keeping his gun hand free.

"Open her up," Kane said to Brigid.

The UTEL radio accurately transmitted her sigh of resignation, then she depressed one of the two keys and the curving hatch slid aside. Kane reeled, trying to balance himself on the balls of his feet as the encapsulated atmosphere within the bullet car roared out onto the surface of Mars. He hadn't expected the rush of the wind to be so powerful. The tremendous velocity of the vehicle as it raced along the rail didn't help him to keep his balance, either.

The thin Martian air whipped at Kane's body, snatching at him, trying to yank him from the little car. With a muscle-straining effort, he stood spraddle-legged, jamming the sides of his boots firmly against the hatch frame. "You got me?" he asked breathlessly.

"Got you," came Grant's response.

Carefully, Kane crooked his elbow, bringing up his

Sin Eater. He couldn't extend the barrel of the weapon very far past the rim of the hatch due to the bullet car's speed. Cupping his right hand with his left, Kane brought a sled into target acquisition and pressed the trigger stud. He maintained his finger's pressure, sending a long, stuttering burst toward the flying craft, doing what he could to account for windage.

The stream of 9 mm rounds stitched the side of the air sled with a pattern of holes, then the block of machinery astern flamed up in a fierce, flaring explosion.

The sled inscribed a crazed trajectory, like a meteor knocked off course. It veered away in an east-to-west parabolic curve, trailing a banner of spark-shot smoke. The craft rolled, but it didn't jettison its pilot, so obviously the sled was equipped with some sort of restraint. The sled lanced into the face of a dune, disappearing in a mushroom cloud of rust-hued grit.

Braced against the bullet car's hatch, Kane felt the concussion of more rounds against the hull and even heard the detonations. Sand fountained up all around the rail, scouring the visor of Kane's helmet. He wiped the dirt away and saw a pair of sleds swoop past.

"Missed us, dickheads!" Kane shouted at them, even though he knew the pilots couldn't hear his words.

He indulged in smug self-congratulation for all of three seconds. While the words of his gibe still echoed within the walls of his helmet, another air sled skimmed into view, flying abreast of the bullet car. The armored figure kneeling within it raised a long, glittering object. The suffused sunlight glinted from the crystalline barrel of a quartz cremator.

Frozen with sudden terror, Kane could only stand and stare with Grant's hand anchoring him in place. He waited for the scorching beam to cleave through his body as cleanly as a white-hot blade through paraffin.

To his complete astonishment, the faceplate of the pilot's helmet suddenly burst outward in a shower of razor-edged shards amid a misting of blood. The EVA-suited figure flailed backward, arms flinging up and hurling the pulse-plasma emitter over the sled's side and onto the Cydonia Plains. The craft lost velocity and altitude. It dropped slowly, the blunt nose plowing a gouge in the sand.

Face clammy with sweat, Kane turned his head to the right, looked down and saw Brigid half prone on the deck, lying between his outstretched legs. The long barrel of the rail pistol in her fist protruded uncomfortably close to the juncture of his thighs.

"Thanks," he said hoarsely.

Brigid backed away from between his legs. "My pleasure."

Kane looked through the forepart of the bullet car as it continued to speed along the rail. He saw no more air sleds. In the distance he was able to discern crumbling ruins around the foot of the immense pyramid. The structures were huge, but dwarfed by the monument. Walls had fallen in and the stone blocks were scoured smooth by windblown sand.

Craning his neck, he looked up, studying the long spire affixed to the pyramid's apex. Like an unimaginably huge needle, it seemed to pierce the wispy clouds.

Grant asked, "Any sign?"

Kane replied, "I think they got the idea to let us go our way."

"Good," Grant grunted. "My arm is getting sore."

He released his grip on Kane's belt and massaged his biceps. It hadn't been that long since his entire left side had been paralyzed, and he still exhibited occasional weaknesses in his arm and fingers.

Before Kane could back away from the open hatch, an air sled roared up from the rear and slammed into the side of the bullet car. The prow battered it like the snout of a killer whale, sparks flying from the impact point. Jarred off balance, Kane teetered on the edge, arms windmilling. Brigid's and Grant's alarmed, angry cries filled his ears. Then he toppled from the racing bullet-car, right onto the port side of the air sled.

He landed hard enough to knock the breath from his lungs and while he gasped in a mouthful of oxygen, he almost slid off. He drove the gloved fingers of his left hand between two rails of metal on the side, wedging them in far enough to secure a grip.

The pilot turned around from the tiny control console and pointed a stunted blaster at Kane. He fired, the muzzle flashes flaring like blossoming fluorescent tulips in the eerie sunlight. Bright brass arced out from the ejector port. Kane swiftly lowered his head, pulling it below the level of the sled's raised lip. Even as he ducked, he identified the gun in the pilot's hand as a decidedly unexotic Ingram M-11 machine pistol.

Judging by the shape and length of the clip, the weapon carried a 16-round box magazine. Due to its light recoil, the M-11 had a very high cyclic rate of fire and Kane guessed the EVA-suited pilot had just burned through half the magazine.

Propping the barrel of his Sin Eater on the edge of the sled rim, Kane squeezed off a triburst. Two of the shots went wild, but one of the bullets struck the pilot, throwing off a flare of sparks and ricocheting away from his armored shoulder epaulet. The kinetic shock knocked his body awkwardly to one side, and the air sled curved off in the same direction.

Kane caught a fragmented glimpse of the pilot's knees fitting within a pair of up raised stirrup-and-cup contrivances bolted to the floor plate. The sled dived down and the pilot struggled to bring up its nose. Still, the craft dropped far enough so Kane's feet hit the ground with a painful jar he felt all the way into the base of his spine. He couldn't help but cry out in pain.

"Kane!" Brigid's voice shrilled into his helmet. "Are you all right?"

"Hell yes!" he half shouted in response as the toes of his boots dragged along the desert, cutting twin furrows across the red sand. "Don't I look all right?"

If Brigid had a response, it was lost when the starboard side of the air sled scraped against the crest of a dune. The violent jounce nearly broke Kane's one-handed grip on the raised lip of the craft. For a long moment he dangled by his left hand, feet hitting the desert floor with little puffs of rust-colored dust. He retracted his Sin Eater into its forearm holster and heaved himself up enough so he could slap both hands around the raised edge of the sled. He pulled up his legs, trying to chin himself onto the deck.

The undercarriage of the sled struck another dune a glancing blow, bouncing Kane straight up, blinded by a pluming contrail of dust. He hung jackknifed over the side of the craft, his upper body on the deck but his legs still dangling over the desert.

A steady vibration ran through the chassis of the sled and in the next few seconds, the flight leveled out, became smoother and faster. The sled flew rapidly upward in a wide spiral. The pilot threw the vehicle into a sudden whirl in the air, turning the craft upside down.

Biting back a curse and a cry of fright, Kane grabbed the rim and hung grimly on. He glanced down, seeing the bullet car still sliding along the track. He estimated it was about fifty feet below, but not getting farther away. He guessed the air sleds had definite ceilings, mechanical limitations on how high they could fly.

"Kane!" Grant's voice boomed inside his helmet. "We're almost to the pyramid!"

"What do you want me to do about it?" he snarled in reply.

The strain on his hands and shoulders was growing painful.

"I don't know," came the gruff response. "But you'd better do something—and damn fast. Otherwise you'll be stuck out here with your new friends."

The pilot rolled the sled back over and turned toward Kane, pointing the Ingram on a direct line with his helmet's faceplate. Kane looked into the stunted bore only inches away and came to a swift, almost insane decision. Flexing his wrist tendons, the Sin Eater sprang into his hand, the long barrel smashing into the frame of the subgun at the same time the pilot squeezed the trigger. The Sin Eater fired a triburst simultaneously and the rounds spit by both weapons collided in midair as soon as they shot from their respective muzzles. A constellation of sparks flashed and flared.

Kane had no idea how many rounds screamed away wild, but he knew that at least one grazed the top of his helmet. His ears rang with the chiming echo of the ricochet. The box-shaped machine at the stern of the sky craft suddenly jumped, parts of the dark casing flying away in flinders. He heard a brief buzz and concluded electromagnetic energy poured out of the shielded engine block.

Oily black smoke curled from the seams, torn apart and scattered by the wind. He felt the buffet of escaping, expanding energies as the sled rocked violently. The craft flung itself on a wild, corkscrewing downward course. Kane could only hang on desperately, teeth gritted, stomach churning.

The pilot frantically worked at the control console and the sled achieved a more or less stable attitude but still followed a steadily declining trajectory. Glancing down, Kane saw the bullet car and track almost directly below. He pushed himself away from the craft and fell.

He fanned his arms as he plummeted downward. In the lesser gravity, it felt as if he dropped for a disquietingly long time. Then, when he hit the flat car squarely with the soles of his feet, he decided he hadn't fallen long enough. The twin impacts jacked both knees up into his lower belly. Over his whoofing explosion of violently expelled air, he heard Grant say, "That's one way to do it."

Dropping onto his hands and knees, Kane tried to drag air into his emptied lungs. Over his strangled gasps he heard Brigid's voice calling his name and urging him to get inside. He craned his neck, scanning the sky for the air sled, and saw it flutter out of sight on the far side of a hill, trailing a banner of smoke.

Kane forced himself to his feet, breath rasping in and out of his straining lungs as he staggered to the rear of the bullet car and climbed along its hull. He fell into the cabin and allowed Grant and Brigid to deposit him in a chair.

"Just in time," Grant told him dourly, taking his own seat. "Thought you were going to be left behind."

"Yeah," Kane rasped. "And wouldn't that have been a damn shame?"

As the bullet car came closer to the pyramid, they saw the great cavity that occupied a large portion of the base. High heaps of debris were piled on either side of it. The track disappeared into the hole. They knew the cavity was the result of explosive penetration made during the Archon attack on the Danaan outpost. Maccan claimed Balam himself had led the assault.

The bullet car plunged noiselessly into the cavity. Lights shone intermittently overhead, small splotches of illumination that did little to alleviate the deep shadows. The track tilted upward at a gradual incline until it reached a ninety-degree slant. The speed of the vehicle didn't slacken.

After a couple of minutes the track angle decreased

in sharpness until the car rode straight and smooth again. Through the foreport they saw walls constructed of individual stone blocks three times the size of the vehicle that carried them. The bullet car's speed dropped rapidly until it slid to a halt beside a broad platform.

The bullet car darkened inside as the foreport went opaque. They all disembarked onto the platform, noting how heavy their bodies felt compared to the trip across the plains. During their first visit, Sindri had claimed that this particular level of the pyramid had been adjusted to accommodate humans, complete with synthetic gravity generators and oxygen circulation pumps. With a clanking of gears, the section of rail supporting the car rotated on a hidden pivot, turning it around 180 degrees, so it faced the way they had come.

They looked around, not seeing any change since the last time they had been here. Grim walls of gray-red cyclopean stone surrounded them. They knew all the levels of the pyramid were immense. Sindri had speculated that different strata of Danaan society occupied the levels, perhaps with their own customs and dialects.

"Do we want to do this with or without our helmets?" Kane asked.

After a moment of consideration, Grant said, "Without. It makes it easier to see if anybody is trying to sneak up on us."

The three outlanders opened the seals and latch flanges of one another's helmets. They tentatively lifted them off, sniffing the air experimentally. Although cold, it smelled fresh. Their breath steamed before their eyes, so they figured the temperature was balmy by Martian standards.

Attaching the helmets to their back-straps, they entered a wide corridor lit by wall-bracketed neon tubes, passing through a series of triangular archways. Cut into the stone above each one was a plate-size spiral glyph, the same kind of cup-and-spiral design that served as something of an unofficial emblem of the Tuatha de Danaan.

The floor slanted slightly upward and the stone blocks were worn smooth as if by the pressure of many feet. The arches opened occasionally to the left and right, but the outlanders kept to the main corridor. They became aware of a low hum of sound ahead of them, almost like the bass register of a piano, which continued to vibrate long after a key had been struck. Presently a brighter light glimmered in the murk just beyond a tall arch.

"Do you think Micah Harwin is still alive?" Kane inquired in a low voice. "Still tending to the transmitter?"

Brigid shook her head. "It's possible, but I don't think it's likely."

A man's voice, frighteningly familiar, echoed hollowly through the shadowy murk of the corridor. "And you would be so right."

Then they heard a laugh, a rising and falling titter with a hint of a sob. The laugh was full of bitterness and even a touch of self-pity, underscored by a note of hysteria.

"Maccan," Brigid whispered.

"None other," Kane muttered. "Just like I expected."

Grant's teeth flashed in a savage grin. "And just like I hoped."

Three figures emerged from an archway behind them. "I'm glad," Maccan said. "A reunion is so much more joyous when all parties involved are happy to see one another. And I can't express how delighted I am to see you again, Kane."

Chapter 20

Kane turned slowly, with a mocking smile of confidence on his face that he didn't feel. Two armed people, a man and a woman in hard suits, flanked Maccan. The man pointed an Uzi at Grant and the woman trained a Gyrojet pistol on Brigid. Their glittering eyes bespoke a total scorn for life, their own and any other's. Although they didn't look alike, in stature they were almost identical.

Both people were honed to a razor-keen tautness of attitude, as if held in check by woven steel leashes. The man's head was shaved and he affected a cup-and-spiral tattoo on his forehead. The woman's face was scarred. Kane figured she was the bull dyke Philboyd had mentioned. A sense of violence moved with both of them, like the clammy touch of a wind blowing from a slaughterhouse.

As tall as the guards were, almost as tall as Grant, who was imposing by any standards, the figure between them was even more powerful and dynamic than the two people, shrinking them into relative insignificance. Whereas the guards wore the drab gray hard suits, Maccan's long, lean body was draped in an armored ensemble that mixed the medieval with the futuristic—or the alien.

From wrist to throat and heel he was clad in supple molded leather, dyed a bright red and decorated all over with plates of silver, each one embossed with a different swirling glyph and intricate interlace design. A long, deep purple cloak fastened to his shoulders with golden torques belled out behind him like the wings of some great bird. A gauntlet made of beautiful silver alloy encased his right hand and forearm. Sparks of blue fire hissed and crackled between the fingers.

The pride and wisdom Grant, Kane and Brigid had all seen in Maccan's high-planed face was still there— as well as deep, abiding loneliness. His eyes were pits of black shadow now, swirling with a malign energy. The notion flickered through Brigid Baptiste's mind that here was a man who had watched the march of history from the sidelines, but who could have had a devastating effect on it had he so desired. An electric aura seemed to surround him, the same kind of energy radiated by dozens of conquerors and men of destiny who had shaken the foundation of the world.

"I apologize for not meeting you at the station," Maccan said in a smooth, friendly voice. "But to be perfectly frank, I issued specific orders that you three should be persuaded to arrive by an altogether different route."

He angled a questioning eyebrow, first at Brigid,

then at Kane. "Am I to apprehend that my representatives were not wholly successful in their techniques of persuasion?"

"You might say that," Grant rumbled. "Just like you might say none of your representatives will be in the persuading mood for a long time to come."

The scar-faced woman bared her teeth in a ferocious snarl. "You'll suffer as they suffered, dung-dog!"

"Dung-dog?" Kane repeated, affecting an attitude and expression of wounded pride. "Is that any way to talk to guests during a reunion?"

Maccan smiled thinly. "It's an epithet Shayd reserves only for native Terrans. She and her companions were born on the Moon and feel somewhat alienated from the planet that birthed their great-grandparents."

"I remember that hostility," Brigid replied disinterestedly. She nodded toward the bald man. "And what are you called?"

"Raschid, brother of Saladin." The man bit out his words with such harsh emphasis they sounded like whip cracks. His dark eyes bored in on Grant and Kane. "My brother whom you two killed."

Neither Kane nor Grant responded to the accusation, even though it was less than accurate. Brigid smiled at the man. "Thank you. Do you know where our friend might be found, Raschid?"

The big bald man blinked in bewilderment at Brigid's pleasant, forthright manner. Automatically he opened his mouth to reply, caught himself, then scowled at her. "On your knees!" he barked. "On your knees before the first prince of the Tuatha de Danaan!"

The three outlanders remained standing, surveying Raschid with expressions of mild amusement. Kane turned toward Maccan. "Now, if we can get back to the main discussion—"

Raschid growled and took a step forward, raising his Uzi. Kane and Grant swung their Sin Eaters in his direction, but he behaved as if he didn't see them or didn't know what they were. Maccan lifted his right hand, which sparkled with little threads of energy. "It is not necessary, Raschid. You may not think it seemly of them, but we will allow our guests to remain standing....for the time being."

Eyeing the pulsing lens on the palm of the metal glove, Kane made a very obvious show of shifting the barrel of his pistol to train the bore directly on it. Softly he asked, "What would happen if I shoot that little piece of costume jewelry on your hand?"

Maccan gazed at him speculatively for a long moment, and the black of his eyes sudden lightened, first to a dull gray, then they acquired a faint pinkish sheen. He didn't answer.

"I don't think any of us want to find out," Kane continued in the same quiet tone. He sensed Brigid and Grant staring in tense concentration at the lens. Shayd and Raschid both leaned unconsciously away from Maccan.

"Usually, I tell people to raise their hands," Kane

went. "But I want you to drop yours. And take off that glove as long as you're at it."

Slowly, Maccan lowered his hand, but he made no move to take off the gauntlet. "I prefer to keep it on. I tend to catch chills easily in this place. That's why I wasn't disinclined to leave it all those centuries ago."

Brigid looked on the verge of asking him to elucidate, but Grant demanded harshly, "Where is Lakesh?"

"Safe," Maccan answered laconically. "As safe as his interphaser. Both of them await my attention."

"For what?" asked Brigid.

Maccan's lips quirked in a sardonic half smile. "That is what you shall learn, along with Lakesh."

"Take us to him," Kane snapped.

"Of course. But first you must disarm."

Grant snorted disdainfully. "That's not going to happen, elf-boy. The plan for the day is for you to send one of your psychotic ass-kissers to fetch Lakesh and his machine. Once that's done, we'll give you about three minutes to convince us why we shouldn't shoot you dead for what you did to our friends and to our home."

The half smile on Maccan's face widened and his eyes acquired a discomfiting yellow shimmer. In a colorless voice he intoned, "Shayd is right—you Terrans *are* dung-dogs."

With a swift scutter and scuffle of bare feet sliding over stone, interspersed with metallic clankings, transadapts boiled out of the shadows. They voiced high-pitched squealing cries of triumph, which under other circumstances might have made Kane and Grant laugh. Fourteen of the little men clustered around the three outlanders, their eyes glittering with hate. From the horde rose a murmuring titter.

Most of the transadapts were armed only with edged weapons, makeshift poleaxes and spears, but they acted as if they not only knew how to use them, but also as if they desperately wanted to. Brigid, Grant and Kane stood in the center of the wheel of sharp steel, their hearts trip-hammering within their chests, their faces composed.

"At least we know what happened to the transadapt population in the colony," Brigid commented blandly. She swung the long barrel of her rail pistol in left-to-right arcs.

A ragged figure pushed through the throng of gnomes and strutted up to the three people. David snickered snidely and said, "Said you'd die if you stayed here."

Kane glanced down contemptuously at David. "Big order, small-timer."

David's face contorted and he shrieked, "On your knees!"

Grant sneered. "In your dreams."

Raising his arms, hooks glinting, he screamed, "I'll rip off your balls and feed them to your woman!"

"Be silent!" Maccan's voice crashed like a thunderclap.

David turned toward him. "But my prince—"

"Enough!" Maccan's eyes glowed like banked embers. "We do not waste our time on crude physical threats. Do you understand?"

David dropped into a groveling posture, his hooks clicking on the stone floor.

Maccan smiled genially at the three people. "Forgive him. He hates humans very much in general, and you three in particular."

Kane smiled condescendingly. "He just likes to threaten and scream and switch loyalties. It's who he is."

Maccan nodded. "I understand. I hope you understand why your own threats will never come to fruition."

Grant shrugged. "Your fused-out gnomes don't worry us as much as you think they should. We've had a lot more experience kicking their asses than you have ordering them around."

Maccan made a tsk sound of sympathy. "You are brave—all of you are brave, but like most humans, your courage derives from rash stupidity."

"That might be so," Brigid said casually. "But we know what you're hoping to accomplish with the interphaser working in conjunction with the infrasound transmitter here in the pyramid."

"What I am hoping is of no importance to you, Brigid. You and your friends are so very close to death that I can only presume you are seeking to distract me by acting as if my intentions are childishly transparent. Please do not bore me further with such a display. All of you, Kane in particular, know I have some small degree of psychic ability."

Brigid recollected that Maccan had denied being a telepath, although he conceded a large number of the Tuatha de Danaan were adept in the art of mind manipulation. He claimed the human mind was very easy to trick, to feed illusions of invisibility and shape-shifting, abilities that folklore attributed to the Danaan. However, Maccan possessed the ability to interact with brain-wave patterns, to sense emotional states, intercepting intent, to receive flashes of insight.

"So what?" Kane demanded derisively. "There are plenty of psi-muties on Earth who could run rings around you—telepathically speaking. So you don't impress us by boasting about it."

Kane spoke the truth as he understood it. Mutants with obvious physical characteristics were dying out, partly due to the long campaigns of genocide waged by the baronies, but primarily because most of the human muties had reached evolutionary dead ends generations before.

The general supposition had always been that the muties, human and animal alike, were the unforeseen by-products of radiation and other mutagenics. Lakesh had indicated otherwise, claiming if radiation and/or chemicals were the sole cause, then logic dictated all human mutants would be similar, nor would the non-adaptive traits have lasted beyond a single generation. Genetic codes scrambled at random couldn't account for the many different monstrosities and deformities among men, women and animals.

According to Lakesh, most of the hordes of muties that once roamed the Outlands were the result of pantropic sciences, the deliberate practice of genetic engineering to create life forms able to survive and thrive in the postnukecaust environment. However, one breed of human mutant that had increased geometrically since skydark was the so-called psi-mutie—people born with augmented extrasensory and precognitive mind powers. As Lakesh had said, these abilities weren't restricted to muties, since a few norms possessed them, as well, but generally speaking, nonmutated humans with advanced psionic powers were in the minority.

Maccan sighed as if Kane's comment vexed him. "Kane, I owe you a bloodletting, but I am not a vengeful man by nature. Nor do I easily forgive. You humiliated me and imprisoned me, and for that you must be duly punished."

Kane rolled his eyes in weary exasperation. "Oh, *please*. Do you have any idea how many assholes with attitudes have uttered that very same lousy cliché—"

Maccan's eyes flamed up as if the fires of hell erupted from the sockets. They instantly filled Kane's field of vision, overwhelming all of his perceptions. The shock was so unexpected, so terrible, he nearly collapsed. Time, space, the universe darkened and tilted.

His surroundings shattered into a kaleidoscope of

flying fragments. He drifted among them and the sudden terror of it dragged a scream up his throat. He clamped his jaws shut on it. Quite suddenly he was in the pyramid again, standing in front of Maccan, surrounded by transadapts.

Kane's heart drummed in his chest and his head ached and his body was filmed with cold sweat. The psychic assault wasn't a fraction of the intensity of the one Maccan had inflicted upon him on the Moon, but he wasn't inclined to make a comparative analysis at the moment. He smiled contemptuously.

"Is that the best you can do?" he asked, trying to minimize the faint tremor in his voice.

Maccan's face lost its facade of gentle good humor. "By no means, Kane. Hasn't it occurred to you that I may choose to punish you by inflicting great pain, a maddening eternal agony on these two friends of yours?"

Kane swallowed hard, realizing anew that Maccan was no ordinary adversary. He briefly relived the terror he had felt of the man during their struggle in the lunar catacombs. He had always secretly feared he would one day cross swords with his superior, and during that fight his fear had seemed to come to life and take physical form.

He knew the statistics for survival in his chosen profession were discouragingly low, but so far he had beaten the odds. He couldn't deny he and his friends seemed to lead exceptionally charmed lives, but he knew his own personal string of good fortune couldn't last forever. He had made too many powerful enemies, brought too much hell in his wake.

Hearing the rapid respiration of Brigid behind him, Kane knew the same uncertainty about Maccan gripped her and probably Grant, as well. But he allowed none of his doubt to show on his face or to be heard in his voice as he said, "Point taken."

He retracted the Sin Eater into its holster and began to unstrap it from around his forearm.

FOR A LONG TIME, longer than Lakesh cared to recall, the damp stone walls, the dim light bulb burning overhead and the hard stone bench had been pretty much all of Mars he had been allowed to see. Set in the wall was a massive metal door with huge strap hinges of thick iron and a heavy lock in the center. The door looked as if it hadn't been opened in centuries and perhaps it hadn't until Maccan had pulled it open to admit him into the cell, many hours before.

He didn't resent being confined as long as he knew it was soon to end. After all, he had spent most of his adult life cloistered in installations like the Cerberus redoubt, so he was accustomed to going for days on end without seeing daylight or enjoying so much as a whiff of fresh air. He couldn't help but sourly note the irony that it was only after the Earth had become a nuke-blasted shockscape that he had come to appreciate the small things about it.

Lakesh had been imprisoned before, in the Cobalt-ville cell blocks, where most of his senses had been taken away from him except pain. Salvo, the crazed Magistrate, had been obsessed with forcing him to admit he was a high-ranking member of the Preservationists. Salvo had failed, but only because the Preservationists didn't exist. Many years before, Lakesh had created the Preservationist menace as a straw adversary, an alleged underground resistance movement that was pledged to deliver the hidden history of the world to a humanity in bondage.

Not that there weren't real-life post-skydark precedents for groups like the Preservationists. A century or more before, a loosely knit organization called the Heimdall Foundation had been formed to keep alive the science of astronomy and astrophysics.

And there was Ireland's Priory of Awen, whose origins could be traced back over a thousand years to its reputed founding by Saint Patrick himself. The Priory clergy, many of whom boasted descent from the Tuatha de Danaan, would no doubt be very distressed by Maccan's behavior.

Still and all, neither Maccan nor any of his people had abused Lakesh since their arrival in the Cydonia compound. However, a hook-handed transadapt made it abundantly clear he wouldn't be averse to employing his prosthetics for mutilation. For that matter, he knew Maccan's bodyguards, Raschid and Shayd, would gladly kill him given the slightest provocation.

Fortunately, Maccan needed his expertise with the interphaser and more than likely his knowledge of hyperdimensional physics, as well. He couldn't help but wonder why, since he was certain Maccan's race had forgotten more about the subject than humanity was ever likely to learn. Of course, he reminded himself sourly, they had taken great pains to ensure humanity would never learn of the system at all.

It was an axiom of conspiracies that someone or something else always pulled the strings of willing or ignorant puppets. Lakesh had expended many years tracing those filaments back through convoluted and manufactured histories to the puppet masters themselves.

The strings led back to the very dawn of human history. Though Lakesh rarely strayed beyond the borders of science, even theoretical, he had made a study of ancient history, scanning very old texts for clues to Archon involvement in human evolution. He did not have to look very deeply before he realized the so-called alien/UFO phenomenon dated back well before the twentieth century, when it gripped public consciousness. In fact, the historical records of nonhuman influence on Earth ran uninterrupted from the very dawn of hummankind to the present day.

Always it was the same: human beings as possessions, with a never-ending conflict bred between them, promoting spiritual decay and perpetuating conditions of unremitting physical hardship. And always, secret societies were created by human pawns to conceal and to protect the true nature of humanity and its custodians—or masters.

Loathing once more rose up within him. Now he knew the Archons weren't the hidden masters of humanity, but custodians, created by two races who didn't belong on Earth, who hadn't evolved there. The Tuatha de Danaan and the Annunaki, despite all their influences on humankind's development, were from outside, and they feared some aspect of humanity's nature. He still didn't know what. Even after all his years of research and study, his work was pitifully incomplete and inadequate.

All he knew was that the Danaan and the Annunaki had created the so-called Archons to contain and control the masses of humankind. Humans, despite all their failings, had at least learned the concept of acknowledging that others of their kind had the right to freedom. True, they forgot easily and had to be reminded often—sometimes violently—but the history of respect for each other was there. Perhaps it was the sense of freedom, the desire to achieve spiritual liberty, that was so feared.

Lakesh sighed and shifted position on the hard bench. He shivered, despite the environmental suit he had been given by his captors upon their arrival in the Cydonia Compound. The temperature was uncomfortably low in the pyramid, perhaps only a few degrees above freezing. The suit's internal thermostats couldn't keep him warm without the helmet to complete the microenvironment.

Regardless of his physical discomfort, Lakesh still retained the sense of awe that almost suffocated him upon his first sight of the pyramid from the bullet car. Walking through the monument was like entering a long-lost world of the past, a world of the god Lugh, of the goddess Danu, of the Sidhe and the otherworld of Tir Na Nog and all of its fabulous wonders.

He didn't need to be informed the pyramid was honeycombed with rooms and passages. The light and the recycled air indicated a power source either activated or installed by Cydonia Compound colonists was still functional. Lakesh briefly wondered at the sheer number of man-killing hours the colonists had devoted to exploring and even excavating the vast monolith.

Thinking about such things kept his mind from wondering about the possibility of rescue or release and replaying his last sight of Domi. He felt rage rise and then subside in him. He was a man of science and couldn't allow raw emotion to sway him now. He sensed with a bowel-tightening prescience that his time in the pyramid was running out.

Metal clanked loudly on the other side of the door, startling him so much he bit back a startled, profane cry. Lakesh quickly stood, resisting the impulse to back into a corner. He watched as the door swung slowly inward on squeaking hinges. Three black shadows glided in, and Lakesh felt his nape hairs prickle in an instant of superstitious dread. Then one of them spoke.

"Thought we'd drop by for a cup of that green Bengali tea you like so much," Kane said.

"Fresh out," Lakesh retorted, deadpan.

Chapter 21

The shadow suits lent Kane, Brigid and Grant a sinister aspect, but the garments had become important items in their ordnance and arsenal over the past few months. Ever since they'd absconded with the suits from Redoubt Yankee on Thunder Isle, the suits had proved their worth and their superiority to the polycarbonate Magistrate armor, if for nothing else than their internal subsystems.

Manufactured with a technique known in predark days as electrospin lacing, the electrically charged polymer particles formed a dense web of formfitting fibers. Composed of a compilated weave of spider silk, Monocrys and Spectra fabrics, the garments were essentially a single crystal metallic microfiber with a very dense molecular structure.

The outer Monocrys sheathing turned opaque when exposed to radiation, and the Kevlar and Spectra layers provided protection against blunt trauma. The spider silk allowed flexibility, but it traded protection from firearms for freedom of movement.

The inner layer was lined by carbon nanotubes only a nanometer wide, rolled-up sheets of graphite with a tensile strength greater than steel. The suits were almost impossible to tear, but a high enough caliber bullet could penetrate them and, unlike the Mag exoskeletons, wouldn't redistribute the kinetic shock. Still, the material was dense and elastic enough to deflect knives and arrows.

"Surely you three didn't arrive in those clothes," Lakesh said.

Kane hooked a thumb over his shoulder toward the doorway, where the woman named Shayd lurked. "We took them off so they could be searched."

"And to keep you from getting ideas about trying to escape," Shayd snapped. "You'd die in minutes."

"How long do we have to stay in here?" Brigid asked.

Shayd's lips twisted in a smirk. "Until one of us tells you to come out."

She didn't pull the door closed, but stood just outside in the corridor, hand resting on the butt of her Gyrojet pistol.

"When did you return from California?" Lakesh asked.

"Yesterday evening," Brigid replied. "So you've been here for about thirty hours, give or take a few minutes."

Lakesh nodded. "And what was the resolution of the mission there?"

"Unsatisfactory," answered Brigid bluntly, and she proceeded to provide him with a brief overview.

Making no comment, Lakesh's only response was to tug absently at his nose. "You don't seem very happy to see us," Kane commented, eyeing him darkly.

"In truth, I don't know how I feel," Lakesh replied frankly. "I had hoped to complete whatever task Maccan set for me, then be returned to Cerberus. But it's apparent now he's been waiting for your arrival before proceeding."

"Proceeding with what?" Grant inquired.

Lakesh shrugged. "I confess I'm not quite sure, but I think it may have something to do with aligning the energy helixes of the interphaser and the pyramid's transmitter."

Kane nodded as if everything now ad made perfect sense. "I see. And Baptiste here thought he was fooling around with a silly theory about mirror matter."

Lakesh's eyebrows rose toward his hairline, and the glance he threw toward Brigid was full of surprise and admiration. "Dearest Brigid, that's *exactly* what I think!" A toothy grin split his face. "You've made up my mind. I *am* very glad you're here."

Grant glowered at him. "Don't get all giddy on us. We're unarmed and outnumbered and at the mercy of a mad god."

Lakesh regarded him reprovingly. "A mad god? I seriously contest any assertion of Maccan's divinity, sane or otherwise."

Grant's lips moved beneath his mustache in a slight smile. "Domi coined the phrase, not me. She—"

"Domi!" cried Lakesh excitedly, eyes alight. "She's all right? You spoke with her?"

"Not for long," Grant muttered, casting his gaze downward. "DeFore sedated her."

Sensing Grant's discomfort at Lakesh's reaction, Kane interjected, "She was conscious when we left, but DeFore had her confined to the infirmary."

Seeing the alarm spreading across Lakesh's face, Brigid said hastily, "Reba says she'll make a full recovery. She took a jolt of infrasound."

The expression of alarm on Lakesh's face changed to one of simmering anger. "I was there—I saw it. Maccan used the Silver Hand of Nuadhu on her. Poor child. As if she hasn't been through enough in her young life."

"So you made the Nuadhu connection, too?" Kane asked, wanting to steer the conversation away from Domi's suffering, particularly with Grant in the same room.

"It was a fairly obvious one to make," Lakesh stated. "Certainly with what we've learned about the Danaan's science of sonic manipulation. Evidently, Maccan's gauntlet emits a tightly focused infrasound envelope, but like the wands in use by the hybrids, it can't propagate destructive waves over an extended distance."

"Oh really?" Kane challenged. "The op center looked as if it had been used for artillery practice."

"Yes," Lakesh snapped impatiently. "That's because most of the damage was caused by conventional firearms."

"Mebbe so," Grant growled. "But his glove is still damn dangerous. I read up on infrasound weapon experiments after our first exposure to the wands. We were very lucky that when the wands resonated with our body cavities our internal organs didn't turn into jelly. Probably the only reason they didn't was because of our Mag armor. So don't try to tell us Maccan's glove is primarily for show."

Lakesh smiled, but without humor. "By no means. I'm not trying to downplay how dangerous it is, but it's not quite the doom weapon of Celtic myth, either. If the situation arises, we ought to be prepared to take advantage of its limitations."

Kane stared at Lakesh, more than a little surprised that the man was advocating violent, life-risking action. He demanded, "What's with this 'we' shit, Lakesh? You know you mean me and Grant."

Kane's surprise quadrupled when Lakesh whirled on him, his face suffused with furious blood. "I said 'we' and I meant it, you self-righteous bastard! If you hadn't been off on your foolish mission to California, more than likely we wouldn't even be having this conversation, certainly not in these surroundings. Don't you dare imply I'm delegating all the risks to you while I sit back and criticize from a safe remove!"

Kane didn't interrupt Lakesh's angry tirade. He listened without flickering so much as an eyelash, feeling the prickles of shame and embarrassment warming the back of his neck under the high collar of his shadow suit. Neither Brigid nor Grant offered words of defense, but he knew he didn't deserve them.

"Reprimand accepted," Kane said quietly. "I was way out of line. We were told how you led the defense of Cerberus."

Lakesh rubbed his eyes with the heels of his gloved hands. Hoarsely he declared, "It was my worst nightmare given flesh and form, friend Kane. Forgive my short temper. Whatever Maccan has planned for us—"

Lakesh broke off when Raschid appeared in the doorway. He tossed the Cerberus team their EVA suits. "Put these back on. You'll need them where you're going."

AFTER THEY WERE suited up, they stepped out into the passageway where Raschid thrust their helmets into their hands. "Don't put them on until you're told."

Maccan stood at the end of the corridor, holding a large aluminum-walled carrying case. All of them recognized it as the container for the interphaser and its support systems. It was outfitted with O-ring seals to make it air- and watertight. He nodded to them and turned smartly on his heel, his cloak swirling in a dramatic fashion.

Kane, Grant, Brigid and Lakesh followed Maccan along a stone-floored path through an arched entrance, flanked by Raschid, Shayd and a retinue of transadapts, four in all, David among them. Raschid and Shayd had their helmets tucked under their arms and they fisted firearms in their free hands.

They strode down a circular flight of stairs worn smooth by thousands of years of feet, passed through another arched portal and entered a vault-walled chamber of huge proportions. Brigid, Grant and Kane had been there before, but Lakesh gaped around in goggle-eyed surprise. The chamber was so vast that its nether end was lost in the shadows. Six circular tiers descended to the center of the chamber, surrounding a column like dais raised six feet from the floor. From it, a metal shaft rose straight up to the shadow-shrouded ceiling.

Rising from the base of the dais, extending at ever-increasing angles into the high shadows, was a taut webwork of silver filaments, hundreds, perhaps thousands of them. They were all connected to the series of circular tiers. A dim glow came down from the pointed roof, glittering from the strings.

As before, Kane had the impression of vast energies being drawn down from the metal spire and disseminated through each one of the silvery threads. The mass of stretched-out strings vibrated gently, continuously, producing a bass note, that he felt rather than heard.

Maccan paused by the metal shaft and asked, "Do you know where you are?"

"The tuning chamber of the Danaan broadcast tower," Brigid answered.

Maccan nodded approvingly. "Exactly."

Kane pointed to himself, Grant and Brigid. "We've been here before. The last time we found an old man living here, trying to readjust the frequency."

"Yes," Maccan stated. "Micah Harwin. I was told of him. No one knows his fate. You understand the purpose my people put this pyramid to, don't you?"

"It transmitted ultrasonic frequency fatal to the Archons, the First Folk," replied Kane. "To keep them from establishing an outpost here."

"And to keep them from absconding with the pyramid itself." Maccan smiled when he said it, so no one knew if he was joking or simply as mad as Domi had suggested.

After a lengthy pause Kane inquired, "You were afraid Balam would steal this monument?"

"Yes," Maccan answered matter-of-factly. "The power it once possessed cut a path like a scythe through the Earth. Millions died by incineration so swift they never knew it."

"Are we talking about the protoplanic force Balam and his people used against your settlement on the Moon?" asked Brigid. "The one which caused a blowback effect?"

"And nearly destroyed the Earth," Maccan declared with a small smile.

"Is that what you're planning to do again?" Brigid's tone was studiedly neutral. "Is that what you need the interphaser for?"

Maccan surprised them all by laughing, softly and bitterly. "By no means. I need the interphaser to go through the looking glass."

He walked quickly and deliberately across the chamber and through another arched portal. The people from Cerberus were pushed ahead by Raschid and Shayd at gunpoint. Only shadows waited ahead and Lakesh stopped moving. "Where are you taking us?" he demanded, his tone harsh and hard with impatience.

Maccan laughed again. "Do you find this place so strange, my friends?"

"No stranger than many other places we've seen," retorted Brigid stiffly.

"I promise to show you a place stranger than anywhere you have ever been before," Maccan declared. None of them doubted his words.

A muted bell sounded and lights flickered, illuminating the murk. They stood in front of a square cubicle, like a three-sided box. They saw it was a lift, with silver fretwork like that of a giant birdcage. Maccan made a sweeping gesture with one arm, indicating they should enter.

The four people didn't move, despite Raschid pressing the bore of his Uzi against Lakesh's back. "Where will this take us?" he asked suspiciously.

"Down. Far, far down," Maccan answered. "To the seat of the broadcast tower. There is insufficient oxygen for you down there, so you may wish to put on your helmets now."

Reluctantly the Cerberus team stepped into the lift and did as Maccan said, slipping the helmets on over their heads and helping one another secure them to the collars of the EVA suits. Raschid and Shayd donned their own headpieces. They weren't surprised that the transadapts took no precautions, since they were bred to function in rarified atmospheres, but they wondered at Maccan.

He seemed to sense their mystification and he gave them a sly smile. "I will find such environmental conditions invigorating, as long as I don't overstay."

The lift began its descent, dropping smoothly down a vertical shaft. As it did so, they felt the lessening of gravity on their bodies. The open side of the elevator afforded them tantalizing glimpses of the other levels of the pyramid—they saw walls tiled in Celtic patterns with blues and reds and ancient knotwork designs, received impressions of huge tables and chairs carved from oak, brilliant-colored tapestries.

On another level, they saw a collection of curving harps, the brass frames gleaming. They passed chambers furnished in a bizarre blend of the traditionally ancient and the technologically advanced, with computer consoles and view screens side by side with flowing tapestries.

They glimpsed displays of broadswords, maces, suits of medieval armor, halberds, poleaxes and battle standards from thousand-year-old military campaigns. There was too much to absorb, much less easily identify.

The elevator continued to sink downward, through the relics of a lost world, of a distant past humanity knew only from legends, folklore and mythology. Kane glanced over at Maccan. His black eyes held a vacant sheen, as if he gazed mournfully down the long track of time. He recalled what the Danaan had said to him on the Moon: "A man is born in one world and there he belongs. But my world is dead. Age and death came at last to everything there. I cannot live with the dreams of my world haunting me at every step."

Maccan suddenly stiffened, his gaze sliding over to Kane, who didn't look away. Maccan stared at him intently, but his eyes didn't change color. "Do not pity me, human," he said.

Kane nodded within his helmet and flicked his gaze to one side. "So noted, prince."

The elevator passed another level and it was the most uninteresting by far, seeming to be little more than a converted warehouse. It looked to be nothing but a dimly lit space filled with stacked crates and boxes, most of which were stenciled with the legend NASA. Others read Parallax Red/Cydonia Compound.

He also spied a number of the air-sleds, a couple of which were filled with boxes. He realized the craft were actually more like dollies or forklifts, rather than actual vehicles, which explained their altitude limitations.

The elevator bumped to a stop. A long passageway stretched before them, made of rough-hewn ancient stones set in huge blocks without mortar. Kane exchanged glances with Brigid, who nodded knowingly. They were at the lowermost level of the pyramid, within a foundation buttress of the enormous structure above. It was dark except for a feeble light glowing ahead, down the throat of the corridor.

Maccan stepped into the passageway and marched deliberately toward the glimmer of light, his cloak streaming out behind him. David pushed against the backs of Kane's thighs with the curved ends of his hooks, saying, "Go."

The transadapt's voice sounded far away. The thin atmosphere at the bottom of the pyramid couldn't transmit sounds very effectively. Kane, Lakesh, Brigid and Grant entered the corridor, followed and bracketed by Shayd, Raschid and the transadapts. Stout stone columns rose from the floor, and red dust puffed up around their feet, the residue of many centuries.

The passageway ended after a few dozen yards at an arcaded opening. They walked through it into a cavernous gallery, which reminded Kane of a stupendously huge well. It was at least a thousand feet in diameter.

The people stood on a wide ledge that circled the well. The walls were formed of a gray, molded substance, which looked like sponge, undulating in curving waves and involutions.

Extending down from far, far above glittered the metal shaft of the Danaan resonator. The shaft terminated in a huge crystal cluster that reminded them all of a huge chandelier. Kane, Grant and Brigid knew the universal power source of the Tuatha de Danaan derived from sculpted crystals.

The cluster hung about a dozen feet above a circular platform made of a highly polished alloy. A wide walkway of the same kind of material extended from the ledge and joined with it.

From the exact center of the platform, directly beneath the crystalline point, rose a slender dais. It wasn't more than five feet tall and terminated in a flat, perfectly square top. Kane couldn't help but think it was the perfect size and shape to hold the interphaser.

A man stood on the platform dressed in an EVA suit much like Lakesh's. The face they saw through the visor bore ugly bruises and flakes of dried blood. When he saw Kane, Grant and Brigid, George

Neukirk's eyes flashed with shocked recognition, but he reacted to Maccan's presence by dropping instantly to his knees, bowing his head, evidently awaiting either deliverance or death.

Chapter 22

Maccan swept majestically out onto the walkway, taking long-legged strides, the aluminum carrying case swinging jauntily at the end of his left arm. Everyone else hung back on the lip of the ledge, looking around nervously. The transadapts gave the distinct impression they had never visited the cavernous chamber before.

Halfway out on the walkway suspended above the pit, Maccan glanced over his shoulder and stabbed four fingers at Lakesh, Kane, Grant and Brigid in an unmistakable gesture for them to join him. They didn't move. David pushed against Kane's leg, shouting, "Get out there!"

The crystalline cluster at the tip of the shaft shivered slightly, emitting a bell-like tone that climbed into an almost painfully high whine they felt vibrating against their eardrums, even through their helmets. The vibrations corresponded exactly with each one of David's words.

"What the hell?" Grant blurted, reflexively touching the side of his headpiece.

Lakesh murmured, "This chamber is like a gigantic ear canal. The acoustics can amplify or modulate the resonances created by any sounds."

With a gloved finger he pointed to the spongy substance on the walls. "That paneling keeps the sounds from escaping or dissipating. It bounces the noise back to the crystal."

Maccan, on the platform, gestured impatiently toward them again. Kane stepped gingerly onto the walkway, glancing over the side. There were no handrails, only an edge that seemed to plunge straight down into darkness. After a couple of steps he realized the substance beneath his feet didn't yield or sag so he marched across it self-confidently.

Inscribed on the floor of the platform in highly polished silver was an intricate, symmetrical pattern of looping, interlaced and interlinking curves. Kane, Brigid and Grant had all seen the design before and knew it was called a Celtic wheel or knot. The various loops and links were arranged in accordance with the compass points, representing the facets and pathways of life. The square-topped dais rose from the center of it.

Maccan laid the case atop the dais and stepped to one side, pushing Neukirk out of the way and saying, "Lakesh, please make your mechanism operational."

Lakesh hesitated a moment, then stepped forward and undid the latches on the case, lifting the lid. He removed the little metal pyramid and its support systems from their hollowed-out foam cushions. Deftly he attached the small power unit and then pressed a seam on its alloyed skin. A small keypad slid out from the base. A faint low-pitched whine emanated from the interphaser, just at the edges of audibility. Maccan watched him, as though he found his activity of only vague interest.

While he worked, Kane stared intently at Neukirk, who affected not to notice. At length he asked, "Who smacked you around like that, George? Somebody else you betrayed?"

Neukirk's eyes flicked toward him. "I didn't betray anybody. I was always in league with Maccan. I wasn't a traitor."

Maccan glanced toward him, almost as if he were surprised to see him there. "You've run a thorough check on the power conduit, George?"

Neukirk ducked his head. "Yes, my prince. It functions perfectly."

"Good. Then I have no further use for a traitor."

Without altering his expression of mild interest, Maccan planted his gauntleted hand against George Neukirk's chest. The man instantly flew backward as though he were performing a reverse broad jump. He hurtled over the edge of the platform and into the darkness below. He uttered one single shriek before he disappeared into the black pit.

Maccan returned his attention to the interphaser, idly scratching at his cheek with his beringed left hand. Kane, Brigid and Grant stared at him, nonplussed by the swift and casual way he had murdered the man. Lakesh seemed to be unaware of what had happened. He completed setting up the pyramid and stepped back from the dais. It emitted a steady hum, like an engine on idle.

Maccan eyed it critically, then nodded graciously

to Lakesh. "Thank you. Now for your efforts, the least I can do supply is an explanation." The pitch and timbre of his voice seemed to have no effect on the crystal mass hanging above them.

Maccan said, "Kane, Brigid, I know you have some knowledge of my people's history on Earth. Do you know why they left?"

Kane recollected the information imparted to him by Fand during their encounters and he answered softly, "Most of the Tuatha de Danaan left Earth around 453 A.D., by the old calendar. The Irish clanspeople had outgrown you. Christianity had come in. Your science was condemned as sorcery and even you mentioned persecutions."

"And before we lived on Earth?" Maccan asked in a gentle voice.

Kane shrugged. "I always assumed your race came from another planet, like the Annunaki."

"We did," Maccan agreed with surprising geniality. "That planet was this one. Mars."

"Mars?" Brigid echoed incredulously. "That's impossible. Mars hasn't been able to support even bacterial life for millions of years."

Maccan smiled patronizingly. "This particular Mars, the Mars of this reflection, has been barren for a very, very long time. But it was not so in my universe."

Grant's eyebrows dropped down, shadowing his eyes. "Are we back to parallel casements again?"

Lakesh took it upon himself to answer. "Not precisely, friend Grant. We're talking about a mirror Mars, aren't we?"

"We are," confirmed Maccan. "Your own primitive scientists undertook mathematical investigations of the theories dealing with the plurality of universes."

"It sounds like the sidereal space routine to me," Grant remarked gruffly.

"The theories are connected," Lakesh said slowly, as if he were finding his way around what to say next. "But there are important differences." He held up four fingers. "There are four known fundamental forces in nature—gravity, electromagnetism and weak and strong nuclear forces. Gravity is quite familiar to most of us. It keeps our feet on the ground, it keeps our planet and all the other planets in our solar system in orbit around the Sun and keeps the Sun in orbit around the center of our galaxy.

"Electromagnetism is no less important. While it is gravity that holds us down, it is electromagnetism that stops us from falling through the floor. Weak and strong nuclear forces are of equal and fundamental importance as all the others."

Nodding approvingly, Maccan said, "Gravity can be described in geometrical terms as a curvature of four-dimensional space time while the other three forces are described in terms of symmetries or an abstract internal space, which has nothing to do with ordinary space time as you understand it."

"And what the hell does that have to do with why you invaded our home and killed our people?" Kane demanded in a half snarl.

Maccan regarded him with a sad smile. "Imagine that for each type of ordinary particle there is a sepa-

rate mirror particle. That is, not only do we have photons, electrons, positrons and protons, but we also have
mirror subatomic particles. In nature's mirror not only
space is reflected but also atoms, molecules, cells. Do
you understand now?"

Before Kane could either deny or confirm his comprehension, Brigid stated matter-of-factly, "I think I
do, Maccan. The relationship between ordinary matter and mirror matter is somewhat like the relationship
between the letters b and d. So, while neither b nor d
is symmetric together they are in fact mirror symmetries, with the two letters interchanging in the mirror
image.

"Therefore the properties of the mirror particles
would turn out to be very similar to ordinary particles.
For example, the mirror particles must have the same
mass and lifetime as each of the ordinary particles—
otherwise the mirror symmetry would be broken."

As she spoke, Kane mentally reviewed what they
had all learned about Maccan's people over the past
couple of years. Obviously the Danaan deeply understood the indivisibility of space and time and of matter and energy. They knew all of them were
interchangeable, one turned into the other and vice
versa, according to the application. The deeper the
Danaan scientists probed into the very composition of
matter—the building blocks of material objects—the
more they found energy and complexities of energy at
the bottom of everything.

Thousands of years earlier the Tuatha de Danaan
had mapped all the quantum pathways, the vortex

points on Earth. According to a priestess of the Priory of Awen, the Danaan bolted into the vortex points and scattered themselves. The Celtic cup-and-ring markings, as well as the knot patterns, were one-dimensional depictions of multidimensional geometrics. He grudgingly admitted the Danaan had earned the right to take pride in their accomplishments. Nor was it completely their fault that primitive Terrans regarded the lordly Tuatha de Danaan as gods from the stars.

"So," Kane ventured, "the Danaan came from a mirror universe, a reflection of this one, not from another planet in this galaxy."

"Yes," Maccan said.

"How?"

"I thought that would be obvious to you by now, Kane." Maccan gestured all around them. "This pyramid is not just a structure, but a vehicle which, for thousands of years, permitted access to this universe that coexisted with mine. My people isolated a technique for translating the reality of one universe into its reflection. We brought our entire culture, our whole race here."

"'Backward and forward and sideways did she pass,'" Brigid quoted quietly. "'Making up her mind to face the cruel looking glass.'"

Maccan threw her a fleeting, appreciative smile. "You are not far wrong. This structure is a kind of transportation device, a giant interphaser or contiguity which was originally built to pass backward, forward and sideways through the two universes."

Kane inhaled a deep breath. "And now you want to

go back through the looking glass, to return from this reflection into another one."

Maccan nodded, pointing to the interphaser, the dais and then to the crystal hanging over the platform. "Yes. By tying in your interphaser with the primary power conduit, the necessary energy will progress through the resonance shaft to form a single conclusionary flow at the apex. The energy flows in a helix spiral pattern exactly opposite and of equal frequency and the intensity on each side of the vortex at any given point will trigger a quantum induction shift by vibrational resonance."

He gestured to the Celtic knot on the floor of the platform. "The shift will then feed into the propagation medium, which will expand the field influence and—"

Grant rudely cut into the torrent of technobabble by demanding, "Why?"

Maccan stopped talking and arched a quizzical eyebrow. "I don't understand the question."

Gesturing to the enormous chamber with both hands, Grant stated flatly, "You left your home universe to come to its reflection. You've been here for thousands of years. There must have been a reason why the rest of the Danaan returned through the—what did you call it, the contiguity?—and abandoned you here without a way to rejoin them."

Maccan's eyes lightened by a shade. "I was not abandoned."

Grant made a wordless utterance of scorn. "You could've fooled me, Mac."

"Do not presume too much," Maccan replied. "You stand there now only because I am indulging a whim. Do not provoke me into changing that whim into wrath."

Brigid chuckled lowly. "The mad god's wrath."

Maccan's reply was sibilantly soft with menace. "And you believe your sex will keep you safe from it?"

"Answer Grant's question, why don't you?" Kane snapped angrily. "Why did the Danaan leave you in this reflection?"

Maccan's eyes acquired a yellow shimmer as his temper rose. "You ignorant savages could not understand our reasons."

"Right." Lakesh spoke in a curiously guttural, contemptuous drawl. "You freely chose to remain here, a magician, a scientist, a prince among ignorant savages. We're not buying it, Maccan."

"Do you wish to share the fate of George Neukirk?" Maccan asked, his voice trembling slightly with the effort to control himself. "He suggested this undertaking to me and as you witnessed, I dealt with his treacherous nature, not his scientific knowledge or devotion to me."

Kane snorted. "So, you betrayed him without a second thought—no big surprise." He swept a hand toward Shayd, Raschid and the transadapts all still waiting on the ledge. "Will you reward their devotion the same way?"

Raschid and Shayd heard his question over their helmet UTEL comm links, but unless they possessed the ability to lip-read, Maccan's response would be a mystery to them.

As it was, Maccan refused to be baited further. Coldly he said, "I do not propose to engage you in a debate as to my motives."

"Fine," Lakesh announced, moving quickly around the dais and locking arms with Brigid Baptiste. "We'll just be on our way. We'll leave you to whatever activities you wish and you can have the interphaser—"

"No," Maccan stated unemotionally.

"No what?" asked Grant impatiently. "No, you don't want the interphaser or no, we won't be on our way?"

"No, you won't be going anywhere. Except with me."

Kane eyed him first speculatively, then suspiciously. "What the hell does that mean, Mac? I thought you were taking a trip back through the mirror."

"I am," replied Maccan. "I will activate the contiguity and translate all of us into the reflection of this world."

"You want us to go with you?" Grant demanded, voice thick with disbelief. "What the fuck for?"

Maccan turned toward him, lifting his gauntleted hand, little bursts of energy flaring between the fingers, energy shimmering within the lens. "Have a care, Grant. My reasons are—"

"Very basic," Brigid broke in, a sneering laugh underscoring her words. "That's why we couldn't figure them out. Maccan, you wanted to extinguish the Sun with the accelerated entropic gradient produced by the DEVIL platform. You wanted to kill yourself, but in your infantile egomania, you couldn't picture the world, the universe, going on without you. So you decided to take millions of lives with you, like an old pagan god who measured the degree of his divinity by the number of lives sacrificed in his name."

Brigid turned to her companions. "Don't you get it? This sick bastard couldn't figure out an appropriately apocalyptic way of committing suicide, one that's worthy of his stature, so he's changed his mind...now he's taking his toys and going home. In this case, *we're* his toys. He still needs worshipers and the handful we represent is a pretty pitiful testament to ten thousand years of strutting around being adored by simple clanspeople—but he'll take what he can get. He probably thinks we'll provide him with more by breeding with one another."

Kane stared transfixed at Maccan, almost overwhelmed by astonishment. He heard himself husk out, "She's right, isn't she, Mac? The reason you never tried to make the transition back to where you came from is because there are no worshipers there. Hell, there might not even be any of your own people there anymore!

"You wouldn't be a god there, and that's probably the same reason you didn't return to Earth after you were resurrected from stasis on the Moon. The people on Earth wouldn't be impressed by the idea of becoming agrarian peasants, kissing the ass of a god who throws temper tantrums every time the barometric pressure changes."

"Is that it?" asked Lakesh hoarsely. "This entire operation—the attack on Cerberus, all the killing, the abduction of myself—isn't so much the desire to go home again as to feed your insane hunger to be worshiped?"

Grant shook his head incredulously. "Is your plan to settle us in the mirror-universe Ireland? To force us into a simple pastoral life where we sacrifice goats to you whenever we want it to rain?"

Maccan regarded them all expressionlessly from beneath lowered brows. "You are all very bright and resourceful." His voice was a barely audible rustle. "You have skills and knowledge that would be useful in building a new world. I found your courage, camaraderie and humor intoxicating...reminders of why I loved humanity so much at one time."

Then his eyes seemed to burst into flame, lighting his face with eerie, hell-hued streaks. Lifting both hands, he curved the fingers into talons. "Why do you seek to oppose me?" he shrieked. "Why defy me, Maccan, Angus Og Bhrogha, prince among the Danaan, killer of the Formori, conqueror of the Fir Bolg, sorcerer, warrior, a legend even in the old days of the Danaan empire?"

Lips curled back over his teeth, he roared words in an unintelligible, consonant-heavy tongue, and the blazing fury of his eyes hammered at Kane who fought the urge to flinch away. Reverting to English, he bellowed, "I reigned in the dim lands ages before your White Christ was born! I died, but not as men die! I slept and awoke again and all the old empires had crumbled to dust or were drowned by the sea! I lived on! What are you humans anyway but shadows in the eyes of the gods? And your arrogant, barbaric race thinks it can survive without its ancient masters?"

Maccan thrust out his arm, the fingers of his gauntleted hand spread wide, energies pulsing and throbbing within the lens. "You will follow me, dung-dogs, or you will die in screaming agony—aye, and all whom you love will perish 'neath my hand as well. *Choose!*"

Chapter 23

Lakesh surprised them all by inquiring nonchalantly, "And what is it like on your side of the mirror, Mac? Better or worse than this side?"

"Worse," Maccan bit out, not lowering his hand. "Much, much worse."

"How so?" Lakesh still affected a mild, inoffensive tone, as if he hoped to deflect Maccan's rage by changing the subject. The tactic seemed to work.

Maccan declared flatly, "You think your planet was devastated by war, but our entire universe was dying. Long, long ago it was much like yours. That was when we of the Tuatha de Danaan rose to grand civilization and glory. The scientific powers of our race so expanded we were able to spread out and colonize the worlds of many stars. It was an age of high technology, of discovery and exploration.

"But that was aeons ago. The inexorable laws of entropy took effect, and as the suns of our universe burned out, we had no choice but to migrate, to retreat. Eventually we realized there was no place to retreat to and save our civilization. But our retreat went on for millions of years, withdrawing from our colonies. A universe does not die overnight."

"Then why return to it?" Brigid asked.

Maccan's lips curved in a bitter half smile. "The laws of entropy will reverse themselves when the cooling of our stars reaches a critical point."

"That's only a theory," said Lakesh, still as calm as if he were having the discussion in the Cerberus dining hall and not on Mars with certain death only inches from his face.

"Human physicists might have believed the second law of thermodynamics was immutable," countered Maccan, "that the flow of energy into lower forms is a one-way, irreversible process. Even your own Einstein admitted that cosmic laws were immutable in appearance only."

Brigid said thoughtfully, "So you postulate the Heisenberg principle of uncertainty might rule in cosmic, as well as atomic physics."

"Yes," Maccan said, slowly lowering his gauntlet. "I'm pleased you understand."

"If indeed the curvature of four-dimensional space collapses," murmured Lakesh, "the immense amounts of free radiation compressed into a small sphere of space time would build rapidly into new nebulae, suns, even planets."

Maccan nodded. "And if I can keep my race alive in some fashion until the critical point is reached, and perhaps it has already been reached, then the Tuatha de Danaan will be reborn."

"For what?" Grant's question came out as a harsh

rasp of anger. "So another cycle of gods and worshipers, masters and slaves can begin again?"

"I don't think you need our help to re-create a universe like that," Brigid said smoothly. "Nor do you need the pleasure of our company."

"I will be the one to make that determination," Maccan retorted imperiously.

She shook her head inside her helmet. "Uh-uh. You're wrong again."

Her hand darted forward and struck the enter key on the interphaser keypad. Almost immediately a glowing funnel of light fanned up from the metal apex of the pyramid. It looked like a diffused veil of flame and it expanded into a swirling borealis several feet above the dais.

At the same time, on the far edges of his hearing, Kane sensed a distant, muffled roar, a sound he couldn't focus on or even really be sure he heard.

Maccan cried out in wordless fury, backing away from the interphaser.

Kane instantly grasped Brigid's strategy—the pyramid obviously occupied a vortex node, a naturally occurring geomantic interphase point of the Martian electromagnetic grid. Activating the interphaser without encoding a parallel set of transition coordinates was tantamount to kicking open a door in a submarine. Energy flooded in to fill the entire cavity within the pyramid.

Maccan shouted something at Brigid, a curse or a command or both. He shifted the pulsing lens of his gauntlet toward her. Moving with a speed surprising for a man his size, Grant's hand shot out and closed around Maccan's slender right wrist from underneath. He wrenched his entire arm upward.

Infrasound leaped from the lens in a rippling flow, striking and engulfing the crystal cluster suspended overhead. The ripple splashed back, striking the lens on the gauntlet. Shrieking in agony, Maccan tried to tear himself free of Grant's grip, his face demonic with rage. A halo of coruscating light surrounded the glove, and Grant guessed the blow back overloaded the gauntlet's delicate circuitry.

Everyone's helmet suddenly filled with a series of painfully loud squeals, pops and the hashy hiss of static. Grant's fingers loosened in reaction to the on-slaught of sound, and Maccan yanked his arm free. He launched a kick at Grant's stomach, his boot landing solidly. Pain streaked through Grant's torso and he staggered backward. He would have plunged from the platform if Kane hadn't caught him.

The volume of the cacophony blasting into their helmets through the UTEL transmitters faded to a strange, whispery echo. The crystalline mass changed color, shifting through all the hues of the spectrum. A twisting tendril of softly shimmering light poured down from one of the points to wrap the apex of the interphaser.

The throbbing, echoing whispers swelled louder and all of them felt a corresponding vibration build in their bodies, from the bones outward.

Lakesh shouted, "We've triggered a feedback pulse,

some sort of resonant power surge. There's no place for the buildup to disperse, so it'll keep bouncing back—"

The rest of his words were cut off by a hand-clapping concussion from the interphaser. A parabolic shock wave bowled all of them off their feet, sent them rolling to the edge of the platform. A great gust of sound battered at their senses, followed by a maddening hum that scratched at their nerve endings. Smoke billowed thickly from the interphaser, streaming from every seam. The dais itself glowed red-hot, plasma crackling in dazzling blue skeins all over the metal surface. Maccan's cloak was on fire, and he shouted shrilly as he beat at the flames enveloping it.

The oxygen in the pit wasn't sufficient to maintain the fire for very long, but before it was extinguished, his cape was little more than a scorched rag. His gauntlet, the deadling Silver Hand of Nuadhu, spit little sparks. Its artfully crafted silver segments were blackened, half-slagged scrap metal. The lens on the palm looked like a cheap bauble made of glass.

Struggling to his feet, Kane saw that the wave of force had extended outward from the platform and flattened all the people on the ledge. Raschid and Shayd stirred feebly. The transadapts lay sprawled and unmoving. Without the hard suits, they had taken the full brunt of the feedback pulse.

A strange dark halo shimmered from the crystal

cluster, expanding like a wave sweeping outward. Kane felt the throb of it within his skull.

Lakesh, sounding half-strangled, gasped, "We must get out of here—the vibrations of the resonator are building to critical mass."

Temples feeling as if they were caught in a vise, Kane began a shambling sprint across the walkway, muttering, "I figured it was something like that."

He glanced back once. From the facets of the cluster, great whorls of color spiraled out, growing in size and brilliance like immense flame flowers blossoming into life. He saw Brigid running after him.

Lakesh stepped onto the walkway, intending to follow Brigid, but a steel-hewed arm encircled his neck from behind and jerked him off his feet.

Maccan sent Lakesh reeling almost to the very edge of the platform, but Grant snatched him by the wrist and hauled him back.

Without a word, Grant closed in on the crimson-eyed Maccan. He threw the first punch, but Maccan brushed it aside with a forearm and sidestepped, avoiding another blow. Grant moved in quickly and pounded two solid punches to the man's midsection. He took them without even so much as a grunt of pain. With his right arm, Maccan aimed another blow at his face. He managed to catch Grant's right wrist and bore down, grinding flesh and tendon against bone, trying to force him to his knees.

Teeth clenched, Grant resisted. He wasn't a small man by any standards, but in Maccan's grip he felt like a child. The Danaan grinned, showing his teeth, eyes blazing like two coals dug out of the hearth of hell.

Grant locked his gaze on Maccan's face and refused to bend. In his mind and heart, it wasn't a struggle between man and man, but between ancient ways and new, between the concepts of master and slave. Anger washed over him like a tide as an image of Domi, barely able to move or to talk, filled his mind.

Unexpectedly, Grant bent at the knees, as if being forced down, then he lunged forward, passing under Maccan's arm on his right side, turning and dragging his arm backward, forcing it in a direction neither human nor Danaan arms were designed to bend.

He twisted it up into a hammerlock and seized a handful of Maccan's long hair with his left hand. He slammed him face-first against the dais, cranked his captured elbow skyward, levering it up until he heard a mushy crack. Maccan screamed a very ungodlike scream of utter agony and sagged to his knees, the side of his face pressing against the conduit. There was a sizzle as of meat on a hot griddle, and he screamed again, throwing himself away from it. His pale face bore a red streak of seared, blistered flesh.

He tried hooking Grant's leg with his own, but Grant simply dropped on top of him, his fist striking him on the point of the chin and bouncing his head against one of the interlacing loops of the Celtic knot design.

His face a half mask of blood and burned flesh, Maccan was somehow able to reach up with his left hand to catch Grant's down-plunging fist. It didn't stop Grant's right fist, which came down like a rock on the side of Maccan's head.

Maccan's head rolled to the side and he didn't move, his grip loosening and falling away from Grant's fist. Panting, Grant crouched atop him, as if suspecting a trick, hand raised to strike him again. But Maccan didn't stir and Grant slowly pulled himself erect, swayed for a second, then staggered out onto the walkway. Lakesh came after him.

"Are you all right, friend Grant?" asked Lakesh anxiously.

Grant opened his mouth to reply, then felt a shattering blow between his shoulder blades that turned the pit into a spinning carousel of light and darkness, pinwheeling crazily away. He heard Lakesh cry out in alarm and anger. He let himself fall, catching himself on his hands and knees, trying to drag air into his laboring lungs.

Lakesh wheeled to confront Maccan and saw the ugly welts of burns on his face and the way his right arm hung dead and useless at his side. But Maccan smiled in savage satisfaction as he pulled back his leg to kick Grant again, to kick him off the platform.

Not having any time to think, Lakesh roared in fury and bounded forward, cannonading his entire weight into Maccan's body. The man stumbled and staggered. For a frantic instant, he tottered on the rim of the platform, clawing with his good hand for a grip to prevent his fall.

An image of Domi with the Silver Hand of Nuadhu

pressed against her forehead flickered through Lakesh's mind, and he kicked the man with all his strength. Maccan screamed and toppled over the side. For what seemed like an eternity Lakesh could hear his shrieks as he plunged down and down. Then it ended abruptly.

Breathing hard, blinking cold sweat from his eyes, Lakesh turned toward Grant and helped the man to his feet. "I ask you again, friend Grant...are you all right?"

"That depends," Grant retorted, teeth set on a groan of pain. "Where's Maccan?"

"Right about now, coming to rest in his own Tir Na Nog, I hope."

A grating, crunching rumble swallowed up the incessant keening hum in their helmets. Both men glanced up as a pouring of powder sifted down from above. Without another word, they began to run across the walkway to the ledge. Kane and Brigid were engaged in a struggle to get past Raschid, Shayd and the transadapts.

The transadapts, hemorrhaging from their ears and nostrils, were in poor shape to put up much resistance. Brigid's right leg whipped up in a swift, spinning crescent kick. The side of her boot knocked one of the gnomes into two of his companions, piling the three of them up in the corridor.

Raschid raised himself to his knees and even through the visor of his helmet, Kane saw that his eyes were glassy. He swung his Uzi around, but Kane kicked him square in the chest, knocking him backward, his subgun falling from his hands.

Kane reached for it, but felt his right leg being pulled out from under him. He went down on top of Shayd. He slapped her Gyrojet rocket pistol aside and lunged again for the fallen Uzi, even as Raschid scrabbled on the floor for it. He kicked free of Shayd and wrestled with Raschid, rolling over into the corridor, slamming into a support column.

At the same time, a dazed Shayd struggled to her feet and bent to retrieve her rocket pistol. Brigid brought her heavy-treaded boot sole down on the woman's wrist. She put all of her weight onto her heel, and Shayd screamed a curse. Her fingers opened around the butt of the tiny pistol, and with her other foot, Brigid kicked it over the side of the ledge.

Shayd lunged upward, catching Brigid at the knees and muscling her over onto her back. The two women rolled into the corridor where Kane and Raschid fought for possession of the Uzi. They collided with the men and the subgun fell from Raschid's hands.

Kane grabbed for the machine pistol, missed and tried again. He secured his hold just as David rose up, hooks held over his head. He was wild-eyed, his ratty hair hanging in his eyes. Shrieking in mad rage, he swung the hooks from shoulder level straight at Kane's faceplate.

Having no choice, Kane lined up the Uzi muzzle automatically and fired a dozen rounds. The stream of 9 mm bullets caught the transadapt in the center of his stomach and rapidly tracked upward, punching him backward, then splitting his head open.

Grant and Lakesh pounded into the corridor just as David's body settled to the floor, both of them wild-eyed. "You fools!" Lakesh bleated. "This place is shaking itself apart! We've got to find a way out of here!"

Kane wasn't sure if Lakesh included him and Brigid in his "fools" remark, but Raschid stopped struggling long enough for him to break free of the man and to climb to his feet. He looked into the pit and saw the hanging crystal cluster surrounded by a bubble of quivering ripples through which coruscating particles of brilliance shot. Rolling multicolored clouds overlapped, engulfing it and the platform.

Shayd staggered to her feet, releasing Brigid. "Where is Maccan?" she demanded, panic thick in her voice.

"Never mind him," Grant snapped. "We've got to—"

Shayd bulled between the two men, shoving them aside. "Maccan!"

Raschid followed her out onto the walkway, reaching for her.

As both people reached the halfway point, a torrent of stone blocks cascaded down from above with a thunderous roar. Great slabs of rock fell and crashed. The four people wheeled and raced down the corridor, the floor quaking beneath their feet. Fragments of rock pattered down all around them. The walls showed cracks, and rocks and mortar, shaken loose from the ancient walls overhead, sifted down. The pyramid heaved and shuddered around them.

"Where are we going?" panted Brigid. "To the train?"

No one had any breath to answer. Everyone was too occupied with trying to maintain his or her balance and footing on the convulsing floor. Blocks of stone dropped like bombs from the ceiling.

They reached the end of the corridor and the lift car. Brigid batted the lever to the up position and fell back against the wall of the elevator, gasping for oxygen. The car rose rapidly to the level above. When Kane glimpsed the scattering of boxes and crates, he slapped the lever to the midposition, locking the lift in place.

"What the hell?" Grant boomed.

"Those air skids, the sleds," Kane said breathlessly. "We can use them to get out of here...we'll never make it to the train before this place buries us alive!"

No one argued with him. They dashed out of the lift and into the warehouse area. The far wall was covered by a massive steel shutter, and Kane's eyes frantically searched for a way to open it. Brigid pointed to an elaborate chain-and-pulley contraption.

Grant bounded to it, giving the device a swift visual examination, and yanked at the handle protruding from its base. With a clanking crash and a shower of rust, the steel panel dropped open, revealing a black, star-speckled sky.

"This was one short-ass day," Kane commented.

"Seemed long enough to me," Grant countered.

"How do you get these things to work?" Lakesh asked in angry, frightened frustration.

Grant, Kane and Brigid turned to see him on his

hands and knees inside an air sled. "I don't have the slightest idea," Kane replied, inspecting another craft.

A huge stone cube tumbled down from overhead, driving up jets of dust. Brigid declared tensely, "We'd better get ideas and fast!"

Kane found controls on the underside of the sled's forepart. They were very simple, consisting of a pair of knobs and a gearshift-like control stick. He kneeled in front of the controls, twisting the knobs experimentally. The sled suddenly rushed up from the floor with tremendous acceleration, flinging him backward and entirely out of the craft.

He hit the floor with an impact that momentarily stunned him, but he glimpsed the sled smashing headlong into the wall above the open portal. The nose flattened and bent back on itself. It dropped atop a stack of boxes and toppled them.

"Shit," Grant hissed softly in disgust, hauling Kane to his feet none too gently.

"At least we know how to make them go," Kane said, voice tight with the effort to keep from groaning. "Let's try 'em again."

The four people climbed into individual air sleds, inserting their knees into special hollowed-out sockets. Flexible metal straps passed around their legs and secured them in position.

Lakesh murmured, "The motive power appears to be an electromagnetic field that alters graviton levels—"

"The knobs control your speed and altitude," broke in Kane impatiently. "You use the stick to steer and for attitude."

A bucketful of rock particles sifted down, rattling against Grant's helmet. "Let's get the hell out of here!" he bellowed.

The air sleds rose from the floor and shot toward the opening in the wall as if they had been launched from catapults. Inestimable tons of thundering stone collapsed behind them and they barely kept a few yards ahead of it.

The craft flew up and out into cold Martian air, not more than twenty feet above the desert. They felt a series of consecutive hammering blasts thundering from behind them. Kane goosed the sled to its highest speed and twisted around to take a look. He saw black cracks a hundred feet across zigzagging through the pitted face of the pyramid. It seemed to implode, crashing inward, block after block collapsing and then scattering in exploding fragments. The walls folded in on themselves, cascading in a contained avalanche.

The four of them followed the trail made by the monorail for the Cydonia Compound, reducing their speed only a trifle. When the domes of the colony came into view, Kane felt it was safe enough to land and look behind them at the pyramid.

Veiled by swirling clouds of dust, the ancient monument of the Tuatha de Danaan settled to the Martian desert like a massive grave marker. A pillar of whirling dust and grit rose toward the sky. They followed its ascent with their eyes.

Phobos was cold and hostile in the infinite darkness of the Martian night, regarding them with indifference. The Milky Way was a silver ribbon of frosty brilliance across the black sky. No one spoke for a long time, then finally Brigid broke the silence. "It was all over for Maccan long, long ago. I can't help but wish this had turned out differently."

Grant grunted. "We fought for every inch of ground we've gained to free ourselves from baronial slavery. If it had ended any differently with Maccan, our fight wouldn't have meant anything."

"How can we judge Maccan by our standards?" Brigid asked.

"Easy," Kane said flatly. "He lies there covered by the same dirt that's at our feet."

Lakesh looked up toward Phobos and murmured, "Shadows in the eyes of the gods, indeed."

James Axler
Outlanders®

SUN LORD

In a fabled city of the ancient world, the neo-gods of Mexico are locked in a battle for domination. Harnessing the immutable power of alien technology and Earth's pre-Dark secrets, the high priests and whitecoats have hijacked Kane into the resurrected world of the Aztecs. Invested with the power of the great sun god, Kane is a pawn in the brutal struggle and must restore the legendary Quetzalcoatl to his rightful place—or become a human sacrifice....

Available May 2004 at your favorite retail outlet.

Or order your copy now by sending your name, address, zip or postal code, along with a check or money order (please do not send cash) for $6.50 for each book ordered ($7.99 in Canada), plus 75¢ postage and handling ($1.00 in Canada), payable to Gold Eagle Books, to:

In the U.S.	In Canada
Gold Eagle Books	Gold Eagle Books
3010 Walden Avenue	P.O. Box 636
P.O. Box 9077	Fort Erie, Ontario
Buffalo, NY 14269-9077	L2A 5X3

Please specify book title with your order.
Canadian residents add applicable federal and provincial taxes.

GOLD EAGLE®

GOUT29

DEATH LANDS®

Hellbenders

*Available in March 2004
at your favorite retail outlet.*

Emerging from a gateway into a redoubt filled with preDark technology, Ryan and his band hope to unlock some of the secrets of post-nuclear America. But the fortified redoubt is under the control of a half-mad former sec man hell-bent on vengeance, who orders Ryan and the others to jump-start his private war against two local barons. Under the harsh and pitiless glare of the rad-blasted desert sun, the companions fight to see another day, whatever it brings....

THE DESTROYER

POLITICAL PRESSURE

The juggernaut that is the Morals and Ethics Behavior Establishment—MAEBE—is on a roll. Will its ultra-secret enforcement arm, the White Hand, kill enough scumbags to make their guy the uber-boy of the Presidential race? MAEBE! Will Orville Flicker succeed in his murderous, manipulative campaign to win the Oval Office? MAEBE! Can Remo and Chiun stop the bad guys from getting whacked—at least until CURE officially pays them to do it? MAEBE!

Available April 2004 at your favorite retail outlet.

Or order your copy now by sending your name, address, zip or postal code, along with a check or money order (please do not send cash) for $6.50 for each book ordered ($7.99 in Canada), plus 75¢ postage and handling ($1.00 in Canada), payable to Gold Eagle Books, to:

In the U.S.	In Canada
Gold Eagle Books	Gold Eagle Books
3010 Walden Avenue	P.O. Box 636
P.O. Box 9077	Fort Erie, Ontario
Buffalo, NY 14269-9077	L2A 5X3

Please specify book title with your order.
Canadian residents add applicable federal and provincial taxes.

GOLD EAGLE®

GDEST135